P9-CEE-788

IT'S A GAME WITH ONE RULE:
KILL OR BE KILLED.

"A tapestry that chills
to the bone."
—*Daily Mail* (UK)

"A fast-paced
roller-coaster ride."
—Life Through Books

"Truly excellent."
—*The Sun* (UK)

"A dark, edgy thriller."
— Will Lavender,
New York Times
Bestselling Author
of *Obedience*

PRAISE FOR
EENY MEENY

"Dark, twisted, thought-provoking, and I couldn't turn the pages fast enough. Take a ride on this roller coaster from hell—white knuckles guaranteed."

—Tami Hoag, #1 *New York Times* bestselling author of *Cold Cold Heart*

"No doubt about it! *Eeny Meeny* debuts one of the best new series detectives, Helen Grace. Determined, tough, and damaged, she must unravel a terrifying riddle of a killer kidnapping victims in pairs to send a particularly personal message. Mesmerizing!"

—Lisa Gardner, #1 *New York Times* bestselling author of *Crash & Burn*

"What a great premise! . . . *Eeny Meeny* is a fresh and brilliant departure from the stock serial killer tale. And Detective Inspector Helen Grace is one of the greatest heroes to come along in years."

—Jeffery Deaver, *New York Times* bestselling author of *The Skin Collector* and *Solitude Creek*

"M. J. Arlidge has created a genuinely fresh heroine in DI Helen Grace. . . . He spares us none of the dark details, weaving them together into a tapestry that chills to the bone." —*Daily Mail* (UK)

"With an orchestration of tension that is always sharp and cinematic, M. J. Arlidge's debut novel grabs the reader by the throat." —Crime Time

"This taut, fast-paced debut is truly excellent." —*The Sun* (UK)

continued...

"A fast-paced roller-coaster ride. Every chapter holds new developments, new murders, new clues. . . . I would highly recommend it for any crime fiction fans, and I am giving it four stars out of five. A truly wonderful debut novel." —Life Through Books

"A thrilling and enjoyable read . . . a shocking twist at the end."

—The Crime Scene

"[A] rip-roaring affair . . . pulls no punches with its opening lines and doesn't let go until the very last. . . . This is the first in what may be a long line of Helen Grace books, and I for one am excited about what else she has to come." —Boy, Let's Talk About Books

"There are so many things about this novel that are expertly pulled off. It has a devious premise. DI Helen Grace is fiendishly awesome. It's scary as all hell. It has an ending that's fair and shocking. And it has a full cast of realistically drawn, interesting characters that make the thing read like a bullet. *Eeny Meeny* is a dark, edgy thriller."

—Will Lavender, *New York Times* bestselling author of *Obedience*

EENY MEENY

M. J. ARLIDGE

NAL NEW AMERICAN LIBRARY

New American Library
Published by the Penguin Group
Penguin Group (USA) LLC, 375 Hudson Street,
New York, New York 10014

USA | Canada | UK | Ireland | Australia | New Zealand | India | South Africa | China
penguin.com
A Penguin Random House Company

Published by New American Library, a division of Penguin Group (USA) LLC. Previously
published in a Penguin Group (UK) edition.

First New American Library Printing, June 2015

Copyright © M. J. Arlidge, 2014
Readers Guide copyright © Penguin Random House, 2015
Excerpt from *Pop Goes the Weasel* copyright © M. J. Arlidge, 2014
Penguin supports copyright. Copyright fuels creativity, encourages diverse voices, promotes free
speech, and creates a vibrant culture. Thank you for buying an authorized edition of this book and
for complying with copyright laws by not reproducing, scanning, or distributing any part of it in
any form without permission. You are supporting writers and allowing Penguin to continue to
publish books for every reader.

REGISTERED TRADEMARK—MARCA REGISTRADA

LIBRARY OF CONGRESS CATALOGING-IN-PUBLICATION DATA:

Arlidge, M. J.
Eeny meeny/M. J. Arlidge.
p. cm.
ISBN 978-0-451-47549-7
1. Policewomen—Fiction.   2. Serial murder investigation—Fiction.   I. Title.
PR6051.R55E38 2015
823'.914—dc23   2014037039

Printed in the United States of America
10 9 8 7 6 5 4 3 2 1

Set in Adobe Garamond
Designed by Spring Hoteling

PUBLISHER'S NOTE
This is a work of fiction. Names, characters, places, and incidents either are the product of the
author's imagination or are used fictitiously, and any resemblance to actual persons, living or dead,
business establishments, events, or locales is entirely coincidental.

EENY MEENY

1

Sam is asleep. I could kill him now. His face is turned from me—it wouldn't be hard. Would he stir if I moved? Try to stop me? Or would he just be *glad* that this nightmare was over?

I can't think like that. I must try to remember what is real, what is good. But when you're a prisoner, the days seem endless and hope is the first thing to die.

I rack my brains for happy memories to hold off the dark thoughts, but they are harder and harder to summon.

We've been here only ten days (or is it eleven?), yet normal life already seems a distant memory. We were hitching back from a gig in London when it happened. It was pouring rain and a succession of cars had sailed past without a second look. We were soaked to the skin and about to turn back when finally a van pulled over. Inside, it was warm and dry. We were offered coffee from a flask. Just the smell of it was enough to cheer us up. The taste was even better. We didn't realize it would be our last taste of freedom.

When I came to, my head was pounding. Blood coated my mouth. I wasn't in the warm van anymore. I was in a cold, dark space. Was I dreaming? A noise behind me made me start. But it was only Sam stumbling to his feet.

We'd been robbed. Robbed and dumped. I scrambled forward, clawing at the walls that enclosed us. Cold, hard tiles. I crashed into Sam and for a brief moment held him, breathing in that smell I love so much. Then the moment passed and we realized the horror of our situation.

We were in a disused diving pool. Derelict, unloved, it had been stripped of the boards, signs and even the steps. Everything that could be salvaged had been. Leaving a deep smooth tank that was impossible to climb out of.

Was that evil shit listening to our screams? Probably. Because when we finally stopped, it happened. We heard a mobile phone ringing and for a brief, glorious moment thought it was someone coming to rescue us. But then we saw the phone's face glowing on the pool floor beside us. Sam didn't move, so I ran. Why did it have to be me? Why does it *always* have to be me?

"Hello, Amy."

The voice on the other end was distorted, inhuman. I wanted to beg for mercy, explain that they'd made a terrible mistake, but the fact that they knew my name seemed to rob me of all conviction. I said nothing, so the voice continued, relentless and dispassionate:

"Do you want to live?"

"Who are you? What have you done to u—?"

"Do you want to live?"

For a minute, I can't reply. My tongue won't move. But then: "Yes."

"On the floor by the phone you'll find a gun. It has one bullet in it. For Sam or for yourself. That is the price of your freedom. You must kill to live. Do you want to live, Amy?"

I can't speak. I want to vomit.

"Well, do you?"

And then the phone goes dead. Which is when Sam asks: "What did they say?"

Sam is asleep beside me. I could do it now.

2

The woman cried out in pain. And then was silent. Across her back, livid lines were forming. Jake raised the crop again and brought it down with a snap. The woman bucked, cried out, then said:

"Again."

She seldom said anything else. She wasn't the talkative type. Not like some of his clients. The administrators, accountants and clerks stuck in sexless relationships were *desperate* to talk—desperate to be liked by the man who beat them up for money. She was different, a closed book. She never mentioned where she'd found him. Or why she'd come. She issued her instructions—her needs—clearly and crisply, then asked him to get on with it.

They always started by securing her wrists. Two studded leather straps pulled taut, so that her arms were tethered to the wall. Iron ankle fetters secured her feet to the floor. Her clothes would be neatly stowed on the chair provided, so there she'd stand, chained, in her underwear, awaiting punishment.

There was no role play. No "Please don't hurt me, Daddy" or "I'm a bad, bad girl." She just wanted him to hurt her. In some ways it was a relief. Every job becomes routine after a while and sometimes it was nice not to have to pander to the fantasies of sad wannabe victims. At the same time it was frustrating, her refusal to strike up a proper relationship with him. The most important element of any S&M encounter is trust. The submissive needs to know that they are in safe hands, that their dominator knows their personality and their needs and can give them a fulfilling experience on terms that are comfortable for both parties. If you don't have that, then it swiftly becomes assault or even abuse—and that was most definitely *not* Jake's bag.

So he chipped away—the odd question here, the odd comment there. And over time he'd divined the basics: that she wasn't from Southampton originally, that she had no family, that she was closing in on forty and didn't mind. He also knew from their sessions together that pain was her thing. Sex didn't come into it. She didn't want to be teased or titillated. She wanted to be punished. The beatings never went too far, but they were hard and unremitting. She had the body to take it—she was tall, muscular and seriously toned—and the traces of ancient scars suggested she was not new to the S&M scene.

And yet for all his probing, all his carefully worded questions, there was only one thing that Jake knew about her for sure. Once, when she was getting dressed, her photo ID slipped from her jacket pocket onto the floor. She snatched it up in a heartbeat—thought he hadn't seen, but he had. He thought he knew a bit about people, but this one had taken him by surprise. If he hadn't seen her ID, he'd never have guessed that she was a policewoman.

together we would survive. Amy stood on my shoulders, her nails cracking as she clawed the tiles, straining to reach the lip of the pool. When that didn't work, she tried jumping up from my shoulders. But the pool is fifteen feet deep, maybe more, and salvation seems forever just out of reach.

We tried the phone but it was PIN-locked and after we'd tried a few combinations it ran out of power. We shouted and screamed until our throats raged. All we heard in response was our echo, mocking us. Sometimes it feels like we are on another planet, with not another human being for miles around. Christmas is approaching. There must be people out looking for us, but it's hard to believe that here, surrounded by this terrible, enduring silence.

Escape is not an option, so now we simply survive. We chewed our nails until our fingers bled, then sucked up the blood greedily. We licked the condensation from the tiles at dawn, but still our stomachs ached. We talked about eating our clothes . . . but thought better of it. It's freezing at night and all that keeps us from dying of hypothermia is our scant clothing and the heat we glean from each other.

Is it my imagination or have our embraces become less warm? Less secure? Since it happened, we have clung to each other day and night, willing each other to survive, desperate not to be left alone in this awful place. We play games to pass the time, imagining what we will do after the cavalry arrives—what we will eat, what we will say to our families, what we will get for Christmas. But slowly these games have tailed off as we realize that we were brought here for a purpose and that there will be no happy ending for us.

"Amy?"

Silence.

"Amy, please say something."

She doesn't look at me. She doesn't talk to me. Have I lost her for good? I try to imagine what she's thinking, but I can't.

Perhaps there is nothing left to say. We have tried everything, explored every inch of our prison, looking for a means of escape. The only thing we haven't touched is the gun. It sits there still, calling to us.

I raise my head and catch Amy looking at it. She meets my eye and drops hers. Could she pick it up? A fortnight ago, I'd have said no way. But now? Trust is a fragile thing—hard to earn, easy to lose. I'm not sure of anything anymore.

All I do know is that one of us is going to die.

4

Stepping out into the crisp evening air, Helen Grace felt relaxed and happy. Slowing her pace, she savored this moment of peace, casting an amused eye over the throng of shoppers that surrounded her.

She was heading for Southampton's Christmas market. Ranged along the southern flank of the WestQuay shopping center, the market was an annual event—an opportunity to buy original, handcrafted presents that weren't on any Amazon wish list. Helen hated Christmas, but every year without fail she bought something for Anna and Marie. It was her one festive indulgence and she always made the most of it. She bought jewelry, scented candles and other trinkets but didn't stint on the comestibles either, snapping up dates, chocolates, an obscenely expensive Christmas pudding and a pretty packet of peppermint creams—Marie was particularly partial to those.

She retrieved her Kawasaki from the WestQuay car park and blasted through the city center traffic, heading southeast toward Weston. She was speeding away from excitement and affluence and toward deprivation and despair, drawn inexorably toward the five monolithic tower blocks that dominate the skyline there. For years they've greeted those approaching Southampton by sea and in the past they were worthy of such an honor, being imposing, futuristic and optimistic. But it was a very different story now.

Melbourne Tower was by far the most dilapidated. Four years ago, an illegal drugs factory had exploded on the sixth floor. The damage was extensive, the heart ripped out of the building. The council promised to rebuild it, but the recession put paid to their plans. It was still technically scheduled for renovation but no one believed it would happen now. So the building remained as it was, wounded and unloved, abandoned by the vast majority of the families who used to live there. Now it was the terrain of junkies, squatters and those with nowhere else to go. It was a nasty, forgotten place.

Helen parked her motorbike a safe distance from the towers and continued on foot. Women generally didn't walk the projects alone at night, but Helen never felt concerned for her safety. She was known here and people tended to steer clear, which suited her fine. All was quiet tonight, apart from some dogs sniffing around a burned-out car, so Helen picked her way past the needles and condoms and stepped inside Melbourne Tower.

On the fourth floor, she paused outside flat 408. It had once been a nice, comfortable council flat, but now it looked like Fort

Knox. The front door was riddled with dead bolts, but more strik-ing were the metal grilles—padlocked firmly shut—that reinforced the main entrance. The vile graffiti—*flid, retard, mong*—that cov-ered the exterior gave a clue as to why the flat was so protected.

It was the home of Marie and Anna Storey. Anna was severely disabled, unable to speak, feed herself or go to the toilet. Anna, now fourteen, needed her middle-aged mother to do everything for her, so her mum did the best she could. Living on benefits and handouts, buying food from Lidl, being sparing with the heating. They would have been okay like that—these were the cards they'd been dealt and Marie was not one to be bitter—had it not been for the local yobs. The fact that they had nothing to do and were from broken homes was no excuse. These kids were just nasty thugs who enjoyed belittling, bullying and attacking a vulnerable woman and child.

Helen knew all this because she'd taken a special interest in them. One of the scrotes—a vicious, acne-covered dropout called Steven Green—had attempted to burn out their flat. The fire crew had got there in time and the damage was contained to the hallway and front room, but the effect on Marie and Anna had been devas-tating. They were utterly terrified when Helen interviewed them. This was attempted murder and someone needed to be called to ac-count for it. She did her best, but the case never went to court for lack of witnesses. Helen urged her to move, but Marie was stubborn. The flat was their family home and had been kitted out specially to deal with Anna's mobility limitations. Why should they have to move? Marie sold what valuables she still possessed to fortify the flat. Four years later, the drugs factory blew up. Before that, the lift had worked fine and flat 408 was basically a happy home. Now it was a prison.

Social Services was supposed to call round to keep an eye on them, but they avoided this place like the plague and visits were fleeting at best. And so Helen, who had little to keep her home at night, would pop in. Which was why she'd been there when Steven Green and company returned to finish the job. He was high as usual and clutching a petrol can that he was trying to light with a homemade fuse. He didn't get the chance. Helen's baton caught him on the elbow, then across the neck, sending him sprawling to the floor. The others were caught off guard by the sudden appearance of a copper and dropped their petrol bombs to flee. Some of them made it; some of them didn't. Helen had been well trained in how to take the legs out from under fleeing suspects. She foiled the attack and not long after had the distinct pleasure of watching Steven Green and three of his closest friends get a substantial prison sentence. Some days the job really did give back.

Helen suppressed a shiver. The dingy corridors, the broken lives, the graffiti and filth were too redolent of her own upbringing not to provoke a reaction. It conjured up memories she'd fought hard to suppress and which she forced back down now. She was here for Marie and Anna—she refused to let anything darken her mood today.

She knocked on the door three times—their special code—and after much unlocking, the door swung open.

"Meals on Wheels?" Helen ventured.

"Piss off," came the predictable reply.

Helen smiled as Marie opened the outer grille for her to enter. Already her dark thoughts were receding—Marie's "warm" welcome always had that effect on her. Once inside, Helen doled out her gifts, received hers and felt utterly at peace. For a brief moment, flat 408 was her sanctuary from a dark and violent world.

5

The rain poured down, washing away her tears. It should have felt cleansing, but it didn't—she was too far gone for that. She plunged madly through the tangled foliage of the wood, not heeding her direction. She just needed to keep going. Away. Away. Away.

Thorns tore at her face; stones lacerated her feet. But on she went. Her eyes scanned desperately for someone, something, but all she could see were trees. For a moment she had a terrible thought—was she even in England still? She screamed for help, but her cries were feeble, her throat too hoarse to function.

At Sampson's Winter Wonderland, families were queuing patiently for Santa's Grotto. The whole site was really just a handful of tents hastily erected on muddy farmland, but the kids seemed to like it. Father of four Freddie Williams had just bitten into his first mince pie of the season when he saw her. Through the driving rain, she appeared ghostly. Freddie's mince pie hung in midair as she limped slowly but deliberately across the site, her eyes fixed on him. On closer inspection, she wasn't ghostly; she was pitiful—bedraggled, bleeding and deathly pale. Freddie didn't want any part of her—she looked mental—but his legs wouldn't move, rendered immobile by the fierceness of her gaze. She covered the last few yards quicker than he'd expected and suddenly he was reeling backward as she launched herself upon him. His mince pie somersaulted into the sky, landing with a satisfying *splat* in a puddle.

In the site office, swathed in a blanket, she didn't look any less mental. She wouldn't tell them where she'd been or where she was from. She didn't even seem to know what day it was. In fact, all they could get out of her was that she was called Amy and that she'd murdered her boyfriend that morning.

Helen jammed the brakes and came to a halt outside Southampton Central Police Station. The futuristic glass and limestone building towered above her, commanding fantastic views over the city and the docks. It was only a year or two old and by any measure was an impressive nick. State-of-the-art custody facilities, a Crown Prosecution Service unit on-site, SmartWater testing facilities—it had everything a modern copper needed. She parked up and walked inside.

"Sleeping on the job, Jerry?"

The desk sergeant snapped out of his daydream and tried to look as busy as possible. They always sat up a bit straighter when Helen entered. This wasn't just because she was a detective inspector; it also had something to do with the way she carried herself. Entering the building clad in her bike leathers, she was six feet of driving ambition and energy. Never late, never hungover, never sick. She lived and breathed her job with a fierceness they could only dream of.

Helen headed straight for the offices of the Major Incident Team. Southampton's flagship nick might be revolutionary, but the city it watched over remained unchanged. As Helen surveyed the caseload, she sagged a little at the predictable familiarity of it all. A domestic argument that had ended in murder—two lives ruined and a young child taken into care. The attempted murder of a Saints fan by traveling Leeds United supporters, and most recently the brutal killing of an eighty-two-year-old man in a botched mugging. His attacker had dropped the stolen wallet while fleeing the scene, handing the police a clean fingerprint and a swift ID. The perpetrator was well-known to Southampton police—just another lowlife who had devastated an unsuspecting family in the run-up to Christmas. Helen was due to brief Crown Prosecution Service lawyers on the particulars this morning. She opened the file, determined that the case against this little thug should be absolutely watertight.

"Don't get too comfortable. Job's on."

Mark, her DS, approached. A handsome and talented copper, Detective Sergeant Mark Fuller had worked hand in glove with Helen for the last five years. Murder, child abduction, rape, sex trafficking—he'd helped her solve numerous unpleasant cases and she had come to rely on his dedication, intuition and bravery. A nasty divorce had taken its toll, however, and recently he'd become erratic and unreliable. Helen was depressed to notice that he once again smelled of booze.

"Young girl who says she's killed her boyfriend."

Mark extracted a photo from his file and handed it to Helen. It had the distinctive Missing Persons stamp on the top right-hand corner.

"Victim's name is Sam Fisher."

Helen looked down at the snapshot of a fresh-faced young man. Clean-cut, optimistic, even a touch naive. Mark paused a moment, allowing Helen to examine the photo, before handing her another.

"And our suspect. Amy Anderson."

Helen couldn't hide her surprise as she took in the image. A beautiful bohemian girl—twenty-one years old at the very most. With long, flowing hair, striking cobalt eyes and delicate lips, she looked the definition of youth and innocence. Helen picked up her jacket.

"Let's go, then."

"Do you want to drive or shall—?"

"I will."

They walked down to the car pool in silence. En route, Helen extracted her DC, who'd been liaising with Missing Persons. The irrepressibly perky Detective Constable Charlene "Charlie" Brooks was a good officer, diligent and spirited, who resolutely refused to dress like a cop. Today's offering was skintight leather trousers. It was beyond Helen's remit to take her to task over her dress sense, but she was tempted to nevertheless.

In the car, the stale alcohol on Mark's breath smelled even

stronger. Helen cast a sideways look at him before rolling down the window.

"So what have we got?" she asked.

Charlie already had the file open.

"Amy Anderson. Reported missing a little over two weeks ago. Last seen at a gig in London. She e-mailed her mother on the evening of the second of December to say she was hitching home with Sam and would be back before midnight. No sign of either since. Her mother phoned it in."

"Then what?"

"She turns up at Sampson's this morning. Says she's killed her boyfriend, then clams up. Won't say a word to anybody now."

"And where's she been all this time?"

Mark and Charlie looked at each other. Mark eventually replied:

"Your guess is as good as mine."

They parked the car in the Winter Wonderland car park and marched to the site office. Entering the tired trailer office, Helen was shocked by the sight that greeted her. The young woman huddling beneath a tatty blanket looked wild, unhinged and painfully thin.

"Hello, Amy. My name's Detective Inspector Helen Grace—you can call me Helen. May I sit down?"

No response. Helen carefully eased herself into the chair opposite.

"I'd like to talk to you about Sam. Is that okay?"

The girl looked up, a horrified expression spread over her

ravaged features. Helen studied her face intently, mentally comparing it to the photo she'd seen earlier. If it hadn't been for her piercing blue eyes and the historic scar on her chin, they'd have struggled to ID her. Her once lustrous hair was lank, knotted and greasy. Her fingernails were long and dirty. Her face, arms and legs looked like a frenzy of self-harm. And then there was the smell—that's what hit you first. Sweet. Pungent. Revolting.

"I need to find Sam. Can you tell me where he is?"

Amy closed her eyes. A single tear escaped its confines and ran down her cheek.

"Where is he, Amy?"

A long silence and then finally she whispered:

"The woods."

Amy categorically refused to leave the sanctuary of the trailer office, so Helen had to use the dog. She left Charlie to babysit Amy, ordering Mark with her. Simpson, the retriever, buried his nose in the bloodstained rags that had once been Amy's clothes, then shot off through the woods.

It wasn't hard to see where she'd been. Her progress through the woods had been so blind, so crashing, that she'd rent great holes in the thick undergrowth. Bits of cloth, bits of skin decorated her path. Simpson hoovered these up, bounding through the brush. Helen kept pace behind him and Mark was determined not to be outrun by a woman. But he was laboring, sweating alcohol.

The lonely building came into view. A municipal swimming baths, long since earmarked for demolition, a sad relic of fun times gone by. Simpson clawed at the padlocked door, then broke away, racing around the building before eventually coming to rest by a broken window. Fresh blood decorated the cracked panes. They had found Amy's cocoon.

Getting inside was tough. Despite the building's derelict state, care had been taken to secure every possible entry and exit. Secure it against whom? Nobody lived round here. Eventually the lock was forced and the usual ballet began, shoes cased in sterile covers skating over the floor.

And there he was. Lying fifteen feet below them in the diving pool. A brief delay as a long ladder was sought, then Helen was in the pool, face-to-face with Amy's "Sam." He was a strait-laced kid, bound for a law firm, but you wouldn't have known that to look at him. He looked like the corpse of any old dosser you might find on the streets. His clothes were stained with urine and excrement, his fingernails cracked and dirty. And his face. His gaunt face was contorted into a hideous expression—fear, agony and horror written in his twisted features. In life he had been handsome and winning. In death he was repulsive.

6

Would they ever stop torturing her?

Amy thought she would be safe at Southampton General. That she would be left alone to heal and grieve. But they were intent on *tormenting* her. They refused to let her eat or drink, even though she begged them to. Her tongue was swollen, they said, her stomach too contracted, and her bowels might tear if solids passed through them. So they'd hooked her up to a drip. Maybe it was the right thing to do, but it wasn't what she *wanted*. When had they ever gone without food for over two weeks? What did they know?

She had a morphine drip too, which helped a bit, though they were scrupulously careful not to overfill it. She operated it with her left hand, punching the button when the pain became too much. Her right hand was cuffed to the bed. The nurses bloody loved that, speculating in loud stage whispers about what she'd done. Killed her baby? Killed her husband? They really were enjoying themselves.

And then—God help her—they'd let her mother in. She went berserk at that, shouting and screaming until her bewildered mum had to retreat on doctor's orders. What the *fuck* were they thinking? She couldn't see her mother, not now. Not like this.

She just wanted to be left alone. She would concentrate fiercely on the things around her, staring at the intricate cotton weave of her pillowcase, gazing for hours on end at the hypnotic glowing filament in her bedside lamp. That way she could zone out, keep her thoughts at bay. And when a vision of Sam *did* spring up from nowhere, she would hit the morphine trigger and for a moment she'd drift away to a happier place.

But she knew in her heart that she would not be left in peace for long. Demons were circling her now, dragging her back to the living death she'd left behind. She could see the police hovering outside, waiting to come in and question her. Didn't they get that she *never* wanted to answer those questions? Hadn't she suffered enough?

"Tell them I can't see them."

The nurse who was busy studying her charts looked up.

"Tell them I've got a fever," Amy continued. "That I'm asleep . . ."

"I can't stop them, love," the nurse replied evenly. "Best get it over with, eh?"

She could never suffer enough. Amy knew that really. She had killed the man she loved and there was no way back from that.

7

"Tell me how you got out of the pool, Amy."

"A ladder."

"I didn't see a ladder there."

Amy scowled and turned away. Pulling the hospital blankets up round her chin, she receded into herself once more. Helen regarded her, intrigued. If she was lying, she was a bloody good actress. She shot a look at Mark, then continued:

"What sort of ladder was it?"

"A rope ladder. It was dropped down just after I—"

Tears stung Amy's eyes and she dropped her head to her chest. There *were* mild burns on the palms of Amy's hands. Consistent perhaps with someone scrambling up a rope ladder? Helen gave herself a mental slap—why was she even considering the possibility? Amy's story was insane. According to her, they'd been picked up on the motorway, drugged, abducted, starved—and then forced to commit murder. Why would anyone do such a thing? On the face of it, Amy and Sam were two good kids, but the answer to this awful crime must lie within their own lives.

"Tell me about your relationship with Sam."

At this Amy started to sob.

"Perhaps now would be a good time to break, Detective Inspector?" Amy's mother had insisted on a solicitor being present.

"We're not finished yet," Helen snapped back.

"But you can see she's exhausted. Surely we ca—"

"All I see is a dead boy called Sam Fisher. Who's been shot in the back. At close range. By your client."

"My client doesn't deny pulling the tr—"

"But she won't tell us *why*."

"I've *told* you why," Amy spat out in response.

"Yes, and it's a great story, Amy. *But it doesn't make any sense.*"

Helen let her words hang in the air. Without having to be told, Mark took his cue to ratchet up the pressure.

"Nobody saw you. Or the van, Amy. The truckers didn't. The traffic cops didn't. The other kids hitching that route didn't. So why don't you cut the crap and tell us why you killed your boyfriend? Did he hit you? Did he threaten you? Why did he take you to that awful place?"

Amy said nothing, refusing even to look up. It was as if Mark hadn't spoken at all. Helen took up the baton, softening her tone.

"Don't think you're the first, Amy. To fall for a nice guy who turned out to be sadistic and violent. It's not your fault—no one's judging you, and if you can tell me what happened, what went wrong, then I promise I can help you. Did he assault you? Were others involved? Why did he take you there?"

Still nothing. Impatience seeped back into Helen's voice.

"Two hours ago, I had to tell Sam's mum that he'd been shot and killed. What she needs, what his little brothers and sisters need, is someone to be held to account for this. And right now you're the only person in the frame. So for your own sake as well as theirs, stop bullshitting and tell me the truth. Why did you do it, Amy? Why?"

There was a long silence. Then Amy looked up, angry eyes flaring through the tears:

"*She* made me do it."

8

"So what do you think, boss?"

For the first time in her life, Helen couldn't answer. Yes or no, guilty or not guilty, Helen Grace always had an answer. But not here. This was something different. All her experience told her that Amy was lying. The abduction story was crazy enough, but the fact that the perpetrator was a lone female was the clincher. Female murderers kill their husbands, their children or people in their care. They don't go for stranger abductions, nor do they favor high-risk scenarios such as the one Amy had described, where they are outnumbered by their victims. Even if this one *had*, how was she strong enough to maneuver two grown adults out of a van and into the diving pool? Helen was more than tempted to throw the book at Amy. Perhaps when she was facing a murder charge, she would finally give up the truth.

And yet, why would she make up such a story unless it *was* true? Amy was a smart, together girl with no history of mental illness. Through it all, her testimony had been clear and consistent. Her description of her "abductor" had been precise—dirty blond crop, sunglasses, short grimy nails—and she'd stuck to it religiously. Right down to the tiny details about how she'd over-revved the van in the low gears. And it was clear that she loved—*really* loved—Sam and was devastated by his death. Everyone described them as inseparable, two halves of a whole. They had met at Bristol University; then each had applied to do a master's degree in science at Warwick so they could stay together, deferring entry to working life and possible separation. They didn't have much cash, but during their time together they had hitched all round the country, seldom holidaying with anyone else.

Forensics had linked her to the gun, so there was no doubt she did it, but they'd also confirmed her story about their captivity. Their physical state—the hair, the nails—plus the human waste in the tank all suggested that they'd been there for at least two weeks before she killed him. Had they given up hope and drawn straws? Made a deal?

"Why him and not you?" Amy had collapsed again, but Helen repeated the question.

Eventually Amy managed to speak:

"Because he asked me to."

An act of love, then. An act of self-sacrifice. What a thing to have on your conscience . . . if it was true. And that was what was nagging at her—the plain fact that Amy was destroyed by what had happened. Not just traumatized. She was destroyed, imploding under the weight of guilt. It was an emotion Helen knew all too well, and in spite of everything she found herself feeling for Amy. Maybe she'd been too hard on this vulnerable young woman.

It couldn't be true. Because *why* would anyone do this? What on earth did they—"she"—stand to gain? She wasn't even there to watch, according to Amy, so what was the point? It couldn't be true. And yet, when Helen replied to Mark's characteristically direct question, she found herself saying:

"I think she's telling the truth."

9

Ben Holland loathed his weekly trip to Bournemouth. To him it was pointless, a day lost. But the firm was very strong on face time between their various offices, so once a week Ben and Peter (Portsmouth) would share sandwiches and coffee with Malcolm and Eleanor (Bournemouth) and Hellie and Sarah (London). They would discuss the finer points of maritime law, banking litigation and international probate—before reverting to bitching about their respective clients. It was sometimes mildly informative, even entertaining, but once you'd factored in the travel from and back to Portsmouth it was all just a colossal waste of time.

This one was proving to be even worse than usual. As was customary, Ben had given Peter a lift to and from the meeting in

Bournemouth, allowing his more senior colleague to drink over lunch. Peter was a partner with a quick brain and a record of getting results. He was also boorish and repetitive and suffered from BO. It was bad enough being in a conference room with Peter. Now Ben was stuck in the car with him for two whole hours. At least he would have been, if they hadn't run out of petrol.

Ben pulled out his phone, swearing under his breath. His eyes widened in dismay.

"No reception."

"What?" replied Peter.

"No reception. You?"

Peter checked his phone.

"Nothing."

A long silence.

Ben tried hard to contain his rage. How many cats had he kicked to be here, in the middle of the New Forest, with Peter, and night falling? Ben had filled the tank up at the Esso station just outside Bournemouth—the petrol was cheapest there—and yet not an hour later the tank had been empty. He hadn't believed the fuel warning sign when it lit up, but anyway he'd been sure he'd have enough to get to Southampton at least. But moments after the fuel warning had first pinged, the car had spluttered to a halt. Sometimes life just keeps kicking you. Would they have to walk to a petrol station? Spend the night together!?

"Platinum service with the RAC breakdown and what use is it?" Peter offered helpfully.

Ben looked up and down the quiet woodland lane. Peter wasn't saying it, but it had been Ben's idea to cut through the New Forest. He always did this, avoiding the M27 around Southampton by using a sneaky shortcut that brought him out at Calmore, but to-day it had backfired badly. Ben had a feeling that this would be mentioned, but only once the ordeal was over. Peter would make great capital out of it. He was just biding his time.

"Are you going to walk or shall I?" asked Peter.

It was a rhetorical question. Seniority rules and, besides, Peter had "bad knees." So it was down to Ben. Looking at the map, he saw that there were some holiday cottages only a mile or two away. Perhaps if he hurried he could make it there before it got too dark. Turning up his collar against the cold, he nodded to Peter and trudged off down the road.

"We'll meet again . . ." sang Peter.

Tosser, thought Ben.

But then, suddenly, a stroke of luck. In the gloaming, Ben could make out two pinpricks of light. He squinted. Yup, no doubt about it. Headlights. For the first time that day, Ben felt his body relax. There was a God after all. He waved his hands vigorously in the air, but the van was already slowing down to help.

Thank goodness, thought Ben. Salvation.

10

Diane Anderson hadn't seen her daughter for over three weeks. And she wasn't seeing her now, even though Amy was pinned to her chest in a suffocating hug. They'd cleaned her up at the hospital—let her have a shower and wash her hair—but she still didn't look like Amy.

The attractive police officer—Charlie—had accompanied them home. She said it was to help Amy, to make her feel safe as she rejoined the outside world, but she was a spy. Diane was sure of that. There to wait, watch and report back. Her daughter wasn't off the hook yet. The two uniformed officers stationed outside their door made that clear. Were they there to protect her, or to stop her from running away? Still, at least they had seen off the press. A reporter from the local rag had resorted to shouting through the letter box, asking in the coarsest terms imaginable why Amy had killed her boyfriend. The fact that the reporter was a young woman made it even worse—what possessed these people?

"Amy shot Sam." That was how the stern one—Detective Inspector Grace—had put it. It didn't make any sense. Amy would never shoot anyone, least of all Sam. She'd never even held a gun before. This wasn't America.

She had turned to her husband, Richard, expecting him to correct the police, clear matters up, but his face had been the mirror of hers: blank shock. For a moment a flash of anger had coursed through her—Richard was never there when he was really needed—before she had pulled herself up and once again confronted the bitter present. Amy *loved* Sam. In many an idle moment, Diane had pondered what it would be like if—when—they got married. She'd always assumed that Amy would follow modern practice and cohabit without getting married. But Amy had surprised her by confiding that she definitely wanted to tie the knot, when the time was right. Typical Amy, though, she would do it with a twist. There was no question of her wearing white, and she was determined that Diane should give her away rather than her dad. Would Richard wear that? Would other people like it or would they think it odd? With a jolt, Diane realized she was daydreaming again. About a wedding that would never happen.

None of it made any sense. Sam hadn't been violent or aggressive, so it couldn't have been self-defense. DI Grace had been infuriatingly tight-lipped about what had happened—"Better Amy tells you in her own time." But Amy hadn't said a word. She was mute. Diane tried to reach her—by making her malt shakes, opening some French Fancies (a childhood favorite), kitting out the bedroom they'd now share with all her old toys and knick-knacks. But none of it had worked. So they sat there, a stilted threesome. Charlie perching on the end of the sofa, trying not to spill her tea, Diane plating yet more unwanted cakes and Amy just staring into space, a shell of the vibrant girl she once was.

11

It was an ambush. The woman was lying in wait, and as Helen got out of her car, she pounced.

"Spare a couple of minutes, Inspector?"

Helen's heart sank. It was beginning already.

"Nice to see you, Emilia, but as you'll appreciate I'm very busy."

Helen moved off but an arm shot out, stopping her in her tracks. Helen glared—*Are you serious?*—and her adversary took the hint, slowly releasing her grip. Unabashed, Emilia Garanita broke into a broad grin. She was a striking figure—youthful and svelte but also broken and disfigured. As a teenager she'd set hearts on fire, but at only eighteen had been the victim of a savage acid attack. If you looked at her profile from the left, she was handsome and attractive. From the right, you felt only pity—her features distorted, her cosmetic eye unmoving. She was known locally as "Beauty and the Beast" and was the chief crime reporter for the *Southampton Evening News*.

"The Amy Anderson case. We know she killed him but we don't know why. What did he *do* to her?"

Helen tried to conceal her disdain—she felt sure it was Emilia who'd been shouting through the Anderson letter box earlier—but it wasn't a wise move to antagonize the press this early in an investigation.

"Was it a sexual thing? Did he beat her? Are you looking for anyone else?" she continued.

"You know the drill, Emilia—as soon as we have anything to say, Media Liaison will be in touch. Now if you'll excuse m—"

"I'm just curious, because you've released her. She's not even on bail. You normally make them sweat a bit longer than that, don't you?"

"We don't make anyone 'sweat,' Emilia. I'm a by-the-book girl—you know that. Which is why all communication with the press will be via the usual channels, okay?"

Helen flashed her best smile and continued on her way. She had won the first skirmish in what would no doubt prove to be a long campaign. Emilia had crime in her blood. The eldest of six children, she had become famous when her drug dealer dad was sentenced to eighteen years' imprisonment for using his children as drug mules. Ever since they were tiny, Emilia and her five siblings had been forced to swallow condoms of cocaine as they journeyed home to Southampton docks from one of their many Caribbean cruises. When her Portuguese father went to jail, his paymasters tried to force Emilia to resume her life as a drug mule to help recover their losses. She refused, so they punished her—two broken ankles and half a liter of sulfuric acid in the face. She'd written a book about it, which eventually took her to journalism. Despite the fact that she still walked with a limp, she was scared of no one and was utterly tireless in her pursuit of a story.

"Don't be a stranger," Emilia called out as Helen buzzed into the police mortuary.

Helen knew that life had just got a little bit harder. But she had no time to ponder that now.

Helen had a date with a corpse.

12

He looked like a ghost. The carefree, handsome face that beamed out from his Facebook page bore no resemblance to the sunken death mask that now confronted Helen. Sam's emaciated body lay on the mortuary slab in front of her, mocking the happy, hopeful person he used to be. It was a profoundly distressing sight.

Helen turned away, distracting herself by checking on the progress of the medical examiner, Jim Grieves. Even after thirty years in the business, Jim still took an age to clean and robe himself for an autopsy. The endless hand washing made him appear like a modern-day Lady Macbeth (albeit an overweight one) and watching his clumsy attempts to sheathe his hands in sterile gloves made you want to march over there and do it for him yourself. Some officers actually had. Others thought he was past it, but

Helen knew better and didn't rush him. He was worth waiting for and there was something vaguely miraculous about the slow transformation from a hefty, heavily tattooed oaf to a gowned, incisive ME who had helped open up many a case for Helen.

"What I am about to say comes with all the usual caveats, as I'm being rushed yet again . . ."

Helen smiled—used to Jim's grumblings—and let him go on. She *was* rushing him, but needs must. Telling Sam's mother about his death had been awful, partly because Helen had been able to tell her so *little*. Olivia Fisher had been widowed some years back, so she had no partner to support her now. Somehow, alone, she had to help her children come to terms with the death of their beloved older brother, and Helen had to give her the tools to do that. So she needed to corroborate or destroy Amy's story fast.

Jim had finished grumbling. He turned to Sam's body and began his summing up:

"Single gunshot to the back. The bullet entered under the right shoulder blade and ended up in the rib cage. I'm using technical terms, so do tell me if there's anything you don't understand, okay?"

Helen let that ride. Jim's sarcasm was a feature of every autopsy she'd ever attended. He carried on without waiting for a reaction:

"Cause of death: cardiac arrest. Possibly caused by blood loss but more likely by the shock of the impact. He was in a bad way even before he was shot. Evidence of emaciation in the torso, limbs and the face—note the sunken eye sockets, the blood around his gums, the hair loss. Bladder and bowels basically empty. The stomach contained fragments of cloth, hair, tile mastic and also human flesh."

Jim moved round the table to lift Sam's right arm.

"The flesh was his own, bitten from his right forearm. By the looks of it, I'd say he managed three or four mouthfuls before he gave up."

Helen closed her eyes, the horror of Sam's last days sinking in, then forced herself to open them again. Jim held Sam's ravaged forearm up for her to get a good look, then gently laid it down again.

"I would estimate he hadn't eaten properly or taken in liquid for at least two weeks, probably more. His body would have been living off fat reserves during that time, and when they ran out, it would have started to leach nutrients from his internal organs. He was a whisker away from total organ failure when he was killed. From what I've been told about the girl's medical state, she was going the same way. Another few days and they both would have been dead of natural causes."

Jim paused once more, this time to ferret through his paperwork.

"Bloods. What you'd expect from someone suffering extreme dehydration on a fast track to organ failure. The only unusual constituent was trace elements of benzodiazepine. I expect you'll also find traces in her blood and stronger traces in their waste."

Helen nodded—forensics had already confirmed traces of the powerful sedative in the excreta recovered from the diving pool. Helen suppressed her growing anxiety, but this was all heading one way now. Jim carried on for another ten minutes; then Helen called time on it. She had all she needed.

Against all the odds, Amy's story was starting to stack up. Forensics had found particles of rope near a corner of the pool, tallying with the use of a rope ladder as Amy's means of escape. Furthermore, their recovered clothes had deep soil stains on them, suggesting Amy and Sam could have been dragged from a vehicle across open ground to the abandoned pool. Could a woman have dragged Sam by herself—all twelve stone of him—or would she have needed an accomplice?

As she headed back to Southampton Central, Helen knew this would consume her totally from now on. She would not rest until she had solved this strange crime. Entering the incident room, she was pleased to see that Mark was already cracking the whip. There were numerous practical and bureaucratic issues that could stymie a major investigation like this and Helen needed things to run like clockwork. Mark was the classic DS—an abrasive but effective instrument—adept at making everyone row in the same direction. He'd rounded up a good team of officers—DCs Bridges, Grounds, Sanderson, McAndrew—in addition to support staff; already the investigation was coming to life in front of her eyes. Mark hurried over when he saw her enter.

"What are we going to tell the press, boss?"

A good question and one Helen had been chewing on since she left Jim Grieves. Emilia Garanita wasn't going to go away and there would be others behind her. A young girl had shot her boyfriend in a deserted location. It was horrific, and thus made good copy.

"As little as possible. Until we're in control of this, we can't let out there's a third party involved. So we call it a domestic but go gently on the detail. The press will infer all sorts of things about Sam and why Amy killed him . . ."

"But we don't want to blacken his name unnecessarily."

"Exactly. He and his mum deserve better than that."

"Okay, let's play it tight for now."

He headed back to work. He was unquestionably rough around the edges—rangy, unshaven, rugged—but on form Mark was a good copper to have on your team. Helen hoped it would last.

Satisfied everything was in hand, she allowed herself five minutes for a cup of tea. She was tired—the interview with Amy had been grueling and the visit to the mortuary even worse. She wanted to tune out for a moment, but her brain wouldn't let her. Sam's awful death had got to her and she couldn't shake the image of his lifeless, twisted face. What a thing for his mother to have to see.

She was so deep in thought that she didn't notice Charlie until she was virtually on top of her.

"Boss. You'll want to see this."

The day had already been full of nasty surprises, but Helen sensed she was about to get another.

Charlie handed her a pair of photos—two smartly dressed business types, one in his thirties, one a fair bit older.

"Ben Holland and Peter Brightston. Reported missing three days ago. They were traveling back from a legal powwow in Bournemouth. Never made it home."

A sickening feeling was creeping over Helen.

"Their car was found in the New Forest. Local plod and the park rangers have scoured every inch of the forest. No sign."

"And?" Helen sensed there was more.

"Coats, bags and wallets still in the car. Their mobiles were found nearby—the SIM cards have been deliberately destroyed."

Another abduction, then. And this one even stranger than the first. Two grown men—smart, strong and able to fend for themselves—had vanished into thin air.

13

How do you wake yourself when you're dreaming? When you're in the midst of a nightmare, how do you climb out of the abyss?

Ben Holland rolled these thoughts round and round. *I must be dreaming. I am dreaming. Perhaps Jennie and I'd hit the liquor store after work and picked up a bottle of Bison Grass? Maybe I'm dreaming a vodka dream right now? Any second now I'll wake up with my head pounding and a stupid smile on my face . . .*

Ben opened his eyes. He'd known all along of course—the smell down there was overpowering. How could you imagine you were anywhere else? And even if you could, then the constant whimpering from Peter would bring you back to your senses. Ever since their abduction, Ben had been a riot of anger and disbelief. But Peter had opted for despair.

"Peter, would you shut up for God's sake . . ."

"Fuck you," was the reply, spat back. *Where are your leadership qualities now?* Ben thought venomously.

They were trapped. It made no sense, but it was true. One minute they had been in the van, relieved and happy; the next they had woken up here. Groggy, bruised and covered in thick, clinging dust. Ben had stumbled to his feet in disbelief, screwing up his eyes to penetrate the gloom and make sense of their surroundings. They were in some sort of giant silo or storage facility, the floor of which was covered with coal. This was what covered them, coal dust creeping into their ears and eyes, making their tongues thick and dirty. Instinctively Ben scrambled toward the sides. The going was tough, the surface constantly shifting beneath his feet, but eventually he made it. Cold, smooth steel. Using the wall as a guide, he stumbled round, hoping against hope for a door, a hatch, some means of escape. But the sides were smooth and, having done a couple of laps, he gave up. Casting his eyes upward, he noticed light spilling through the joint of a massive hatch. This was how they had fallen into this strange hell.

It was then that Ben became aware of the cuts and bruises that covered his face and torso. It was a good twenty-foot drop down from the hatch and the compacted coal wouldn't have made for a soft landing. Suddenly everything hurt. The shock was wearing off and his battered body was protesting. A noise made him turn. Peter was stumbling toward him—his face a picture of dull, stupid astonishment. He was looking for explanations, but he would get none from Ben. And it was as they were standing there, exhausted and hopeless, that the phone rang.

They both froze for a moment, then simultaneously scrambled for it, Ben just getting there first.

After they'd been given their deadly ultimatum, they both laughed maniacally, as if the whole thing were some preposterous joke. Slowly, however, the laughter evaporated.

"Let's call the office." Suddenly Ben needed to be out of this pit.

"Good idea. Call Carol—she'll know what to do," said Peter, feeding off Ben's energy.

Ben punched in the familiar numbers. But the phone was PIN-locked. Four small digits separating them from freedom.

"What shall we try?"

Already Ben's eye was drawn to the battery sign at the top right of the screen, flashing low.

"We've only got a few goes at this. What shall we try?" Ben's voice was tight, the impossibility of their task starting to register.

"I don't know. One two three four?"

Ben's look was withering.

"Well, I don't fucking know," Peter responded angrily. "What year were you born?"

It was desperate, but as good as anything else. Ben tried Peter's birth year, then his own. He was attempting a third combination when the phone died in their hands.

"Shit."

The word echoed around the vault.

"What now?"

The pair stood quiet, staring forlornly at the locked hatch above them. Light seeped in through the cracks, illuminating the gun nestling quietly on the floor between them.

"Nothing. There's nothing . . ."

Ben's words petered out as he turned and retreated into the dark. Slumping down in the coal, he was suddenly overwhelmed with despair. Why was this happening to them? What had they *done*?

He shot a glance across at Peter, who was pacing up and down, muttering to himself. Ben had never liked Peter, but he didn't want to kill the guy, for God's sake. Perhaps the gun wasn't real? He got up to check, but the look Peter shot him made him sit straight back down.

Ben sat there in his own private hell. He had never been very good with enclosed spaces. He always liked to know where his escape route was in any given situation. But now he was trapped—and, worse than that, trapped underground. Buried alive. Already his hands were beginning to shake. He felt light-headed and sweaty; lights danced in front of his eyes. He hadn't had a panic attack for years, but he could feel one coming on now. The world was closing in on him.

"I've got to get out." Ben was stumbling to his feet. Peter turned, surprised and unnerved. "Please, Peter, I've got to get out. *Help! Somebody please help!*"

He shouted and screamed to try to ward off the attack, but felt faint and stopped. Surely someone would find them and rescue them? They *had* to. The alternative was unthinkable.

14

Mark Fuller left the nick shortly after Charlie had dropped her bombshell. A whole new line of inquiry had opened up, but for now it was the data compilers and uniformed officers who would carry the load. A massive double- and triple-checking of facts was taking place and it would only be once the two men's disappearance was confirmed as suspicious that Criminal Investigation Department officers would be deployed. Tomorrow looked like it would be a long day for Mark, Charlie and the rest of the team, so Helen had sent them home to rest up. But Mark had no intention of sleeping.

Instead, he drove across town to suburban Shirley, parking up in a quiet residential street. He never used his own car, so as not to give himself away. The beaten-up Golf with the tinted windows was designed to deflect attention from its true purpose, and it worked—passersby wrote it off as another teenager's attempt to soup up an old wreck. It was the perfect vantage point from which to watch undetected.

A seven-year-old girl appeared in the window and Mark sat up, his eyes glued to her. She surveyed the street outside, then pulled the curtains to, shutting out the world. Mark cursed his luck—some days Elsie stood at that spot for twenty minutes or more. Her gaze would flit now here, now there, and over time Mark had convinced himself that she was looking for him. It was a fantasy, but it fed his soul.

The sound of high heels on the pavement made him slide down in his seat. Stupid, really—no one could see in. But shame makes you do strange things. He couldn't let her discover him like this. He watched as the trim thirty-two-year-old marched up to the house. Before she could get her key in the lock, the door opened and she was gathered into the arms of a tall, muscular man. They kissed each other long and hard.

And there it was in a nutshell. His ex-wife swept off her feet by another man—with Mark left out in the cold. A wave of fierce anger ripped through him. He had given that woman *everything* and she had stamped on his heart. What had she said when she called time on their short marriage? That she didn't love him enough. It was the most debilitating of character assassinations. He hadn't done anything wrong. He just wasn't *enough*.

They had married too young. Had a baby too quickly. But for a while the chaos and emotion of first-time parenthood had glued them together. The shared fear that their baby would stop breathing if left unattended, the sleep-deprived paranoia that you were doing a bad job, but also the immense joy of seeing their little girl grow and thrive. But slowly Christina had grown tired of the rigors of parenthood—the deadening routine, the privations—and had thrown herself back into her career. Which made her arguments during their bitter custody hearings all the more obscene. She played the mother card to the hilt, contrasting her loving nature, ordered existence and well-paying job with Mark's unpredictable and dangerous life as a Southampton copper—not forgetting to throw in some choice anecdotes about his drinking. And what had she done when she'd got sole custody of Elsie? She'd gone straight back to work full-time and handed over care of their child to her live-in lover. The woman who had once claimed to love Mark with all her heart had turned out to be a deceitful and vindictive little shit.

Christina and Stephen had gone inside now and all was quiet. Elsie would have had her bath and would be dressed for bed. Snug now in her Hello Kitty dressing gown and slippers that Mark had bought her, she'd be curled up in front of the CBeebies bedtime story. It was too young for her really, but she had a sentimental attachment to it and never missed it. Suddenly Mark felt the anger subside, subsumed by a terrible sadness. He too had found parenthood tough—the never-ending round of baths, bed, stories, playdates and more—but he would have given anything to be back in the midst of it now.

It was stupid to come here. Mark gunned the engine and sped away from the house, hoping to leave his troubles right there in the street. But as he drove they clambered round his brain like monkeys, goading him with his failure, his insignificance, his loneliness. Heading for home, he suddenly changed direction, shooting down Castle Way. There was a pub near the docks that ran illegal lock-ins. As long as you were in there by midnight, you could drink all night. Which was exactly what he intended to do.

15

The Brightston home was an imposing Victorian semi in affluent Eastleigh. Helen paced outside, angry and frustrated. She had arranged to meet Mark here at nine thirty a.m. It was now nearly ten o'clock and there was still no sign of him. She left her third voice mail on his phone, then cut her losses and rang the bell. Why did he have to be such a fuckup?

The door was opened by Sarah Brightston, a handsome woman in her mid-forties. Expensively dressed, immaculately made up, she betrayed no emotion at finding the police on her doorstep, ushering Helen inside.

"When did you report your husband missing?" The pleasantries had been concluded, so Helen cut to the chase.

"Two days ago."

"Even though he hadn't come home the night *before* that?"

"Peter is a lover of life. Too much so sometimes. Those trips to Bournemouth were a jolly and it would've been just like Peter to get the whole team pissed, then sleep it off in a local B&B. But he's not a callous man—he would have called the following morning to talk to me, talk to the boys."

"And do you have any idea where he might be now?"

"Silly sod's probably lost. They must have broken down and tried to walk to a garage. Probably had too much to drink and twisted an ankle or something—that'd be just like him. He's never been very coordinated."

She spoke with total conviction—there was no doubt in her mind that her husband was alive and well. Helen admired her fortitude, but was also intrigued.

"How many people do you have out looking for them?" Sarah continued.

"Every available officer."

This much wasn't a lie at least. The search *was* in full swing, but they'd found nothing and as each hour passed Helen's fears for their safety grew. The road the two men had been on would have led them out of the forest at Calmore—a long but unchallenging walk. The weather was cold but fine, so . . .

Helen knew in her heart that Amy's ordeal and Peter's disappearance were connected, but she'd forbidden anyone else from suggesting that—this was still officially a missing persons inquiry. Helen hadn't told Sarah that she was a murder cop by trade. Time for that later.

"Did Peter have anything on his mind? Was anything troubling him?" Helen resumed.

Sarah shook her head. Helen's eyes roamed over the well-appointed interior. Peter's legal wage was generous and Sarah worked in the antiques trade, so they weren't strapped for cash.

"Had anyone asked him for money recently? Have you noticed any changes in your financial circumstances recently? More money? Less?"

"No, everything was . . . normal. We're comfortable. Always have been."

"And how would you describe your marriage?"

"Loving. Faithful. Strong."

She emphasized the last word, as if slighted by the question.

"Any problems at work?" said Helen, changing tack.

Peter and Ben worked for a prestigious solicitors' firm with a particular interest in maritime law. There was a lot of money involved in their long-running cases, particularly where shipping was concerned. Their disappearance could have benefited someone.

"Had he felt under any particular pressure on a case?"

"Not that he told me."

"Was he working longer hours than usual?"

A small shake of the head from Sarah.

"Did he discuss his individual cases with you?"

Sarah claimed ignorance of Peter's caseload, so Helen made a mental note to follow this up with his firm. But all the while, she had the nasty feeling that she was clutching at straws. Scanning the walls for inspiration, her eyes alighted on a framed photo of Peter on a sunny beach, the smiling paterfamilias at the heart of a group holiday bundle. Sarah followed her sight line and filled her in on the details, going on to outline their future plans—a family trip to Boston at Easter. Sarah was unwavering in her belief that Peter would turn up and that things would once more return to normal. Helen wanted to believe that too, but she couldn't. In her heart of hearts, she feared that Sarah would never see her husband again.

16

It was the middle of the night and Peter Brightston was frozen to the bone. He always wore lightweight suits even in winter because of his tendency to perspire—a habit he bitterly regretted now. Somewhere in the New Forest was Ben's car and in it was the lined coat that Sarah had bought him for his birthday. Swearing violently, he pulled his suit jacket a little closer round him.

As he breathed out heavily, his frosted breath danced in front of him. It was virtually all he could see—it was pitch-black outside tonight. He could sense Ben was nearby, but couldn't see him. What was he doing? Ben was an okay bloke basically, but he wasn't good in confined spaces. He had nearly fainted earlier, in the throes of some sort of panic attack, and he screamed in his sleep. The steel walls that enclosed them amplified his night terrors, giving the whole scene a nightmarish feel and inducing a dull, nagging panic in Peter's guts. Would anybody find them in time? Or would they die in this sorry hole?

Peter cast a glance in Ben's general direction, then, taking advantage of the darkness, slipped his hand into his pocket. He never traveled without a packet of soft mints—it didn't do to go home stinking of booze—and slowly, cautiously he eased the last sweet from the now empty wrapper. Quickly he dropped it into his mouth. He'd had half a packet in his pocket when they'd been dumped here. He'd worked his way through them without telling Ben. He was sure Ben would have done the same, so why not? Any pangs of conscience he felt had been stilled by the gnawing hunger in his stomach. He swirled the sweet round and round his mouth, letting the sugar slowly dissolve and trickle down his throat. It was warm, sweet and comforting.

What would he do now? His meager supplies were exhausted. And he couldn't sleep, which only made him hungrier still. What the hell was he—were they—going to eat now? Coal? He laughed bitterly, then swallowed it. The echo sounded weird and he was strung out enough already. *I have to keep calm.* He'd had two heart attacks in the last five years and he didn't need another one—not down here.

He'd been shocked at first by their incarceration but had been pretty active since, desperately trying to find some means of escape. The sides of the silo were rusty in places, and after a lot of tugging he'd managed to wrench off a two-inch-long metal splint. It was something to work with. He'd banged on the sides with it, tried to punch a hole in the wall with it, even attempted to use it as a form of crampon to help him climb to safety. But it was all hopeless, and he'd slumped to the floor in defeat.

Suddenly tears were rolling down his face. The thought of dying in an airless hole away from his boys filled him with an inconsolable despair. He had led a good life. Done good things. Or tried to. He didn't deserve *this*. No one deserved this. Pushing the coal angrily aside, Peter fashioned himself a little hollow and settled down for the night. Was Ben asleep still? He'd gone quiet now and Peter couldn't be sure. Should he have comforted Ben during his night terrors? Would Ben hold it against him that he hadn't? Would it affect his thinking now that they were . . . Peter let the thought fizzle out—didn't want to go there. But the truth was, he had no idea what Ben was thinking or feeling. He knew him as a colleague, but not as a man. Ben had always been very coy about his past—why was that? Was *he* the reason they were here? Fired by the thought, Peter was about to call out to Ben, then suddenly bit his tongue. Best not to accuse him of anything—there was no telling how he would react.

As he lay on his freezing bed, Peter berated himself for never having bothered to get to know Ben better. But the bald truth was that you could never really know someone else.

And it was that thought that was going to keep Peter awake all night.

17

The incident room was a buzz of activity. Pictures of Amy and Sam were being pinned up on the board, alongside maps covering their route from London to Hampshire, diagrams and photos outlining the design of the abandoned pool, lists of friends and relatives and so on. Sanderson, McAndrew and Bridges were hitting the phones, following up potential witnesses, while computer operators input the pertinent details into HOLMES 2, cross-referencing the particulars of this abduction with the tens of thousands of crimes stored in the vast police database. DC Grounds stood over them, diligently scanning the results.

Mark hovered in the doorway, unable to step inside. His head pounding, he was assailed by wave after wave of nausea—the sheer busyness of the room made his head spin. He was tempted to turn and run, but he knew he had to face the music. He stepped inside, heading straight for Charlie's desk.

"Just in time," she said brightly. "Team briefing starts in ten minutes. I was going to bluff through it, but now you're here . . ."

Mark really liked Charlie on days like this. Despite his wretched behavior and general lack of professionalism, Charlie never judged him. She was always supportive and loyal. Mark felt a pang of remorse for having let her down.

"Why don't I grab you some coffee? You can freshen up and get ready to bang some heads together," she continued.

Charlie was climbing out of her seat to do just that when Helen's voice rang out loud and clear.

"DS Fuller. Nice of you to join us."

Mark's heart sank. His reprieve had been short-lived. Turning on his heel, he took the long walk of shame to Helen's office. The team acted busy, but everyone had one eye on the condemned man.

Mark shut the door behind him and turned to face Helen. She didn't offer him a chair, so he remained standing. She clearly wanted him to be visible to the rest of the team. Mark's shame ratcheted up another notch.

"I'm sorry, boss."

Helen looked up from her work.

"Sorry for what?"

"For missing our meet. For being unprofessional. For . . ."

Mark had prepared a speech on the way to the station, but now it eluded him. He racked his brains for it, but it danced away out of reach. His head pounded harder, his dizziness grew—he just wanted to be away from here.

Helen was staring at him, but her expression was hard to read. Was that anger? Disappointment? Or just boredom?

A long silence. And then finally she spoke.

"So."

Mark stared—uncertain what she wanted from him.

"Are you going to tell me what's going on? You're late. You're drunk. For a young man, you look like shit."

There was no arguing with that, so Mark remained silent. He knew from experience not to interrupt Helen when she was in full spate.

"I know you've had a tough time, Mark, but I'm telling you now that you're a whisker away from blowing it here. Whittaker would love an excuse to get rid of you, believe me. I don't want that to happen, so tell me what's going on. We're up against it and I need my deputy here both in body and in spirit."

"I went out and had a couple of drinks—"

"Try again."

Mark's head pounded faster, harder.

"Okay, a lot of drinks, but I was meeting a couple of mates and—"

"Try again. And if you lie to me once more, I'm going to pick up the phone and call Whittaker myself."

Mark stared at the floor. He hated the harsh spotlight on his drinking, could sense the disapproval. Everyone knew Helen never drank, so how to admit that he was smashed every night without appearing completely pathetic?

"Where did you go?"

"To the Unicorn."

"Jesus. And?"

"I drank there from eight p.m. to eight a.m. Lager, whisky, vodka."

There it was—out and on the table.

"How long?"

"Two months. Three maybe."

"Every night?"

Mark shrugged. He couldn't actually bring himself to say yes, though it was obvious that that was the answer. It was clear now—to Helen as well as Mark—that he was well on his way to alcoholism. He caught a glimpse of his reflection in the glass wall behind Helen. In his mind's eye he was still the handsome guy of a year ago—tall, rangy, with thick curls—but he was in a deep pit now and it showed. His skin was lifeless, his eyes dull. An unshaven, shambolic mess.

"I don't think I can do this anymore."

It just came out. He hadn't meant to say it. He hadn't wanted to say it. But he really needed to talk to someone. Helen had always been fair with him. He owed it to her to be honest.

"I don't think it's fair to you or the team to drag this out . . ."

Helen regarded him. For the first time today, Mark noticed a softening in her expression.

"I know how you feel, Mark, and if you want some time off, that's fine. But you are *not* quitting on me."

There was a steely determination in her voice.

"You're too good to throw it all away. You're the best DS I've ever worked with."

Mark didn't know what to say. He had been expecting derision, but her tone was kind and her offer of help seemed genuine. It was true that they had been through a lot together—solving the

Paget Street murders last year had been the high point of Mark's career—and a close professional bond had grown between them over time. In many ways her kindness was worse than a bollocking.

"I want to help you, Mark," she continued. "But you're going to have to work with me here. We are in the middle of a murder inquiry, so when I say I want you somewhere at nine thirty a.m., you'd bloody better be. If you can't do that—or don't want to—then I will get you transferred or suspended. Do you understand?"

Mark nodded.

"No more vodka breakfasts," Helen continued. "No more lunchtime trips to the pub. No more lies. If you trust me, I'll help you and we can get through this, but I need you to trust me. Do you trust me?"

Mark raised his eyes to meet hers.

"Of course I do."

"Good. Then let's get on with it. Team briefing in five minutes."

And with that she resumed her work. Mark left her office, wrong-footed but relieved. Helen Grace never failed to surprise him.

18

Biking home to her city center flat, Helen replayed the conversation with Mark in her head. Had she been too hard? Too soft? Was she repeating mistakes she'd made before? She was still chewing on it when she shut her front door behind her. Slipping the chain on, she headed straight for the shower. She'd been up for forty-eight hours straight and she needed to feel clean again.

She faced forward, the water pummeling her neck and breasts, before she turned round. The steaming hot water struck her back and immediately pain coursed through her body. It was agony at first, but slowly the stinging subsided and Helen once more felt calm.

Toweling herself down, she walked back into the bedroom. Now dry, she dropped the towel to the floor and looked at herself in the full-length mirror. She was an attractive sight naked, but few had seen her like this. Cautious of intimacy and wary of the inevitable questions, her encounters had mostly been casual and short-lived. Not that the men had cared—by and large they had seemed extremely pleased to find a woman who would go to bed with them and didn't hang around afterward.

Opening her wardrobe, Helen eschewed the rows of jeans and shirts in favor of sweatpants and top—she was due at a Box Combat class later and there seemed little point in changing twice. She paused briefly to take in the police uniforms, neatly preserved in pristine suit bags, that she used to wear when she was on the beat. Those days had been the making of her. The first day she tied her hair back, strapped on the stab vest and hit the streets was one of the happiest of her life. For the first time ever she felt she belonged. That she mattered. She reveled in the way it changed how she looked and felt—the sexless anonymity of the uniform allied to the security and strength it provided. It was like a disguise, but one that everyone recognized and appreciated. There was a small part of her that longed to be back there, but she was too ambitious and restless to have remained a rookie PC—police constable—for long.

Leaving nostalgia behind, she made herself a cup of tea and headed into the lounge. It was a large, spartan room. Not much in the way of pictures on the walls, no magazines left lying around. Neat and tidy, with everything in its place.

Helen selected a book and started to read. The bookshelves groaned with books. Books on criminal behavior, serial offending, a history of Quantico—all of them well thumbed. She didn't really do fiction—Helen didn't believe in happy endings—but she did prize knowledge. As she thumbed through a favorite tome on criminal psychology, she lit a cigarette. She'd tried to quit many times but had always relented, so now she'd given up trying. She could endure the self-censure for the rush it still gave her. Everyone has a dirty habit or two, she told herself.

Suddenly Mark popped up into her head. Had her words had the desired effect or was he in the Unicorn right now, drowning his sorrows? His dirty habit could cost him his job or even his life—she profoundly hoped he could pull himself back from the brink. She didn't want to lose him.

Helen tried to concentrate on her book, but she read the words without taking in their meaning and soon had to double back to pick up the thread of the logic. She had never been good at being idle—it was one of the reasons she worked so hard. Helen drew harder on her cigarette—she could feel those familiar unpleasant feelings creeping up on her again. Stubbing out her cigarette, she dumped the book on the coffee table, grabbed her gym bag and ran down to her bike. Perhaps she would call in on the incident room en route to the gym—maybe something had turned up. Either way, she would keep herself busy for a couple of hours and that way the darkness would not win.

19

I can't remember when I first saw my father hit my mother. I don't really remember things I see anyway. It's sounds I remember most clearly. The sound of a fist on a face. Of a body crashing into the kitchen table. A skull hitting a wall. Whimpering. Shouting. The endless abuse.

You never become inured to it. But you come to expect it. And each time it happens you get a little bit angrier. And feel a little more helpless.

She never fought back. That's what pissed me off. She just took it. Like she deserved it. Is that what she really thought? Whatever— if she wasn't going to fight him, I was. The next time he started on her, I'd get involved.

I didn't have to wait long. My dad's best mate Johnno died from a heroin overdose and after the funeral my dad drank for thirty-six hours nonstop. When my mum tried to get him to stop, he head-butted her—broke her bloody nose. I wasn't having that. So I kicked the stupid tosser in the balls.

He broke my arm, knocked my front teeth out and choked the life out of me with his belt. I really thought he was going to kill me.

A therapist once suggested that this was the root cause of my inability to form meaningful relationships with men. I just nodded, but really I wanted to spit in her eye.

20

Is it possible to die of fear? Peter hadn't moved in hours.

"Peter?"

Still nothing—hope sprang up in Ben's heart. Perhaps his heart had given out, overwhelmed by theatrical self-pity. Yes, that's what it was. And wouldn't it be great? The perfect solution. Survival of the fittest.

Ben immediately felt black. Wishing someone dead. Pitiful to even think of it, given what he'd been through. And anyway, even if he *was* dead, would it count? Would he be released? He hadn't killed him after all.

Ben's thoughts strayed back to his abductor. He hadn't recognized her—she was striking with those long black tresses and plump pink lips—so why had she chosen them? Was this some sick reality TV joke? Would someone jump out soon and reveal the gun to be full of blanks? The tone of her voice on the phone suggested otherwise. She wanted blood.

Ben started to cry. There had been so much bloodshed in his life already that it seemed the ultimate cruelty to end his days like this.

Now. Why not? Just to see if Peter is dead or not. He looks dead, so where would be the harm?

"Peter? . . . Peter?"

Ben eased himself to his feet. It was impossible to do it quietly, so he did it ostentatiously, loudly. Stretching and yawning, he said:

"I'm going to have to take a shit, Peter. Sorry."

Nothing.

Ben took a step toward the gun. Then another.

"Did you hear me, Peter?"

Ben bent down slowly. His ankle joint clicked—the noise echoing around the silo, bugger it—and he paused. Then slowly, quietly he picked up the gun. He shot a glance at Peter, expecting him to rear up in alarm, but he didn't. He wished he would. At least then it would be a fight.

The safety catch was obvious, so he released it. Then he pointed the gun at Peter's back. No, not like that. He might miss. Or just injure him. Fuck knows what a ricochet might do in this metal can. Kill them both? Yeah, that would be a good joke.

Stop prevaricating. Ben took a step closer.

"Peter?"

He really is dead. Still, I'd better do it, to make sure. To make sure I get out. And suddenly a thought of Jennie flitted through his mind. His fiancée. *Who'll be in pieces. Who I'll see soon. Who'll forgive me.* Of course she'd forgive him. He only did what had to be done. What anyone would have done.

Another step closer.

Ben lowered the gun so the barrel was almost resting on the back of Peter's head. *This is it,* he thought, and began to squeeze the trigger. Which was when Peter suddenly reared up, driving a metal splint right through Ben's left eye.

21

Helen never made it to the gym. As soon as she stepped into the incident room Charlie collared her. The chirpy DC had her serious face on. After a brief, hushed conversation, the pair marched straight out again. "Lesbian night at the gym," DC Bridges quipped, trying but failing to hide the fact that he fancied the pants off the very heterosexual Charlie.

Helen and Charlie bustled their way through the city center traffic to the Forensics Unit. The five-minute journey could take twenty-five at rush hour, and with Christmas shoppers and revelers flooding Southampton, today was going to be one of those days. Office party season was in full swing. Helen snarled in frustration at the coaches clogging up the bus lanes. She stuck on the blues and twos and begrudgingly a way was cleared for her. She sped away, plowing straight through a freshly deposited pool of vomit—spraying the surprised culprit in the process. Charlie suppressed a smile.

Ben Holland's silver Lexus was up on the stand and awaiting inspection when Helen and Charlie entered the Forensics Unit. Sally Stewart, stalwart of the unit, was waiting for them.

"Charlie's already talked you through the basics, but I thought you should see this for yourself."

They walked underneath the car and looked up. Sally shone her pen torch at the right rear wheel arch.

"Pretty dirty, as you'd expect, given the amount of miles your driver did every week. But this wheel arch looks—and smells—dirtier than all the others. Why? Because it's been marinated in petrol."

She gestured them out again, and once they were all clear Sally lowered the car so it was almost at eye level.

"Here's why."

Assisted by her deputy, Sally carefully eased the wing off the right side of the vehicle. The innards of the luxury car were duly revealed and now Sally's torch zeroed in on the petrol tank. Helen's eyes widened.

"The fuel tank has been punctured. It's not a big hole, but because of its position on the underside of the tank would empty it completely over time. Judging by the deposits on the wheel arch, I'd say the tank was pretty full when your pair left Bournemouth. It would have emptied swiftly and steadily—by my estimation at a rate of about 1.5 liters per minute, which means your driver would have run out of fuel roughly halfway through the New Forest. Though why he was going that way beats me."

Helen said nothing. Her brain was already whirring, trying to process this development.

"Your next question is, was it made accidentally? Anything's possible, but I'd say no. The puncture hole is too clean, too round—like someone hammered a small nail through the bottom of the tank. If it *was* sabotage, it was simple and effective."

And with that, she moved on. Hers was not to reason why—she was just there to provide the facts. Helen and Charlie looked at each other—it was clear they were thinking the same thing. Having just filled the tank, Ben wouldn't have been watching the fuel gauge and probably wouldn't have realized until too late that he was almost out of fuel. Even when the fuel warning light did come on, Ben would only have had a minute or two left before the tank was completely empty.

"She must have known," Helen thought out loud. "She must have *known* that Ben and Peter did that journey every week. That Ben always filled up at the Esso station. She must have done her research—the size of the tank, rate of fuel consumption, size of the required hole . . ."

"So they would grind to a halt exactly where she wanted them to." Charlie finished Helen's thought for her.

"She was *stalking* them. That's our starting point. Get on to Amy's family—any signs of unwanted attention, suspicious break-ins, anything. Same goes for the Hollands and Brightstons too."

It was their opening move. Helen hoped it would pay dividends, but had the feeling that this game would be long, hard-fought and deadly. It was clear that they were dealing with someone who was organized, intelligent and precise. The motive for these crimes remained a mystery, but the caliber of this killer was no longer in doubt. The biggest question now was, where were Ben and Peter? And would either of them be seen alive again?

22

Hours after the event and the adrenaline was still pumping. Anger hadn't yet given way to guilt, so Peter Brightston paced up and down, abusing his victim. The guy was going to *shoot* him—shoot him in the back of the head. What did he fucking expect?

He laughed bitterly as he remembered giving Ben his job at the firm—over and above better-qualified candidates—because he'd liked his balls, his drive. And this was how he repaid him? They guy hadn't thought twice—he was just going to blow his head off. *Prick.* Still, he'd got his comeuppance—howling in agony as Peter had driven the splint home.

Peter's fist gripped the weapon on which Ben's blood was slowly congealing. Even though the worst was now done, Peter wouldn't—couldn't—relinquish it.

It was self-defense. Of course it was. He had to keep telling himself that. And yet, he'd fashioned his weapon so carefully, so quietly, surely he was kidding himself that he hadn't planned it? He knew Ben didn't like him. Disrespected him. Made jokes about him behind his back. Was there ever any doubt that Ben would put himself first? Peter had known that and had planned accordingly. It was the only sensible thing to do. He had a wife and kids. What did Ben have? A fiancée whom the world acknowledged to be brainless and grasping. Their wedding promised to rival Katie Price's for naffness—a pink carriage, meringue dresses, ponies and pageboys, a sub-*Hello!* affair that would be talked ab—

Ben is dead. Blood is seeping from the hole in his face. There will be no wedding.

Silence. The most horrible, lonely silence Peter had ever experienced. A killer alone with his victim. Oh, God.

Then a blinding light. The hatch yanked open, the midday sunshine streaming in, burning his eyes. Something heavy falling onto his head.

A rope ladder.

His lungs flooded with fresh air, with oxygen, and his whole body convulsed with a sense of euphoria. He was free, he was alive. He had *survived*.

He limped along the quiet country road. Nobody came down here anymore, so what chance did he have of finding a rescuer? Even though he had gained his freedom, he still suspected that it was all a trick. That she was laughing at him as he dragged his protesting body along the road. That he would be hunted down. Peter had reconciled himself to dying in that dark hole—could it be that she was actually going to honor the bargain they'd made? Ahead Peter spotted signs of life and picked up his pace.

He laughed when he saw it. *Welcome* in a jaunty typeface above the convenience shop door. It was so friendly it made him cry. He crashed through the doors to be greeted by a sea of alarmed faces—pensioners and schoolkids shocked by this hideous vision. Face splattered with blood and stinking of piss, Peter careered toward the till. He fainted before he got there, crashing into a promotional display of Doritos. Nobody moved to help him. He looked just like a corpse.

23

Dunston Power Station stood proud on the western edge of Southampton Water. In its heyday the coal-fired plant had provided electricity for the south coast and much beyond. But it had been mothballed in 2012, a victim of the government's determination to reboot Britain's energy supply. Dunston was old and inefficient and couldn't compete with the low-carbon alternatives that were being built elsewhere in the UK. Staff had been reemployed and the site sealed off. It wasn't due to be decommissioned for another two years, so for now it was just an empty memorial to a glorious past. The huge central chimney cast a long shadow over the crime scene and made Helen shiver as she walked toward the police cordon that flapped violently in the sea breeze.

Mark's steps fell in time with Helen's as they hurried across the site. He had made a point of driving her here from the station. He hadn't been drinking and seemed a bit more rested. Perhaps Helen's words had made a difference after all. As they walked side by side, Helen's eyes darted now this way, now that, processing the possibilities.

The site had been alarmed, but after copper thieves had trashed the alarm system for the umpteenth time, the decision was taken not to bother with it anymore. Everything that was worth nicking had been taken already. Which meant all "she" had to do was remove the chain on the main gate and drive in. Would there be tire tracks? Footprints? The hatch at the top of the underground coal silo was easily accessible once you were on the site, and while too heavy for an individual to lift, it could easily have been yanked open by a van with a chain. Deep tire grooves near the silo suggested that that was exactly what had happened. That left the transportation of the victims.

"How did she get them from the van into the pit?" said Mark, reading her mind.

"Ben's pushing six foot, but lean. What do you think? Twelve stone?"

"Sure. It's possible a woman could drag that deadweight on her own, but Peter . . ."

"Got to be fourteen stone. Maybe more."

Helen bent down to get a better look. The ground near the hatch opening was certainly very disturbed, but was that the result of both victims being dragged in or a terrified Peter scrambling out?

This was obviously bad practice. An experienced copper knows never to make snap, instinctive judgments about the nature of the crime or the identity of the perpetrator. But Helen *knew* that this was the second murder. Even if one ignored the evidence of sabotage on Ben's car, Peter Brightston's story was so close to Amy's that the link was undeniable. The pain, guilt and horror etched on Peter's face when they picked him up was the same as on Amy's. These guys were living calling cards, a flesh-and-blood testament to somebody else's sadism. Was that the point of all this?

It was obvious now that they were dealing with a serial killer. Helen had done the courses, read the case studies, but still nothing had prepared her for this. Normally the motive, the connection to the victim, was easy to fathom, but not here. This wasn't an antiwoman thing, wasn't a sex crime, and there seemed to be no correlation in age, gender or status between the victims. Helen felt herself being sucked into a long, dark tunnel. A wave of depression assailed her and she had to pinch herself to snap out of it. She would catch the person responsible. Of course she would.

Helen and Mark approached the mouth of the pit. Helen called for a ladder to be brought over—she was eager to get down there quickly, to know the worst. The hatch was already open, so she peered inside. And there in the gloom lay the body. The man Peter had murdered. Ben Holland.

"Do you want to go down or shall I?"

Mark's question was well-meaning and he was straining not to be patronizing. But Helen had to see this for herself.

"I'm fine. This won't take long."

Carefully, she climbed down the ladder into the body of the silo. The smell was strong down there. Gas fused with coal dust and excrement. The forensics team had found strong traces of a powerful sedative, benzodiazepine, in Sam's and Amy's excrement. They'd probably find it here too. Helen turned her attention to the body. He was lying facedown, a pool of blood congealed around his head. Taking care not to touch him, Helen knelt down, craning round to look at the victim's face.

Disgust and then surprise. Disgust at the bloody hole where his left eye used to be. And surprise at the realization that this was not Ben Holland.

24

Jake was shocked to see her again so soon. Up until now, she'd been fairly predictable: one hour-long session per month. He'd been tempted not to answer the buzzer when it rang—it was after eleven p.m. and all encounters had to be prebooked for safety reasons. But when he'd seen her face on the screen, he'd been concerned. Concerned and intrigued.

Something was up. She didn't look at him when she entered the flat and made no mention of the late hour. Normally, he got a brief smile or a hello at least. But not tonight. She was distracted, looking inward, even less communicative than usual. She put the money on the table and removed her clothes without looking at him. Then she took off her bra and knickers—standing naked in front of him. This wasn't really on—this kind of thing usually led to propositions. He was a dominator, not a whore. He provided a service, but not that kind of service.

He had his speech ready as she walked toward him, but she sailed straight past, toward his armory of goodies. Another rule broken—only he was allowed to choose the method of punishment. That was part of the gig—the submissive didn't know exactly how they were going to be punished. But Jake said nothing; something in her actions brooked no argument tonight. Jake felt a little frisson of fear and excitement. It was as if the game were being turned back on him and for once he was not the one in charge.

She ignored the crops, heading straight for the studded whips instead. She ran her fingers along them before selecting the nastiest. This was only for the hard-core masochists, not really her thing, but she gave it to him and marched over to the wall. He shackled her. Still not a word had been spoken.

He felt oddly tentative, as if he didn't know what game he was playing. So his first strike was a bit soft.

"Harder."

He obliged, but it wasn't enough.

"*Harder.*"

So he let her have it. And this time he drew blood. Her body flinched at the pain, then seemed to relax as a trickle of blood ran down her back.

"Again."

Where was this going to end? He couldn't tell. The only thing he knew for certain was that this woman wanted to bleed.

25

"Tell me again what happened."

Amy shut her eyes and hung her head. Charlie seemed like a
nice person and had handled her with kid gloves, but why did she
have to do this? Since she'd been released from police custody, she
had tried anything and everything to *stop* thinking about it. Her
mother had followed her around like a bloodhound to begin with,
but had backed off after Amy had flipped out. Momentarily free of
her shadow, she'd hunted out leftover party booze and her mum's
"secret" stash of Valium, and when they didn't work she resorted to
her dad's sleeping pills. Big mistake. In her dreams—nightmares—
Sam was ever present. Smiling at her. Laughing. It was unbearable
and she'd woken up screaming—to find herself by the front door
rattling the chain, desperately trying to escape. She'd decided there

and then to stay awake for the rest of her life—never giving in to sleep—and to avoid all human contact. But here were the police again, reminding her of her horrific betrayal.

"You were hitching. It was raining. A van pulled up."

Amy nodded mutely.

"Describe the van to me."

"I've already made a statement. I—"

"Please."

A heavy, breathless sigh. A feeling of suffocation. And suddenly tears were springing up again—Amy forced them down.

"It was a Transit van."

"What make?"

"Ford? Vauxhall? Something like that. It was white."

"What did she say to you? Exact words, please."

Amy paused, unwillingly climbing back inside the memory.

" 'You need rescuing?'—that's what she said. 'You need rescuing?' Then she opened the passenger door. There was space enough for three in the cab, so we got in. I wish to fuck we hadn't."

And this time she did cry. Charlie let her for a second before handing her a tissue.

"Did she have an accent?"

"Southern."

"Any more specific than that?"

Amy shook her head.

"Then what did she say?"

Amy went through it again, beat by beat. The woman had said she was a heating engineer on her way home from an emergency callout. Amy didn't remember seeing a logo or name on the van— perhaps there had been; she wasn't looking. She'd talked about her

husband—who was useless at all things practical—and her kids—
two of them. She asked them where they were going on a cold
winter's night, then offered them a drink.

"What words did she use?"

"She noticed I was shivering a bit and said, 'You could do
with warming up.' That was it. Then she offered us her flask."

"Was the drink hot? What did it smell of?"

"It smelled like what it was. Coffee."

"And the taste?"

"Fine."

"What did she look like?"

When would this end?

"She had short blond hair. She wore mirror sunglasses on her
head. Overalls. Stud earrings, I think. Short, grimy nails. I could
see them on the wheel. Dirty hands. Only saw her face from the
side. Strong nose, fullish lips. No makeup. Height, average. She
looked normal. Completely fucking normal, okay?"

And with that Amy walked out of the sitting room and straight
upstairs, choking with tears, struggling to breathe. Assailed by the
most awful guilt, she allowed herself a flash of anger. Sam had got
it easy. He was dead. *His* suffering was over. But hers would endure.
She would never be allowed to forget what she'd done. Looking
down to the paving stones below from her attic bedroom window,
Amy wondered if Sam would welcome her if she decided to join
him. Suddenly she was seized by the idea and tugged at the handle,
but the window lock was on and the key had vanished. Even her
family was torturing her now.

26

"What did she look like?"

Peter Brightston shivered. Ever since they'd picked him up, he'd been shivering. His whole body was quaking, beating out the rhythm of his trauma in some weird, primal way. Helen was certain he was going to keel over at any moment. But the hospital doctors had given them the all clear to talk to him, so . . .

He wouldn't look at her. Just stared down at his hands, pulling at the IV tubes that emanated from him like tentacles.

"What did she look like, Peter?"

A long beat and then through gritted teeth:

"She looked bloody gorgeous."

Helen hadn't been expecting that.

"Describe her."

A deep breath, then:

"Tall, muscular . . . black hair . . . raven black hair. Long. Down to below her shoulders. Tight white T-shirt. Good tits."

"Face?"

"Made up. Full lips. Couldn't see the eyes. Tinted glasses—Prada ones."

"You sure, Prada?"

"I liked them. Made a mental note. Thought I might get Sarah a pair for our anniversa—"

Then he started to sob.

They got a bit more out of him eventually. The woman had been driving a red Vauxhall Movano that belonged to her husband. She lived with her chap and three kids in Thornhill. They were in the midst of moving to Bournemouth and were saving cash by doing the removals themselves, hence the van. She was talkative, breezy and mischievous, which was why she'd offered up her husband's hip flask, badly hidden as ever under the road atlas in the glove compartment. Peter had of course accepted and then slung it Ben's way. At which point in his testimony, Peter froze once more.

Helen left Charlie to babysit him. Charlie was good with men. She was more conventionally pretty than Helen and had an easy, unthreatening manner—no wonder men flocked to her. In her meaner moments, Helen felt her bland, but she certainly had her uses and would be a good copper in time. But Mark was her sounding board and that was who she needed now.

The White Bear was tucked away in a side street behind the hospital. Helen had deliberately—provocatively—chosen the venue as a test and so far Mark was doing okay, nursing a diet tonic. It was strange meeting in a pub—made it almost like a date, and both felt it. But there were bigger things to occupy them.

"So what are we dealing with?" Mark opened the conversation.

He could tell Helen's mind was spinning, trying to comprehend the latest unexpected developments.

"Ben Holland is not Ben Holland. His real name is James Hawker."

Whenever Helen thought of James, she always conjured up the same image—a blood-splattered young man looking utterly lost. Catatonic with shock.

"His father was a businessman. He was also a fantasist and a fraudster. Joel Hawker lost everything in a bad deal and decided to call time on himself and his family, rather than face the music . . . He killed the horses first, then the family dog, before setting fire to the stables. Neighbors called 999, but I got there first."

Helen's voice wavered a little as she remembered the scene. Mark watched her intently.

"I was a beat copper back then. I saw the smoke and heard screaming from inside the house so I barged my way in. The wife was dead, the eldest daughter and her boyfriend too, and he was setting about James with a carving knife when I arrived."

Helen paused before continuing:

"I took him down. Beat him longer and harder than I needed to. I got a commendation for it, but also a warning as to my future conduct."

Helen managed a rueful smile, which Mark reciprocated.

"But I didn't care. I wished I'd beaten him harder."

"So James changed his name?"

"Wouldn't you? He didn't want that kind of notoriety following him the rest of his life. He went to therapy for a bit, tried to deal with it, but really he wanted to pretend it hadn't happened. I tried to stay in touch with him, but a year or two after the murders he dropped me. Didn't want to be reminded of it. I was sad, but I understood and I wanted him to do well. And he did do well."

It was true. James had got himself educated, got a good job and eventually found a girl—benign, harmless—who wanted to marry him. From such a miserable, head-fucking start, he'd managed to make a good life for himself. Until someone had forced his colleague to stab him through the eye. Sure, it was self-defense, but that was what made it worse. James/Ben loathed violence—what must he have been going through to try to kill Peter?

It was too twisted, too unlucky for words. And yet that was what they were dealing with.

"Do you think they're connected? Joel Hawker's murders and Be— James's death?" Mark interjected, breaking into Helen's thoughts.

"Maybe. But Amy and Sam weren't part of that. Where do they fit in?"

Silence crept over them. Perhaps there were connections to be made, but they were hard to see right now.

So what were they left with? A pair of sadistic, motiveless murders that seemed utterly unrelated and a perpetrator who was either a scruffy blond heating engineer or a busty, mischievous housewife with long raven tresses. What they were left with was a mess and they both knew it.

As Mark scanned the pub, he felt the craving growing. All

around him men and women were laughing, joking and drinking. Wine, beer, spirits, cocktails, chasers—poured down their necks with abandon.

"You're doing really well, Mark."

Helen's words snapped him out of it. He eyed her suspiciously. The last thing he wanted was pity.

"I know it's hard, but this is the beginning of the end. We're going to get you better. We're going to do it together. Okay?"

Mark nodded, grateful.

"You can tell me to F off and go to Alcoholics Anonymous instead and I'll understand. But I don't think they know you. They don't know what we go through day after day. What it does to us. Which is why I'm going to help you. Whenever you need company, whenever you need help, I will be there for you. There will be times—loads of times—when you really, really want to drink. And that's okay—it's going to happen whether you like it or not. But here's the deal. You only ever drink in my presence. And when I tell you stop, you stop. Right?"

Mark didn't disagree.

"That's how we'll beat this thing. But if I find that you've broken that rule, that you've lied to me, then I'll drop you like a stone. Right? Good."

She disappeared to the bar and came back holding a bottle of lager in her hand. She pushed it across the table to him. Mark's hand was shaking slightly as he picked it up. He put it to his lips. The cool lager slid down his throat. But then she was taking it from him. For a moment, he wanted to hit her. But then the alcohol reached his stomach. And all was better again momentarily.

He realized now that she was still holding his hand. Instinctively, he started to caress her hand with his thumb. She pulled it away.

"Let me be clear on one thing, Mark. This isn't about 'us.' It's about you."

He'd misread the situation. And now he felt foolish. Stroking the hand of his superior officer. What a prick. They left soon after. Helen watched him drive off—presumably to make sure he didn't slope back into the pub. The warm, lagery optimism of the afternoon was dissipating now and Mark felt empty and alone.

As dusk fell, Mark's Golf pulled up outside what was once his family home. Elsie would be up in her bedroom now, cuddling Sheepy, bathed in the green glow of her night-light. He couldn't see her, but he knew she was there and that filled him with love. It wasn't enough, but it would have to do—for now.

27

Detective Superintendent Michael Whittaker was waiting for Helen when she arrived back at Southampton Central. He was a charismatic forty-five-year-old—outdoorsy, tanned, fit—a favorite with his female clerical staff, who dreamed of bagging this powerful and successful bachelor. He was also canny, with a keen eye for anything that might help, or hinder, his career. In his day he had been an excellent thief taker—until a nasty shoot-out at a botched bank raid had left him half a lung lighter and flying a desk. Unable to be on the ground directing operations, he was prone to throwing his weight around when he felt things were going too slowly or were spinning out of control. He had survived—and prospered—for so long by always remembering to keep an eye on the details.

"How does she do it?" he barked at Helen. "Is she operating alone or does she have help?"

"Hard to say yet," Helen replied. "She works under the radar and never leaves a trace, which suggests she's working alone. She's meticulous, precise, and I suspect unlikely to involve someone else in such a carefully planned operation. She's using drugs, not force, to subdue her victims, so again that would imply that she doesn't need or want help. The obvious next question is how does she shift them? They are transported in a Transit-type van where they can be easily concealed while subdued, until they get to their destination. She chooses remote, forgotten locations for their imprisonment—so there's little chance of her being spotted moving them from the van. Does she need help to shift them? Possibly, though all four of her victims have pressure burns around their ankles. Which could suggest they'd had their ankles tied together and then were dragged. They have abrasions to their legs, torsos and heads that could fit with being pulled across rough ground, but it would be tough going. Even if you tied cord or a rope round Peter Brightston's ankles, say, he's still fourteen stone of deadweight to drag behind you. Possible, but difficult."

"What about the vans?" Whittaker replied, affording Helen little respite.

"Nothing concrete. Amy's unsure what make her van was, and there are no traffic cameras near her site to help us. Peter's sure he was abducted in a Vauxhall Movano, but dozens of those are stolen every month in Hampshire alone. It's red, which helps a bit, but she could have repainted it. As they were picked up in the New Forest and transported via country lanes to Dunston Power Station, we haven't got any traffic cameras or CCTV footage to help us."

Whittaker sighed.

"I hope I haven't overpromoted you, Helen."

His tone was even.

"I had hoped you might take over from me one day . . . but cases like this can damage careers. We need arrests, Helen."

"Understood, sir."

"That bitch Garanita has been camping out in the bloody atrium, winding up the rest of the local hacks. A couple of the nationals got in on the act this morning. The idiots in Media Liaison have a prolapse whenever the *Times* rings and they come running straight to me. What are we telling them?"

"Sam's death is being treated as a domestic. We're not looking for anyone else, et cetera. Ben's death is being spun as an accident. Story is that he and Peter Brightston were at Dunston on firm business, there was a tragic accident, and so on. The press seem to be buying it for now."

Whittaker was silent. He would never admit that *his* superiors had been roasting his nuts, but Helen knew how it worked. Shit runs up and then runs down harder in cases like these.

"It may well break at some point, so we could go public if we felt that was the right thing to do. Tell the press there's a third party involved. Enlist the help of the public—"

"Too soon," Whittaker interrupted. "We haven't got enough. We'd look like imbeciles."

"Yes, sir."

Helen could sense his anxiety—and his displeasure—and was surprised. He was usually cooler than this. She wanted to allay his fears—she'd always been able to do so in the past—but she had nothing to offer here. Whittaker had a tendency to knee-jerk when the pressure was on. And that wasn't what Helen needed right now. So she worked hard to reassure him—talking him through the vast efforts that were being made to trace the killer—and slowly he began to relax. He had always trusted Helen, and if anyone could keep things on track, she could. Although someone like Whittaker would never admit it, Helen was exactly the kind of officer that top brass love. Female, teetotaler, a workaholic, with no interest in having babies. No danger of alcoholism, backhanders, maternity leave or any other unpleasantness with Helen. She worked like a dynamo and single-handedly boosted their clear-up rate. So even if she did bullshit them occasionally, they would put up with it, because she was up there with the very best.

She talked such a good game that for a second Helen was buoyed up by her words. But as she biked home, that false confidence started to evaporate. It was Christmas Eve tomorrow and the whole of Southampton was seized by the festive spirit. It was as if there had been a collective decision to ignore the lurid headlines in the *Evening News* in favor of out-and-out celebration instead. Salvation Army bands pumped out seasonal tunes, gaudy lights flashed happily above the shops and you could see excited smiles on the faces of kids everywhere. But Helen didn't feel any Christmas cheer. The whole thing seemed like a gaudy and inappropriate pageant to her. Out there somewhere was a killer who killed without conscience and never left a trace. Was she busy stalking her next victims right now? Were they already imprisoned and begging for mercy? Helen had never felt so lost. There seemed no solid ground in this case, no safe assumptions. More blood would be spilled and for now all Helen could do was wait and see who would be next.

28

It's funny the things you remember, isn't it? Why does that reindeer stick in my mind? He was pretty crummy even for that time, a mangy felt reindeer with whacked-out eyes. He looked as if he was dead. But I couldn't stop staring at him as we waited in the long queue. Perhaps I'm drawn to hopelessness. Or maybe not. You can overanalyze these things.

It was Xmas and for once life was okay. Dad had done a flit—did he have another family to be with at Christmas? I never found out—so it was just the girls at home. Mum was drinking, but I'd worked out a plan to keep her from getting too wasted. To save her legs, I'd offer to get the booze myself. I'd hop down to the corner shop, pick up a few cans, but get something solid too. Bread, crisps, whatever. When I got back I'd sit with Mum while she drank. I think she *felt a bit awkward drinking in front of me, and without Dad there to egg her on she cut back on the booze little by little until she was hardly drinking at all. I was never close to her, but we were okay that Christmas. Which was why she took us to the shopping mall.*

Muzak, cheap decorations and the smell of fear. As far as the eye could see parents were panicking, boxed into a corner by a festival that had come round too quickly yet again. Our shopping list was short—very short—but it still took a long time. Making sure the security guard in BHS was otherwise engaged before Mum stuffed clothes and tacky costume jewelry up our jumpers. Our "treat" was to go and see Santa afterward. Given that the guy who did it was a teacher at the local Catholic school, the treat was probably all his.

I've got such a vivid memory of his face. He sat me on his knee and, with his best Yo Ho Ho, asked me what I wanted most of all for Christmas. I smiled, looked him in the eye and said, "I'd like my dad to die."

We left rather quickly after that. Santa gossiping with the appalled mothers—bitches who loved throwing insults at white trash like us. As we hurried past, I gave that mangy reindeer a belting right hook. Didn't get to see the damage—we were out the door before security could catch us.

I'd expected Mum to hit me or at least shout. But she didn't. She just wept. Sat down at the bus stop and wept. Pity, really—it's one of my happiest memories.

29

Her visit was an unexpected pleasure. They hardly ever had visitors—who in their right mind would come here?—and those who did come were usually up to no good. Thieves or thugs. The police were seldom to be found here and you could forget about Social Services. What a joke they were.

Her mother had jumped when the doorbell rang. Marie was so engrossed in *Strictly*, she hadn't heard the footsteps coming down the hall. But Anna had. Whenever Anna heard noises outside, her heart beat a little faster. None of the other flats were occupied, so unless it was junkies seeking an empty flat or Gypsies on the sniff, then it could only mean they were coming for *them*. The footsteps slowed, then stopped outside their front door. She wanted to alert her mum and grunted as best she could, but

Flavia was doing the fox-trot and Marie was hooked. Then the doorbell rang—clear and confident. Marie shot a look at Anna—a moment's hesitation—then decided to ignore it.

Anna was glad. She didn't like visitors. Didn't like surprises. And yet she was curious. Because the footsteps down the corridor were light and clip-cloppy. Like someone was wearing heels. That made Anna chuckle inside. She hadn't heard anything like that since the whores moved on.

The doorbell rang again. Just once—polite but insistent. And then they heard her voice, calling their names, asking if she could speak to them. Marie turned down the TV—perhaps if she couldn't hear them, she'd think they were out and would go away. Pointless, really—the light and noise from their flat were like a beacon in the darkness. Then the doorbell rang for a third time and this time Marie got up and padded to the front door. Anna watched her go—she hated being left alone. What if something happened out there?

But then Marie came back, followed by a pretty woman clutching some plastic bags. She kind of looked like a social worker, except she wasn't depressed and her clothes were all right. She looked around the room, then walked over to Anna and knelt down to her level.

"Hi, Anna. My name's Ella."

She had such a warm smile. Anna liked her instantly.

"I was just telling your mum that I work for an organization called Shooting Stars. You might have seen our ads in the local newspaper. I know your mum likes to read it to you."

She smelled lovely. Like roses.

"Every year we bring Christmas hampers to families like

yours that find it hard to get out and about. How does that sound? Good?"

"We don't do pity in this house," Marie interjected sharply.

"It's not pity, Marie," Ella said, rising. "It's just a helping hand. And you don't have to take it. There's plenty of others who'd love to get their hands on these goodies, believe you me!"

The word "goodies" seemed to do the trick. Marie sat quietly as Ella took the tins and packets out of the bag. It was a real treasure trove—Turkish delight and chocolate ginger on top of all the usual stuff, plus soups and smoothies and liquid sherbet for Anna. A lot of thought had gone into it—Anna was surprised anyone cared enough to go to so much trouble. Ella couldn't have been more attentive, asking Marie a load of questions about Anna: What did she like to have read to her? Was she a fan of Tracy Beaker? What did she watch on TV? Anna basked in the attention.

This year they'd got lucky. This year they were on someone's radar. Marie was chuffed and the party spirit descended briefly as she went in search of the sherry. Anna looked at their visitor. She was smiling and nodding, but now she seemed tense. Anna thought that perhaps she was on a tight schedule, but she couldn't have been, because when Marie came back Ella insisted on opening up the mince pies. She didn't have one herself, but was keen for Marie to tuck in. They were freshly made—a bakery on St. Mary's Road had cooked up dozens of them for free in a fit of Christmas spirit.

Ella seemed to relax after Marie had polished one off. And it was then that things started to go strange. Marie started to feel unwell—faint and nauseous. She tried to get up but couldn't. Ella hurried over to help, but then suddenly and without warning pushed Marie down onto the floor. What was she doing?

Anna wanted to yell and shout and fight, but could only grunt and cry. Now Ella was pinning her mother down on the floor. She was tying her hands roughly behind her back with nasty-looking wire. *Stop, please, stop.* She was shoving something in her mouth; she was shouting at her. Why? What had she done wrong? Then "Ella" looked at Anna. It was as if she were a different person. Her eyes were cold now, her smile even colder. She walked toward Anna. Anna struggled inside, but her useless body was frozen and helpless. Then the woman put a bag over the young girl's head and everything went black.

30

Sandra Lawton. Age: 33. Stalker.

Helen scanned the file. Sandra Lawton was a romantic ob-sessive who when spurned turned nasty. She already had three convictions for putting a person in fear of violence by harass-ment. Safe to say her treatment didn't seem to be working and her belief that smart, educated men in positions of authority se-cretly wanted to sleep with her was as strong as ever.

Helen scrolled on to the next one. Sandra was nuts, but she wasn't violent.

Isobel Screed. Age: 18. Cyber stalker. Again, Helen rejected her. This girl was a slip of a thing who spent her life abusing soap actresses via text and Twitter. She threatened to cut their wombs out and so on, but by the looks of it never left her bedsit, so she could be ruled out. The classic cyber coward.

Alison Stedwell. Age: 37. Possession of an offensive weapon. Actual Bodily Harm. Multiple harassment charges. This was more promising. A serial, experienced offender who had attempted to fire a crossbow at a coworker she'd been stalking before she was arrested and later institutionalized. She was out in the community again now, under supervision apparently, and hadn't offended for several months. Was she capable of putting something like this together? Helen slumped in her chair. Who was she kidding? Alison might be a nasty piece of work, but she wasn't exactly subtle in her techniques—her stalking was visible and deliberately so—nor was she a looker. Peter Brightston's description of a raven-haired beauty could in no way apply to the gappy-toothed blob that stared back at Helen from the screen. Another one to scratch off the list.

She'd been using HOLMES 2 for hours now, searching out every British female stalker convicted in the last ten years. But it was fruitless. The individual they were hunting was exceptional, a far cry from the clumsy stalkers Helen was looking at now. Their stalker must have shadowed her victims for weeks, so as to discover Amy and Sam's propensity for hitching, as well as the ins and outs of Ben and Peter's weekly trips to Bournemouth. To have plotted their abductions in ways that allowed them to be executed on remote roads, in areas with no mobile phone reception, was impressive. But also to find locations to hold them in where they wouldn't be found or heard, where they could go slowly mad with hunger and terror, was something else. Such an individual wouldn't be buried away in the bowels of HOLMES 2;

she would be a living legend already, the regular subject of police seminars and literature.

After the discovery about Ben's car, Helen and Charlie had reinterviewed Amy, Peter and their families, searching for any evidence of stalking. Amy and Sam were easygoing types, not watchful in the slightest, who lived on a busy student campus. Nothing—or nobody—had stood out as odd. Peter Brightston said he would have noticed an attractive woman following him, but it sounded like empty bluster—he had had no reason to be suspicious or on his guard. Ben was a different kettle of fish; he had been by nature cautious and careful, but he was not around to ask anymore and his fiancée insisted he hadn't expressed any fears to her in the run-up to his abduction.

The one small break they did have came as a result of Ben's car. The killer had had a very narrow window in which to punch a hole in Ben's fuel tank. A matter of three to four hours at the most, as the group meeting at the Bournemouth office was shorter than usual that day. Ben usually parked in the office car park, but that was full because of a client lunch on-site, so he'd parked in a lot round the corner. Instinct told Helen that anything out of Ben's normal routine could have posed his killer a problem and so was worth investigating. CCTV showed Ben and Peter parking on the fourth floor, not far from the lifts. They left, and five minutes later a female figure in a lime green Puffa and white Kappa cap walked past. Was she scouting the scene? Probably, because moments later a gloved hand suddenly appeared in front of the security camera, spray-painting out its view on the world. Helen had asked for the footage to be analyzed, enhanced if possible, and had set Sanderson the task of checking CCTV footage from the vicinity of the lot to work out the suspect's route into the building, but for now they had to work with what they'd got. It wasn't much, but it was a fleeting view of their killer and it seemed to confirm everything Amy and Peter had told them about her. Not least the fact that she was a she. There had been some in her team—Grounds and Bridges particularly—who'd questioned whether a woman was really behind all this. But they had their answer now.

Helen shut down HOLMES 2 and headed out and round the corner to the Parrot and Two Chairmen pub. It was the station's Christmas do today and despite the fact that Helen viewed the event as wholly inappropriate in the circumstances, she had to go. It wasn't done for senior officers to duck it—crazy, really, as the last thing rank and file want when they're letting their hair down is their bosses hanging around.

Helen saw her team and pushed her way through the crowd to find them. They were all uncomfortable at being off the case when there was still so much to do, but they were making the best of it. Mark especially was in good spirits, proudly sporting his diet tonic like a trophy of sobriety. Still, he looked well on it—his lean face had more color, his eyes more sparkle. He greeted Helen warmly and seemed keen to include her in the group banter about the nightmare of New Year's, etc. He was laying it on a bit thick, she thought, and on more than one occasion Helen caught a knowing look from Charlie.

"So who fancies a kiss under the mistletoe?"

Whittaker. He was a different man out of the office. Gone were the anxiety and politicking, replaced by an effortless bonhomie.

"So many pretty girls, so little time," he said, casting mock lascivious glances at the assembled females.

"Been there, done that," Helen replied wryly. "I wouldn't write home about it."

"Charlie, then," Whittaker continued. "Make my Christmas."

Charlie blushed to her roots, unsure how to handle the humorous advances of a slightly tipsy detective superintendent.

"She's married, sir. Or as good as," Helen interjected.

"I heard she was still living in sin, which must mean there's a chance," Whittaker said, unabashed.

"I'd move on, sir. Plenty more fish in the sea."

"Pity. Still, you've got to know when you're beaten." His eyes settled on the young and attractive DC McAndrew.

"If you're desperate, I'd happily oblige," Mark threw in. Helen laughed, as did the others, but Whittaker wasn't amused. He'd never seemed that keen on his male officers—it was the women that interested him.

"Think I'll pass. If you'll excuse me . . ."

And he headed off to find others to molest. The conversation resumed, DC Sanderson asking everyone where they were spending Christmas. Helen took this as her cue to leave.

She was surprised to find she'd been in the pub for well over an hour. It had actually been quite refreshing—a moment for her brain to shut down—but now, as she walked back to the station through the cold night air, her mind was once more full of the case. She wanted to follow up the benzodiazepine link. Where was the killer getting her supply? Could that be a route to her?

Helen returned to the empty incident room and once more continued her hunt for the killer who would not be caught.

31

Her fury was reaching fever pitch and she wanted to scream until her lungs burst. The last few days had been terrifying and confusing for Anna, but her mother's refusal to talk to her now was making everything a million times worse.

When Ella had put the bag on her head, Anna's first thought was that she would suffocate—she was unable to move her head at all, and if her airways were covered, then she would die a slow, inexorable death. But luckily the bag was loose fitting and made of some kind of natural fiber, so she could breathe. Reprieved, she'd listened, straining to hear what was happening. Were they being robbed? Was her mother being murdered? But there was nothing, no sound at all apart from the front door being closed and the sound of the grille going on. Was it Ella going? Her mother going? *Please, God, don't leave me here alone like this,* Anna prayed. But no one had answered her prayers, and so she'd sat there, a little girl all alone, swathed in an awful darkness.

She sat like that for hours; then, suddenly, a blinding light as the bag was pulled off her head. She closed her eyes in pain, then slowly opened them, struggling to acclimatize to her freedom. While she'd been sitting there she'd been imagining all sorts of horrible scenarios—the flat turned over, her mother murdered—but as she looked around now, everything seemed relatively . . . normal. Nothing had been taken and it was once more just her and her mother in the flat. At first Anna was relieved, waiting for Marie to explain that the madwoman had stolen some stuff and gone and that they were okay again. But her mother said nothing. Anna grunted and gasped for attention while her eyes swiveled in their sockets, desperately trying to make eye contact. But Marie wouldn't look at her. Why not? What had happened to make her too ashamed to look at her own daughter?

Anna started to cry once more. She was only fourteen—she didn't know what this was all about. Yet her mother didn't look up or try to comfort her. Instead, she left the room. It was three, maybe four days since Ella had arrived and in that time her mother hadn't said one meaningful thing to her. She'd read to her, taken her to the toilet, urged her to sleep, but she hadn't *talked* to her. Anna had never felt so unloved. And so utterly in the dark. She had always been a burden—Anna knew that—and had always loved her mother unreservedly for the patience, love and tenderness she showed her. But she hated her now. Hated her with all her heart for the cruelty she was inflicting on her.

She had gone beyond starving. Her stomach cramped constantly, she was light-headed, her mouth was so dry she could taste blood in it. But her mother refused to give her any food. Why? And why wasn't she feeding herself? *What the hell is going on!?*

A sound from the hall. A terrible battering and screaming. Fists pounding, her mother wailing. Suddenly Marie was back in the room. She marched straight past Anna, looking crazed and ragged.

She was opening the window. Because they were in a tower block, the windows were hinged in the middle and opened only a bit so you couldn't throw yourself out—a smart move given the desperation of the inhabitants. But you could get a bit of a breeze on your face if that was what you wanted.

Now Marie was shouting, begging for help. Yelling for someone—anyone—to come and rescue them. And it was then that Anna knew. They were prisoners. That's what her mother wasn't telling her. Ella had locked them in, imprisoned them. They were trapped.

This was why her mother was shouting at the night. Hoping against hope that someone would pass by and hear her. That someone would care. But Anna knew from experience not to count on the kindness of strangers. As her mother slumped to the floor, defeated, Anna finally realized that they were entombed in their own home.

32

Should they cancel Christmas? It had been Sarah's first question to Peter once she'd got him home from the hospital. She didn't ask about his health—she could see he was making slow but steady progress—nor did she want to talk about what had happened. Nobody wanted to talk about *that*. But she did want to know what to do about Christmas. Would Peter like to have it at theirs as normal, with the usual assortment of cousins and parents? A kind of life-goes-on, we're-glad-you're-alive Christmas. Or did they want to acknowledge that life had suddenly become very dark and that there was no cause for celebration?

In the end, they'd decided to carry on as normal. Every fiber of Peter's being wanted to avoid friends and relatives. He couldn't stand their solicitous cooing and the unasked questions that filled their heads. But the thought of being alone with Sarah at Christmas was even more terrifying. Every second he was left alone was a second in which dark thoughts and darker memories could start to proliferate. He must keep his mind occupied, focus on the good things, even if it was all so much hypocrisy, tedium and anxiety.

At first, he'd been tempted to hate his wife. She was clearly at sea, unsure how to handle her killer husband. She couldn't compute what had happened, so fluttered around doing a million small things to show that she cared—all of which were entirely pointless. And yet as the days passed, Peter realized that he loved her for all her small kindnesses and because she clearly didn't *blame* him for what had happened. He managed a smile when he realized she had banned crackers this year. She had no clear idea what had happened in that hellhole, but she felt instinctively that her husband would not like loud bangs this year. She was right, and for that—and many other things—Peter was grateful.

The gang turned up as usual, and by God were they jolly. They skipped past the uniformed police officers guarding the front door as if they weren't there, positively oozing Christmas cheer in a way that was both manic and forced. Lots of booze was given and received as if everyone had collectively decided they needed a stiff drink. The presents just kept on coming as if a moment's pause in proceedings might prove fatal. The piles of unwrapped gifts grew until they threatened to take over the room.

Suddenly Peter felt claustrophobic. He got up abruptly and slipped from the room. Heading into the kitchen, he tried to unlock the back door, but was all fingers and thumbs. Cursing, he eventually managed it, then strode out into the freezing garden.

The cool air soothed him and he decided to have a cigarette. Since returning from the hospital he'd resumed the habit he'd kicked several years ago, and of course no one had dared comment. A small victory.

Suddenly Ash was beside him. His eldest nephew.

"Needed a break. Don't suppose I could bum one of those off you, could I?" he said, gesturing toward Peter's cigarettes.

"Sure thing, Ash. Knock yourself out," Peter replied, handing Ash the packet and his lighter.

Peter watched him clumsily lighting his cigarette. Ash wasn't much of a smoker and he was an even worse actor. Peter knew immediately that Ash had been sent out there to keep an eye on him. At the hospital, the doctors had spent over an hour discussing Peter's mental state with Sarah, filling her already overanxious mind with a host of nightmare scenarios. Which meant that Peter was pretty much on suicide watch, though no one would put it like that. Silly, really—he didn't have the energy for anything like that at the moment, though God knew it had crossed his mind enough times. Ash chattered on and Peter grunted and smiled, but he might as well have been talking Mandarin. Peter didn't give a toss what he was saying.

"Shall we go back in?"

Ash really didn't look like he was enjoying his cig, so Peter put him out of his misery. They stepped back inside to join the festive fray. The meal had been cleared away and the board games were out now. There was no escaping this one, so Peter settled down for more slow torture. He tried his best to be jolly, but his mind was elsewhere. Somewhere across town Ben Holland's fiancée was having a black Christmas, hating her life—hating the man who had killed her love just weeks before their wedding. How could she carry on? How could any of them carry on?

Peter smiled and rolled the dice, but inside he was dying. It's hard to enjoy Christmas when you've got blood on your hands.

33

The smell of spice was intoxicating and Helen breathed it in deeply. The one element of Christmas that Helen positively enjoyed was her defiant swimming against the tide. She'd never liked turkey and thought Christmas pudding was one of the most unpleasant things she'd ever tasted. She took the view that if you don't like the festive season, then you should embrace your feelings and go the other way. So while others fought in toy shops and spent eighty pounds on a free-range bird, Helen chose a different path, going as far in the opposite direction as she could. And her takeaway from Mumraj Tandoori on Christmas Day was the highlight of her annual rebellion.

"Murgh zafrani, Peshwari nan, aloo gobi, pilau rice and two poppadoms with extra chopped coriander on the side," Zameer

Khan rattled off as he packed Helen's order. He was a local fix-
ture, having run his popular restaurant for over twenty years.

"Perfect."

"Tell you what. Because it's Christmas and that, I'll throw in
a couple of After Eights as well. How's that sound?"

"My hero," said Helen, scooping up her takeaway and smiling her thanks.

It was a large order and Helen always ended up eating left-
overs on Boxing Day, but one of the joys of Christmas Day was
spreading out this Indian feast on the kitchen table and slowly,
deliberately loading up her plate with it. Clutching her haul,
Helen headed back into her flat. Inside, there were no decorations or cards—in fact, the only new additions to the flat were
the case files on Amy's and Peter's abductions that Helen had
brought home to review. She had spent most of the night poring
over them without a break and she suddenly realized she was
starving. She cranked up the oven and turned to get a plate to
heat up. As she did so her arm caught the takeaway bag, brushing it off the work surface. It hit the quarry tile floor at speed and
the flimsy cardboard containers burst open, scattering pungent
food everywhere.

"Shit, shit, shit!"

Helen had cleaned the floor only that morning and the
lemon of the floor cleaner merged with the Indian oils to pro-
duce an acrid, unpleasant odor. Helen stared at it for a moment
in shock; then suddenly tears were pricking her eyes. She was
furious and upset and wanted to stamp on the stupid shit, but
she just about managed to rein in her violence, fleeing to the
bathroom instead.

Lighting a cigarette, Helen sat on the cold rim of the bath. She was angry with herself for her overreaction and drew hard on the cigarette. Usually the nicotine was soothing, but today it just tasted bitter. She threw the cigarette into the toilet in disgust, watching its spark die out in the water. It was a fitting image for her state of mind. Every year she thumbed her nose at Christmas and every year it punched her in the face. Swirls of dark feelings swam round her now like evil flurries of snow, reminding her that she was unloved and worthless. Slowly these thoughts started to take possession of her, and as the depression began to eat into her brain, she shot a glance at the bathroom cabinet and the razor blades that were discreetly hidden inside.

The blade sliced into the turkey, allowing the clear juices to run free. Charlie, paper hat perched on her head, was in her element. She loved everything about Christmas. As soon as the leaves started to fall, Charlie's excitement began to build. She was always very organized, buying all her presents in October, ordering the turkey in November, so that when December finally came she could enjoy every second of it. The drinks parties, the carol singers, wrapping up presents by the fire, cuddling up in front of a festive movie—it was the highlight of her year.

"Can we open our presents yet?"

Charlie's niece, Mimi. Impatient as ever.

"Not until after Christmas lunch. You know the rules."

"But that's *ages*."

"It'll make it all the more exciting when it finally comes." Charlie wasn't going to bend on this one—Christmas was all about idiosyncratic family rituals.

"Who you kidding?" Steve interjected. "You're just delaying the inevitable anticlimax."

"Speak for yourself," said Charlie, cuffing her boyfriend. "I put a lot of effort into my Christmas shopping. If you don't do the same, that's your lookout."

"You'll eat those words later. See if you don't," was Steve's smug reply.

Charlie already knew what she was getting from Steve: lingerie. He'd been dropping hints for some time, and, besides, their sex life was extremely active at the moment. More than anything else, Charlie wanted a baby. She felt it was her time—in truth, it was the one present she really wanted. It hadn't happened yet, even though they'd been trying for a while, and for the first time Charlie's anxiety had started to grow. What if there was something wrong with her? The thought of not having a family was awful—she'd always wanted two or three kids at least.

Still, it was Christmas, and not a time for unpleasant thoughts, so Charlie pushed her concerns to the back of her mind. It was Christmas Day, the best day of the year, so as she doled out the Christmas turkey she beamed her biggest smile and did her best to spread as much Christmas cheer as she could.

Not long to wait now. Already Mark's mood was starting to lift at the thought of seeing Elsie again. This year Christina had ceded Boxing Day to him—first thing tomorrow he'd be picking his little girl up for a fun-packed festive day. It had been a truly shitty year, but at least it was ending on a high. He had booked ice-skating, cinema tickets, a table at Byron's for cheeseburgers— it was going to be the mother of all blowouts.

The prospect of a day out with Elsie had just about managed to keep him upright through the last thirty-six hours. As usual, he'd dropped his presents for her round at Christina's house on Christmas Eve. Elsie wasn't there—she'd gone to a Christingle service with her mum at the local church—so Stephen was home instead. He took the presents politely, then asked Mark if he wanted to come in for a drink. Mark had wanted to punch his teeth in—how *dared* he play host in what used to be *his* home? What were they going to talk about? What Santa was going to bring them for Christmas? He didn't know whether Stephen had done it on purpose—he looked genuine enough, but perhaps he was a good actor—but Mark didn't stick around to find out. When the red mist descended, Mark knew from experience that it was best to walk away. His blood had been boiling ever since and he'd more than once berated the hands on the clock for moving so slowly, but . . . finally his time was coming. *All good things come to those who wait.*

Christmas was done for another year.

34

Marie lay on her bed, staring at the ceiling. Would this be the last thing she saw? This discolored, uneven excuse for a ceiling? It had never bothered her before, but she'd been staring at it for over a week now and it aroused an anger in her that was as fierce as it was absurd. She shouldn't even be in here—she should be in the front room with Anna. From the moment it had happened, she knew she had to tell her the truth, but how to find the words? It was so awful, so unbelievable, what could she say to her? So she'd kept quiet. Day after awful day. Her daughter knew nothing about the deadly ultimatum or the gun that she'd hidden in the bedside table. Anna was a riot of misery and confusion and she would have to stay that way because Marie would not—could not—tell her the truth.

She was a bad mother. A bad person. She had to be to have invited such misfortune upon them. She had chosen a wrong 'un to marry and conceived a child who could barely function. Without giving any cause for offense, she had provoked endless abuse and countless acts of random violence. And now this. The cruelest of blows and the one that would finally end their sorry story. She had given up wondering why this was happening to them—it was just the way it was. She'd given up fighting too. The phone line had been dead since Ella left, the doors were locked from the outside, and no one responded to her cries. Once she thought she'd seen a figure—a child perhaps—when she was shrieking out of the window. But it had hurried off. Perhaps she'd imagined that. When you're stuck in a perpetual nightmare, it's hard to know what's real and what's not.

Anna was crying again. It was one of the few functions of which she was capable and it cut Marie to the quick. Her daughter was lonely and scared—two things Marie had sworn she would never be.

Marie found herself on her feet. Walking toward the door, she stopped. *Don't do this. But I must.* She knew it, really. Their only weapon against the world was their love and their solidarity and Marie had stupidly smashed that because of her own fear and cowardice. It was pitiful, pathetic. Having determined not to tell Anna the truth about their predicament, now she knew she had to. It was her only weapon. Their only hope.

Still Marie paused. Trying to find the words to excuse her cruelty, her silence. But it was impossible to find the words, so, summoning up the courage, she left the bedroom and walked into the living room. She'd expected to be greeted by Anna's accusatory glare, but, miracle of miracles, the girl was asleep. Her crying had finally worn the young teenager out, and for a brief moment she was free of their nightmare. Anna was at peace.

What if she never woke up? Marie was suddenly exhilarated by this thought. She knew she would never shoot her own daughter—that was an impossibility. But there were other ways. In the years since Anna was diagnosed, Marie had read of numerous instances where mothers who had been unable to cope with their child's severe disabilities had taken their lives. They said it was to end their child's suffering, but it was to end theirs too. Society viewed them with sympathy, so why not her too? Anything would be better than slowly starving to death here. Their bodies would rebel against them soon anyway, so what choice was there?

Marie found herself back in her bedroom. Heading to the bed, she picked up the thin pillow and turned it over in her hands. Her mind was racing now. Would she have the courage to do it? Or would her nerve fail her? Vomit suddenly rose into her mouth—she dropped to her knees and was violently sick in the bin. Picking herself up, she found that the pillow was still clutched tightly in her hands.

Best not to hesitate. Best not to waver. So Marie quickly marched out of her bedroom and back into the room where her daughter was slumbering peacefully.

35

I shouldn't have done it, but I couldn't resist. I'd searched in vain for ways to hurt him. Never been able to. And then suddenly it fell right into my lap . . .

My mother had found it rooting around the bins at the edge of the projects. Funny little mongrel with a white patch over one eye. Cute, if a bit mangy. She'd given it to my dad as a birthday present. I think she thought he might hang around if he had something to care for. A simple plan, but it kinda worked. Okay, so he still went off for days at a time, drinking, fighting and shagging the local slags, but he doted on that mutt. He was forever petting it, while the rest of us watched on, ignored.

It's funny, but once you know you're going to do something bad, everything immediately feels better. You feel light-headed, euphoric, free. No one else knows what you're planning. No one can stop you. It's your dirty little secret. The days before I did it were some of the happiest of my life.

In the end I opted for poison. The caretaker in our block endlessly moaned about the rats—however much powder he put down, he couldn't get rid of them. So it wasn't tough to half-inch a tube of the stuff. I thought this was the best way. The mutt was a greedy little beggar, could never resist a feed. So I made him a very special one. The cheapest, shittiest dog food laced with rat poison. He scoffed the whole lot.

I laughed later when I saw the mess. Dog shit and dog puke all over the kitchen floor. The life poured out of him from both ends and within a couple of hours he was dead. Mum was fucking terrified, wanted to bin it before Dad got back, pretend the mutt had run away or something. But he'd bunked off early and caught her in the act.

He went mental, knocking her around, screaming at her. But she was as confused as he was. In the end, he found the empty rat poison tube in the rubbish outside. Stupid mistake, really, but I was still young. He exploded back into the room clutching the tube and, silly cow that I am, I smiled. And that really did it.

He stamped on my head, kicked me in the stomach, booted me between the legs. Then he grabbed my neck and held my head against our three-bar fire. On and off, on and off. Don't know how long he went on for. I passed out after twenty minutes.

36

The decorations were coming down and life was getting back to normal. There's something peculiarly sad and depressing about an office still swathed in tinsel after the Christmas festivities have passed. Some people like to keep them up until well into January, but Helen wasn't one of them and she'd tasked a pliant constable with removing every last bauble and streamer. Helen wanted her incident room back the way it should be. She wanted to refocus.

Predictably, Whittaker wanted an update, so Helen headed straight to his office. The press coverage of Sam's murder seemed to have calmed down a bit—a large seizure of cocaine at Portsmouth Harbour had distracted the local crime reporters for now—and Whittaker was happy enough, so their catch-up was brief for once.

Returning to the incident room, Helen could tell immediately that something was up—there was a tension in the atmosphere, with no one quite daring to meet her eye. Charlie hurried over, then paused, unsure how to start. It was the first time Helen had ever seen her tongue-tied.

"What's happened?" Helen demanded.

"Sanderson just took a call from uniform."

"And?"

"They're down at Melbourne Tower."

Oh, God no.

"A mother and daughter found dead in their flat. Marie and Anna Storey. I'm so sorry."

Helen looked at her as if she were mad—as if she were playing a sick joke on her—but Charlie's face was so solemn and pained that Helen knew immediately that she was telling the truth.

"When?"

"Call came in half an hour ago. But you were in with the chief and—"

"You should have interrupted. For God's sake, Charlie, why didn't you come and get me?"

"I wanted more details first."

"What details? Why?"

"I think . . . we think that this might be the third abduction."

With the eyes of her team on her, Helen tried her damnedest to keep her composure. She instigated the usual procedures, but her mind was already halfway across town. She had to get down there to see for herself if it was really possible. Biking to Melbourne Tower, she thought of all things—good and bad—that they'd been through together. Was this really the end that had been waiting for them all along? Was this their reward for the years of struggling through?

Some days life really kicked you in the throat. Helen had felt sick when Charlie told her the news. She desperately wanted it to be a mistake and wished with all her heart that she could turn back time and somehow make it *untrue*. But she couldn't—Marie and Anna were dead. A team of demolition experts doing recon on the housing project had spotted a weird SOS message, daubed on a bedsheet and hung from a fourth-floor window. They investigated but couldn't raise anyone, despite the fact that the lights and TV were still on, so they rang the police. The attending constables had been none too pleased—it had taken them ages to get the iron grille off and the front door was so dead-bolted it took repeated attempts to barrel-charge it. They'd been convinced all along that the whole thing was a waste of time—that the inhabitants were deliberately hiding or high on drugs or some such. But on entering, they'd found a mother and daughter lying together on the living room floor.

Their first thought was suicide. Lock yourself in and do the deed. Except, on further investigation, they hadn't found any keys—to the dead bolts or indeed to the padlocks that secured the grilles. Stranger still, the victims had a loaded gun. It was lying on the floor beside them, unused. There were no ligatures, no empty bottle of pills or bleach—no visible signs anywhere of suicide. An examination of the exterior showed no signs of forced entry and nothing seemed to have been taken. It was all very odd. They were just . . . dead. The flies that circled their bodies suggested they had been dead for some time.

Helen told uniform to search the block and surrounding grounds—"We're looking for a mobile phone"—while she joined

Forensics with the bodies. She'd never lost her cool in front of fellow officers, but she did now. It was too appalling seeing the pair of them like that. They had been through so much, suffered so much, and yet always the love had been there. There had always been smiles and laughter, even amid the daily degradation and abuse. Helen was convinced this wasn't suicide on these grounds alone, and the presence of the gun put it beyond doubt.

Helen walked into the tiny kitchen to recover her composure. Idly, she flicked open the cupboards, the fridge. No food. Not even tinned or preserved food. The whole space had been cleared of anything edible and yet . . . the bin was empty. There were no wrappers or bottles lying around. As the thought started to lodge in her mind, Helen felt vomit rising. She forced it down and marched over to the sink. Turned on the tap. Nothing. As she'd expected. Picked up the phone. Dead. Helen sank down onto the nearest chair.

"You think this is her doing?" Mark had entered the room.

Helen nodded, then:

"She locked them in. Took their food, cut off the water, cut off the phone, left them the gun. We won't find any keys to the dead bolts or the padlocks because she took them with her . . ."

Mother and daughter trapped in their own home, unable to escape, unable to rouse anyone who might be concerned about them. It was the most lonely way to die. If there was any consolation in the fact that "she" hadn't won, hadn't succeeded in making Marie kill her own daughter, Helen didn't feel it now.

37

Today had been the darkest of days. The worst since it happened. Today was the day of Ben's funeral. At first, Peter Brightston had avoided his victim like the plague—didn't want to know how his fiancée and friends were suffering or what they thought. But as the days passed he found himself spending more and more time online, checking out Ben's memorial page, the messages on his Facebook page, climbing inside the life he'd destroyed.

Three days ago, he'd seen details of the funeral being posted by Ben's best mate. It didn't sound like it was going to be a big affair and Peter found himself wondering who from the firm would go. The partners would all attend, and most of Ben's team of course. But would the PAs go too? Would Peter be the only person who wasn't there? For a mad moment he wondered if he *should* go, before dismissing it out of hand. If Ben's friends saw him, they'd tear him limb from limb. And who could blame them? And yet a big part of Peter wanted to be there. To say good-bye. To say sorry.

He'd thought about writing to Ben's fiancée, but Sarah had talked him out of it. She was right, of course. In a fit of pique, he'd defied her and sat down to write to Jennie—but he hadn't managed a single word. All the things he wanted to say—*I didn't want to do it, I wish I could turn back the clock*—all sounded so empty and pointless. What he wanted, what he felt, didn't matter to her. What mattered to her was the fact that he'd stabbed her fiancé in the face to save his own skin.

Had it been worth it? Peter wasn't sure anymore. After the adrenaline and shock had worn off, he'd felt nothing but a crushing emptiness, as if he'd lost his sense of taste, smell, touch, and was now merely existing rather than living.

What was he going to do with his life now? Could he go back to work? Would he be accepted? Anything would be better than going slowly crazy at home.

If only Ben had pulled the trigger. He could have done it. He'd had the time. Did he hesitate because he was a chicken or because he was moral? If he'd pulled the trigger, then it would have been *him* drowning in a sea of guilt while Peter would be safe and sound under the ground.

Selfish bastard.

38

Everybody has to draw the line sometime. And for Jake that time was now. This was not pleasant or fun or even professional anymore; it was a nasty situation that was getting out of control. He'd been with a client when she turned up, but she didn't seem to care. She had sat outside his flat, face turned to the floor, while Jake finished his session. But the mood had been well and truly broken and he'd had to promise his disgruntled client a free session just to get him out the door. This kind of thing wasn't good for business—the S&M scene on the south coast was a small world and word would soon get around.

She apologized, but she didn't mean it. She was incoherent and emotional. Jake wondered if she'd been drinking and asked her as much. She didn't like that, reminding him that he was a dominator, not a doctor. He'd let that one go, didn't want to provoke her, and suggested a short, mild session today as a way of calming things down. Then perhaps they could talk.

But she wasn't having any of that. She wanted a full one-hour, no-holds-barred session. She wanted as much pain as he could muster. More than that, she wanted abuse—she wanted him to tell her that she was evil and ugly, a useless piece of shit who should be killed or worse. She wanted him to *destroy* her.

When he refused, she got angry, but he had to be honest. Some people he would have happily degraded—whatever floats your boat—but not her. It was not just that he liked her; it was also that he knew instinctively that this wasn't what she needed. He'd often wondered if she took therapy elsewhere—if she didn't, he was tempted to suggest it. Rather than escalating their sessions to yet another level of extremity, Jake felt it was time to draw a line and suggest some complementary avenues for her to explore.

"Are you fucking kidding me?" Helen exploded. "How dare you tell me what to do?"

Jake was taken aback by the force of the explosion.

"It's just a suggestion, and if it's not for you, that's fine. But I don't feel comfortable going in this dir—"

"You don't feel *comfortable*! You're a bloody whore, for God's sake. You're comfortable with whatever I pay you to do."

She was marching toward him, and for a moment Jake thought she was going to attack him, such was the level of her fury. He always had a Taser tucked away close by, but he'd never had to use it. How ironic would it be if he had to use it now on *her*? But thankfully, just as Jake was edging toward it, she turned on her heel and marched out of the flat, slamming the door fiercely behind her.

Jake fought the urge to go after her. They weren't friends; she was just a client. He'd crossed that line before and lived to regret it. Best cut her off now and not look back. He had liked her but hadn't asked to be abused. He was too long in the tooth to put up with that. With a sigh he dropped the blinds and shut her out of his life for good.

39

Helen punched her speed up to a hundred miles per hour and roared into the fast lane. It was late now and the ring road was virtually empty. She reveled in the freedom, gunning the throttle harder and harder. The speed was soothing—for a moment the awful, heartbreaking events of the last few days slipped from her mind.

Only a couple of miles to go. The thought of what lay ahead focused her. She had a job to do. And she had to do it well—lives hung in the balance. Three of the victims—Ben, Marie and Anna—had been known personally to her. Surely that was too much of a coincidence. Was the fact that she knew them important? Or was there something in their past traumas that had made them worthy of the killer's attention?

Amy was the stumbling block. Helen had never met her and as far as she was aware Amy had no criminal record. Same went for Sam. So if the connection to Helen was important, why had *they* been chosen? It was late and Amy's mother wouldn't thank her for calling round with more questions, but there was no other way.

Her father opened the door, primed to deliver a volley of abuse. Emilia Garanita and her colleagues had been a constant presence in their lives since Amy had returned home and the Andersons were reaching the breaking point. On seeing it was Helen, he swallowed his reluctance and let her inside.

She was ushered into the living room and made to wait while Diane Anderson went to fetch her daughter from her bedroom. Helen scanned the walls, looking for inspiration. A handful of happy family photos—Mum, Dad and precious daughter—stared back at her, mocking her ignorance.

Amy was the picture of truculence, clearly unhappy to be forced back into her nightmare. She had actually been asleep—a rare occurrence—and Helen had to work very hard to warm her up. Slowly, as Amy came to realize that maybe she wasn't being cast as the bad guy, she started to rally, answering Helen's questions honestly and openly. Amy had never been in trouble with the cops and had certainly never met Helen before. Had Sam ever got into trouble? Not that she knew of. He wanted to be a lawyer and was always very clear that one brush with the law could put paid to his chosen career. Some people had thought he was a bit dull as a result, but Amy had valued his solidity and reliability. He had always been there for her—until she had shot him in the back.

Amy was clamming up again—her guilt once more forcing

its way into her consciousness, dragging her down to the bottom again. Her mother wanted to accompany her to her bedroom, but Helen insisted she and her husband stay to answer her questions. Diane Anderson was terse in her response, and for once Helen's patience snapped, and she threatened Diane with arrest unless she sat down and did as she was told. She complied and for the next thirty minutes Helen peppered the couple with questions about their lives. Had they ever been in trouble with the law? Had they ever met Helen before in any capacity? But with the exception of a drunk-driving offense by the husband, Richard, three years ago, there was nothing. What about a connection to Ben? Or Anna and Marie? Helen probed, but she knew it was hopeless—they came from completely different backgrounds and moved in different worlds.

Richard Anderson showed her out. She had turned up late at night and blotted her notebook with them for no tangible gain. There must be a connection—Helen was sure of that—but for now it remained as elusive as ever.

40

She was locking up her bike in the station's car park when she heard footsteps coming up behind her. She flinched when she felt an arm on her shoulder, but there was no need—she sensed who it was.

Mark had left countless messages on her mobile. He was worried about her.

"You okay?"

It was a hard question to answer, so Helen simply nodded.

"You shot off so quickly from Marie's flat. I didn't get a chance to talk to you."

"I'm fine, Mark. I was shaken at the time, but I'm okay now. I just needed a bit of time to myself."

"Sure, sure."

But he wasn't sure. She was so brittle, yet so remote. She'd been in tears at the house, which had shocked everyone, but now she was back to her usual elusive self. He didn't think she was a primal screamer. He'd never seen her at the gym. She had no boyfriend, husband or children, so what was her release? At least his was obvious—going for the booze. She was just a bloody enigma, refusing to give away anything of herself. It frustrated the hell out of him.

"Thank you, Mark."

She laid her hand on his arm, gave it the briefest of squeezes and then walked into the station. For a moment, Mark felt like a teenager again, stupidly elated by the tiniest of things.

"Let's review what we've got."

Helen had called the whole team together in the incident room to sift the evidence.

"Witnesses?"

"Nothing so far," DC Bridges responded. "We're still on-site, but it's mostly junkies after a reward or attention seekers. Someone saw a dark car, someone saw a motorbike, someone else saw a UFO . . . The hotline's had plenty of action but it's basically old ladies and kids having a laugh."

What did Helen expect? Marie and Anna must have been there for nearly two weeks—why would anyone remember anything that far back?

"Okay, what about the ME's report?"

Charlie dived in—there was no point dressing this up. "Both victims were emaciated and severely dehydrated. Anna Storey died of asphyxiation. A pillow with traces of her spittle and snot on it was found close to her body."

Helen tried not to react. Marie *had* killed her daughter after all—albeit with tenderness. That somehow made it worse.

Charlie continued: "Marie Storey died of cardiac arrest following multiple organ failure. Brought on by starvation and the effects of dehydration."

Mark saw the effect these simple words were having on Helen—and everyone else in the team—so he jumped in with his crumb of good news.

"There's no CCTV anywhere near those projects—vandalized ages ago. Forensics have dusted the flat from top to bottom without any joy, but they did find a partial footprint on the edge of one of the flowerbeds by the tower entrance. A high heel estimated to be a size six. Uniform is doing the rounds with an image of the woman in the lime green Puffa and Kappa cap—see if it jogs any memories."

"Good. What about the gun?" Helen continued.

"Still loaded when found. No sign of use," said DC McAndrew, picking up the baton. "It's a Smith and Wesson, probably from the early 1990s. The Ben Holland gun was a Glock and the gun that killed Sam Fisher was a modified Taurus."

"Where's she getting them from?" Helen countered. "Is she ex-military? A cop? Let's check if any of the guns harvested in last year's amnesty have gone missing."

McAndrew scuttled off to do Helen's bidding. With no hard evidence to speak of—the sedatives used were over-the-counter stuff, the phones no-contract pay-as-you-go—and little in the way of witness statements to describe this killer chameleon, all they had to go on was pattern and motive. *Why* was "she" doing this? She forced her victims to play a diabolical game of Eeny Meeny

Miny Moe, confident in the knowledge that the shooter would ultimately suffer much more than the victim. Was the ongoing trauma of the survivor the point, the pleasure? Helen opened the question to the floor. If so, would the killer circle back to watch these trauma victims, to enjoy her victory? Perhaps they should be putting extra manpower/surveillance on Amy, Peter, etc. Costs would rocket, but it might be worth it.

"How could she know which one would be killed?" Charlie asked.

"Good question. Does she really know the pairs so well that she can predict the victim?" Helen replied.

"She can't do, surely?" DC Sanderson replied.

Helen agreed:

"It seems unlikely. She couldn't possibly predict how people would react under that sort of pressure. Which begs the question: Are the victims chosen completely at random?"

This was more likely. Some serial killers groom and stalk, but most select their victims based on opportunity rather than identity. Fred West picked up hitchhikers, Ian Brady abducted truant children, the Yorkshire Ripper struck at random . . .

Except . . . Helen knew three of the victims personally. Helen offered this to the room, but received a muted reaction. What had she been expecting? A blinding theory laying the blame at her door or a robust and firm denial that her knowledge of the victims was important? She got neither because, as Mark pointed out, Helen had never met Amy before. He was right, of course— it was an interesting theory but didn't stack up properly. Amy was the odd one out—there was no pattern.

"What about if she chose them because they were easy targets?"

Charlie intervened once more. "Because they were isolated and vulnerable?"

A murmur of agreement from the team.

"Amy and Sam were a quiet couple. She's not much of a social animal and neither was he. They were private, with a few close friends. Ben Holland kept himself to himself. He'd grown more confident over time and got engaged, but he still lived alone, even though his wedding was just a few weeks away. Anna and Marie were all alone in the world. Perhaps the killer targets them because she *can?*"

Helen found herself nodding, but again it wasn't a foolproof theory. It wasn't as if they wouldn't be missed. Amy was very close to her mother and Sam's mum was an active part of his life. Ben was engaged to be married—he certainly would have been missed. Anna and Marie weren't on anyone's radar of course, but Social Services would have found them in the end.

The key was to find a link between the victims. Or prove that they were abducted simply because they were in pairs.

Helen called the meeting to an end. Tasks had been allotted— trawling databases for anyone with past convictions who might bear a grudge against Helen or killers with a penchant for elaborate sadism or game playing—though in her heart Helen didn't expect them to turn up anything.

It was a riddle—pure and simple.

41

Everyone was surprised when Peter Brightston suddenly announced he was returning to work. His fellow partners had urged him to take three months off—six if he wanted—motivated in part by concern, but more by the fear of how people would react to having him back. Peter was boorish, but people were basically fond of him, if only because he knew the law inside out.

But he had stabbed Ben. Killed a colleague. And there was nothing in the HR manual about how to deal with that. The sense was that he wasn't going to be charged—the police had been coy but intimated that it was some kind of terrible accident. And Peter had toed that line, failing to give any of them the details they craved yet feared.

When he turned up after a few weeks' rest and recuperation, it was against the advice of his doctors and counselors. But Peter was determined—January was always a busy month for the firm—and what could they do? Oust him when he hadn't been charged with anything? End his twenty-year association with the practice and throw him on the scrap heap because of an accident? The truth was, no one knew what to do, so predictably they did nothing.

He arrived first thing on a Monday morning. Prompt as always. The office was strangely hushed that day, as Peter sent a few e-mails and made the odd cup of coffee. But no one had scheduled meetings with him—*Ease yourself back in gently, Peter*—and his colleagues soon found excuses to shoot off to the Bournemouth office or take a client out on a long lunch. After all the buildup to his return, the polite inquiries about his health and well-being lasted only half an hour and then it was back to normal.

Except for the empty chair. Ben's post hadn't been filled—the funeral had only just taken place after all—so his desk and chair sat vacant. His personal effects had been bagged up and returned to his fiancée, so the whole workstation looked naked. An empty hole where a life had once been.

It was in Peter's sight line. It was in everyone's sight line. An insistent reminder of what had happened. Everyone—from management down to the canteen workers—had expected it to be hard for Peter. What no one expected was that, at three thirty p.m. on his first day back, Peter would head up to the office roof, shout his wife's name, then jump over the safety rail to his death.

42

Japan? Australia? Mexico?

We had a globe when we were kids. One that lit up. God knows why or where we got it from. We weren't an educated bunch and my mother's geography extended as far as the nearest liquor store. But I loved that globe. It was the seat of all my fantasies. Running your hand over its smooth surfaces, jumping continents in seconds, it was easy to imagine that I was free.

I imagined myself hitching a lift to the port, knapsack filled with provisions—Jammie Dodgers a must—for a long journey. I'd climb up the slippery anchor chain, with links as large as your whole body, and once on board slip into the lifeboat and under cover. My body would thrill as I felt the giant vessel moving clear of land, and *as it journeyed across oceans and past continents, I would be safe and snug in my little hidey-hole.*

Eventually, we'd land in some far-off exotic location. I'd slide down the chain and plant my feet on new ground. My new ground. The start of a whole new adventure.

Sometimes fantasy veered dangerously close to reality. I'd take a couple of plastic bags and fill them with cheese triangles, Club biscuits and a mildewed sleeping bag.

And I'd slip out the door, closing it gently behind me. Along the pissy walkway and down onto the street. Freedom.

But something—or someone—always brought me back home before I'd got out of the projects.

You always brought me back.

43

Rubberneckers are an easy target, aren't they? They are ghouls, feeding on the misfortune of others. And yet which of us can say we wouldn't look? That we haven't looked as we crawled past a motorway pileup or idled by a police cordon. What are we looking for? Signs of life? Or signs of death?

Peter Brightston had certainly pulled a big crowd, eager to see what fourteen stone of flesh and bone looks like as it collides with the pavement. Helen and her team arrived only minutes after the paramedics. But unlike the poor souls whose job it was to scoop up his remains, Helen, Charlie and Mark were not interested in Peter. He'd been seen by coworkers jumping—there could be no question of coercion; it was an open-and-shut case of suicide. No, what interested Helen was the rubberneckers. Those who had come to enjoy the carnage.

Something told Helen that the killer wouldn't abandon her victims once she'd set them in motion. Peter's suicide was surely the climax of all her hopes and dreams. The living calling card unable to cope with the guilt forced upon him by his abductor. The killer didn't even have to do anything this time. Just sit back and enjoy her handiwork. Surely, though, you'd want to see it?

Which was why they'd brought cameras. From various discreet positions—some elevated, some on street level—they scanned the crowds, recording the masses' morbid interest in a middle-aged man's despair.

Reviewing the footage later was a depressing affair. They'd caught the moment when his wife, Sarah, had turned up. She was raving, frantic. She hadn't yet taken in Peter's abduction and bizarre reappearance. She hadn't been able to penetrate his all-encompassing gloom ever since—she'd tried counselors, but his armor was too strong. And now this. Her entire world—and her place in it—had been destroyed in a matter of weeks. Before, it had been a world of comfort, private education, skiing trips, a sense of serenity and contentment. Now the world was a dark place, full of evil, sadism and danger.

"Let's fast-forward a bit," Helen suggested, and no one disagreed.

The images sped up briefly, then settled back down to normal. An endless parade of paramedics and gawpers.

"We're looking for a woman of medium height between five-four and five-eight in height, slender build. Strong nose, fullish lips. Medium to large bust. Pierced ears." Mark reminded the group what they were looking for.

But even as he said it, he wondered if they were wasting their time. Even if they saw the killer, would they know her? They had the e-fits as compiled by Amy and Charlie up on the board, but they were rough and ready, with different-colored hair and so on. Would they look the killer straight in the eye and not know her?

Shortly after, the footage came to an end.

"What do you want to do now, boss?" Charlie asked.

They had watched it twice without anyone spotting anything of interest. But it was hard to be across everyone—there were so many people on-screen—so after a moment's hesitation, Helen replied:

"Let's watch it one more time."

They settled in for another viewing. Mark offered his Oreos around—they all needed a sugar hit and were grateful for a crack at his secret stash of goodies. They fixed their eyes on the screen once more and tried to concentrate harder than ever.

"There."

Charlie said it so loud, she made Mark and Helen jump. Charlie spooled the footage back before replaying it. Then suddenly she paused it.

"Look there."

She was pointing to a woman deep in the crowd who was watching the paramedics loading the body bag onto a trolley.

"If I just zoom in a bit, we might get a better picture—"

"Who is she?" Helen interrupted.

"I've seen her before. At Ben Holland's funeral. She was

alone and disappeared as soon as the service was over. I didn't think much of it at the time, but actually I don't think I saw her speak to anyone there."

The woman's face loomed large on the screen now. Was this their first view of their serial killer? They studied the face closely. She was thin faced, with a prominent-ish nose, blond bob, well dressed, respectable. She *could* be the woman in the e-fits. It was so hard to tell with those things—you so wanted them to fit that sometimes your eyes played tricks on you.

As they drove to the Anderson household, Helen felt a profound sense of relief. And something else too: hope. Finally, she had something to work with. She stared at the printed image of the suspect as Mark drove—who was this woman?

They were let into the Anderson household with the usual bad grace. Funny how victims come to resent the police intrusion, even when they need your help. Seated in the living room, Helen wasted no time getting to the point.

"We have an image of a suspect, Amy. And we'd like you to take a look at it."

Now there was an interest in their presence. Helen noted Amy's parents exchanging a look—were they beginning to hope too? She handed Amy the printout. She examined it closely, then closed her eyes, willing the memory of her abductor back into her mind's eye. Silence. She opened her eyes again. Stared at the image once more.

A long, long silence, then:

"It could be her."

Could?

"How sure are you, Amy?"

"Hard to say. I'd have to see her in the flesh to be sure, but it definitely could be her. The hair, the nose . . . yes, it could be her."

It wasn't perfect, but it was enough for now. Amy handed the picture to her parents, who were only too eager to see the bitch who'd kidnapped their daughter. Helen wanted to snatch the image off them—this was no time for pass the parcel.

"I know her." Diane Anderson's voice rang out crisp and clear.

For a moment, no one said anything. Then Helen said:

"You're saying you've seen her before?"

"I've met her. I've spoken to her. I *know* who she is."

Helen looked at Mark—a link between the victims at last. It had taken them a long time—too long—to get here. But now they had a prime suspect. Helen felt a surge of adrenaline fire through her and for a brief moment remembered why she'd become a cop in the first place.

44

Her excitement was short-lived. As she exited the Anderson house, Helen clocked Emilia Garanita's telltale red Fiat, parked sideways across the drive, blocking her departure. And here was Emilia approaching, a butter-wouldn't-melt smile pasted on her face.

"Do you know what you get for obstructing police business, Emilia?"

"But I can't talk to you any other way, can I?" she replied innocently. "You never return my calls and your Media Liaison people know less about the case than I do, so what's a girl to do?"

"Move it." Mark was growing impatient but his reward was a look of utter scorn.

"I want to talk to you about Peter Brightston," Emilia continued.

"Tragic."

"Odd that he should kill himself so soon after Ben's accident. It was only an accident, right?"

"That's what we believe."

"Only some colleagues at his firm are spreading rumors that he *killed* Ben. Would you care to comment on that, Inspector?"

"People will always speculate, Emilia—you know that." Helen refused to play the game by somebody else's rules. "If anything changes, I'll let you know, but it's not an active line of—"

"What did they fall out over? Love? Money? Were they gay?"

Helen pushed past.

"You're wasting my time, Emilia. And the last time I checked that *was* a criminal offense."

Helen and Mark climbed into the unmarked car. Mark pointedly started the engine, staring daggers at Emilia. She looked down her nose at him, then slowly walked back to her car. Helen was relieved and pleased that Anna and Marie hadn't featured in their discussion. It had been put out as natural causes and no one seemed to be challenging that—yet.

As they drove away, Helen glanced in the rearview mirror to make sure she wasn't following them. For once, Emilia had decided discretion was the better part of valor and had given up the chase. Helen breathed a sigh of relief. There was no way she could have an audience for what she was about to do.

45

Hannah Mickery was in the middle of preparing a dinner party when Helen arrived on her doorstep. She was every bit as respectable and attractive as she looked on her Web site. A good example of what money can do for you. The bottles of Clos Vougeot that had been decanted in anticipation of her guests' arrival reinforced the overall feeling of wealth.

She had so much and Helen would have thought she was extremely eligible. Yet she lived alone. This was the first curious thing that struck Helen. Later, in the interrogation room, Hannah Mickery insisted it was because of her work. That she gave so much to her clients that she seldom had time for socializing or dating. The dinner party that Helen had ruined had already been postponed twice because of her unpredictable job. The feeling of resentment toward Helen for the intrusion snapped sharp in the room.

She had her lawyer flanking her. He was expensive too. Mickery always waited for him to intervene and only if he didn't would she answer the question. They made a strong, considered, credible team. They'd be hard to discredit if they ever got this to trial.

She insisted that she'd been at the site of Peter's demise only because of her link with Ben. She was a therapist who had spent time with Ben after the horrendous events of his childhood. Murder was the worst type of case, worse even than suicide—that at least has a tragic dimension in its sheer futility and desperation. But how do you coach a young man through his father's destruction of their family? How do you deal with the fact that someone you loved has ripped your life apart and left you all alone in the world?

Hannah felt she'd made progress with the young Ben—or James, as he was then. And when he'd stopped visiting her three years later, he was kind of back on his feet. Functioning.

"Did you stay in touch?" Helen interjected, already irritated by the fond tone of Hannah's recollections.

"No, but I kept up to speed with his life. Through Facebook and the like."

"Why?"

"Because I liked him. I wanted him to survive. I was thrilled when I heard he was getting married."

"And how did you feel when you 'discovered' that he'd been murdered?"

"I was devastated. Obviously."

Said without feeling, Helen felt.

"And when I heard from a friend that his killer had committed suicide, I . . . well, I couldn't believe it."

"So you had to see it with your own eyes."

"Yes, I suppose so. It's not very nice, not very laudable, but I did want to see."

"Is it true that you'd offered your services to Peter Brightston after his escape from captivity?"

There was a pause. A sideways glance at her lawyer, and then a yes.

"Despite the fact that he'd killed your friend Ben?"

"Peter was clearly in a bad way. And he'd been released without char—"

"How did you know he was in a bad way? Did you see him after his release?"

A longer pause this time. A really long one, then:

"I went to his house once. I rang the bell and asked to see him. I offered my services but he wasn't interested."

"How did you know where he lived?"

"It wasn't hard to work it out. From what they said in the papers."

"So you stalked him to his house?"

"I'm not sure I like that term, Inspector," her lawyer intervened.

"My apologies, Sandy. I had no idea you were so sensitive. How long did you treat Diane Anderson for?" Helen said, returning her attention to the suspect.

"A couple of months. I'd been recommended to her by a colleague. Her best friend had died very suddenly and she needed help. But in truth her heart wasn't in it. I think she felt seeing a therapist was 'weak.' "

"Did you meet Amy during that time?"

"No. Though I was obviously aware of her."

"So there's no reason why Amy would recognize you?"

"Inspector . . ." her lawyer intervened. He could see where that was heading. But Helen made her answer the question anyway.

"No, we'd never met."

They moved on to alibis. Hannah was at home on the night of Amy's abduction—no witness, as she was working alone on her paperwork—but claimed to have been with a client when Ben went missing. She didn't have a secretary or assistant, so that one would have to be confirmed or denied by her client.

"Tell me about Marie Storey."

They hadn't been expecting that one.

"You treated her a few years ago, following the suicide of her husband."

Mark had found this one. Funny how the team was slowly coming together on this case.

More discussions with the lawyer, then:

"I was assigned her case by Hampshire Social Services. Her husband had killed himself with bleach, as I recall. Couldn't cope with the cards life had dealt him. The mother, Marie, was stronger, though. Had to be, for Anna."

"You remember their names well."

"I've a good memory."

Helen let that sit.

"Have you seen them recently?"

"No."

"Spoken to them?"

"No. I read about their deaths, obviously. I assumed in the

end that it had got too much for Marie. The papers were pretty vague on the details."

"Why did you stop treating her?"

"Cutbacks at the Health Trust. It wasn't my decision."

"How do you view your clients? As just that—clients? Or as patients? Friends?"

"I view them as clients. People I can help."

"Do you ever find that you dislike them?"

"Never. They can be frustrating, but that's to be expected."

"You really never find yourself disliking their weakness, their self-pity, their 'woe is me' act?"

"Never."

She parried well—like a professional—and shortly afterward her lawyer called time on the interview. They had to let her go. Had nothing to charge her with. But Helen didn't mind. During the time she'd been interviewing Hannah, Mark had applied for and got a search warrant for her house and office. There was more than one way to skin a cat.

One female suspect. With links to three very different victims. Someone who knew them—and their vulnerabilities—intimately. Now all they needed was proof. For the first time since the investigation started, Helen sensed that they were finally getting somewhere.

46

It was a strange sort of celebration. She clutching a Coke and he nursing a slowly warming tonic. Not very rock 'n' roll. But it felt good nevertheless. Neither had ever confronted a case like this before. Multiple murders were rare and when they happened tended to be spree killings. An explosion of anger that destroyed all but died out quickly. The level of care and planning that had gone into these murders was something else. Although no copper would ever admit it, these sorts of crimes were deeply unnerving. They made you feel that your experience counted for nothing, that your instincts were wrong, your training pitifully inadequate. These sorts of crimes broke the system that kept your faith intact.

But now they had a lead. Nothing cut-and-dried yet, but coppers are always happy when they have a strong scent. Something—or someone—to prosecute. Mark watched his superior as she chatted animatedly about the case. She'd always been attractive, but now there was something more. A warmth, a sense of optimism and hope, which was usually hidden from view. It was her smile that was the revelation. Seldom seen, but not easily forgotten.

He could sense his growing attraction to her and was determined to resist it. He would never again let any woman have that kind of hold over him. And yet he wanted to penetrate her armor and find out more about her. What did she dream of when she was little? Was she popular? Was she rich? Did the boys like her?

"Did you grow up round here?"

A poor opener, but Mark had never been good at chat. She shook her head.

"Sarf London. Can't you tell?"

Was she flirting with him?

"You haven't got an accent."

"I ironed it out. Good friend of mine in the force told me early on that the posher you sound, the quicker you rise. Just prejudice, really, but everyone thinks you're more intelligent."

"That must be where I went wrong."

"You're not so bad."

She *was* flirting with him.

"I had no idea you were so devious."

"Well, you don't know me very well yet, do you?"

Was that a come-on or a put-down? *I really am out of practice,* thought Mark. Helen headed off to the bar and came back with a pint of lager. Mark watched her, excited, aroused, torn—his desire for her jostling with his desire for the alcohol. She offered him the glass.

"We've had a good day today. So have some. You know the rules—as long as I'm here, it's okay."

He took the glass from her. And drank. But just a sip—wanted to show her that he was in control, that he wasn't weak. He'd hated himself and his life for so long. Now that he was climbing out of the abyss, he was going to show strength. He handed her back the glass. She smiled at him—warm and encouraging.

"Why did you join the force, Mark?"

Now it was her turn to ask the questions.

"Because no one else would have me."

She laughed at that one.

"Seriously. I completely messed up school. It was a good one—grammar school and that—but I just couldn't get into it. Couldn't pay attention. Just wanted to get out of the classroom."

"To chase the girls?"

"And the rest. After two years of sniffing glue and setting light to phone boxes, my old man kicked me out. I spent three nights on my sister's floor, then thought, 'Fuck this.' So I joined up."

"My hero."

"My dad nearly had a heart attack. Assumed it was a joke. But I surprised everyone. I liked it. Liked the fact that every day was different. That you never knew what was coming at you. And I liked the craic with the boys. We didn't have female superiors in those days."

She raised an eyebrow. Then slid off to the bar to buy another round. So this clearly wasn't just a quick drink after work, then. Mark wondered how he should play this, but was none the wiser by the time she'd returned. Her cleavage winked at him as she placed the drinks on the table. Whether this was accidental or not was impossible to tell.

"How about you? Why'd you join?"

A brief pause, then:

"To help people."

Brief and to the point. Was that all? Then:

"When I walked into Ben's house. Saw the carnage. And helped save that boy from a similar fate. That was it for me. I couldn't stop. Couldn't walk away after that."

"You're good at it. Saving people, I mean."

She looked at him intently. He hesitated, then continued:

"I would have quit by now, if it wasn't for you. I didn't tell you this, but I'd written the letter. Was ready to hand it in. To give up. But you saved me. Saved me from myself."

Said with passion and from the heart—for a moment Mark felt ashamed of his openness, his nakedness. But it was true. Without her, who knew where he'd be? She looked at him, suddenly earnest. Had he messed this up? Then she leaned across the table and kissed him.

Outside, he smiled as he offered her the cheesiest line he could think of.

"Your place or mi—"

"Yours."

47

Mark's flat was a mess. He hadn't planned on seducing his superior that day and the vestiges of last night's meal were still in evidence. Still, he'd changed the bed linen that morning and it felt clean and crisp as they sank down onto it.

She'd never been one for small talk. And the same was true now. Usually the man sets the pace in these things—or tries to—but that was not the case here. Mark was both surprised and aroused by how firmly his boss took the lead.

"I'd offer you a drink, but . . ."

She didn't bother to reply. She just crossed the flat and kissed him. Then, dropping her coat on the floor, she asked him which direction the bedroom was in. Once inside, she shoved him down onto the bed and reached for his belt.

Mark had made love many times, but he realized that this was the first time that he'd been made love *to*. Angry at being made to submit, he tried to spin her round. Now that he was aroused he suddenly wanted to dominate her—fuck her, bully her—but she pinned him back down, straddling him forcefully.

Was she loving him or just taking her pleasure from him? Mark suddenly realized that this mattered to him. That even now as she was lowering herself onto him, causing a sweet shudder to ripple through both of them, he wanted this to mean something, rather than just be a bit of fun. Men were supposed to be dissociative about sex. Able to turn off their emotions and think with their dick. But Mark had never been like that.

Again he tried to maneuver her so that he could be on top, but she pushed him back down aggressively. Clearly she wasn't ready to go there yet, so Mark decided to submit. The battle over, their lovemaking became more relaxed, more tender. Helen slowed the pace and finally their bodies moved in tandem. To Mark's surprise, she seemed to be enjoying it. Enjoying *him*. Brushing her nipples over his lips, Helen slid her hand between her legs, pleasuring herself as she rocked back and forward on top of him.

Mark was fighting desperately now to hold off his orgasm. It's one thing to screw your boss. Quite another to screw her badly. Or too briefly. So he fought, conjuring all sorts of dull and mundane images to suppress his excitement, but as Helen picked up the pace again, sensing his orgasm, it was only going to end one way.

He wanted to apologize. But wasn't sure whether it was warranted. She helped him out.

"That was nice."

Mark once again felt all his doubt disappear. He held her

close and warm and to his surprise she didn't resist. She nestled into his side to dwell in postcoital happiness.

As they lay there, the sheet barely covering them, Mark ran his eye over her body. In the throes of passion, he'd felt scratches on her back, but hadn't paid any heed to them. Now, less distracted and more curious, he looked at them in more detail. He was shocked. The rest of her was so soft, so clean, so . . . perfect.

She must have sensed his thoughts, because she pulled the sheet up over her back. Conversation closed before it had even started. They lay together in silence for a while. Then she turned to him and said:

"This is between us and no one else. Okay?"

It wasn't an order, nor was it fearful. No, it was beseeching, almost tentative. Mark was surprised again on this, the most surprising of days.

"Of course. Totally."

Then she went off to shower, leaving Mark full of questions.

48

Helen marched across the street to her bike. She knew Mark was watching her from the window above, but she didn't acknowledge him. She wasn't playing games—she just wasn't ready for cheery waves or blowing kisses yet. Still, it felt good to have his eyes upon her, and she slowed her pace deliberately to enjoy it for a few seconds more.

She clambered onto her Kawasaki and turned the ignition. Her bike leathers and helmet were another form of armor for Helen, a space where she could exist alone and unmolested. But today, for the first time in ages, she felt she didn't need it. That she didn't have to hide from the world. What had happened with Mark had been unplanned and unexpected—which was probably why it had felt so right. When Helen had time to think, things often got overcomplicated and then didn't happen at all. But today was just right. She wondered what Mark was thinking. Perhaps he thought she was odd—he wouldn't be the first. Or maybe he found her intriguing. That was the best that she could hope for at this stage and she would definitely settle for that.

It was time to leave. The crazy fool was still watching, the curtain only vaguely hiding his naked form. For his sake as well as hers, she knew she'd better go. So she revved the throttle and sped off down the road. As the wind whipped her body, she realized that today she was feeling decidedly unusual.

She was happy.

49

Martina pulled off her bra and thrust her naked breasts toward the other girl. Caroline—was that her name?—responded, licking her nipples with feverish, theatrical desire. Martina threw her head back groaning, and her eye was immediately caught by a dent in the roof of the van. How had that got there?

She'd done this so many times that it was impossible to keep your mind on the job. While your body was bucking and cavorting for someone else's pleasure, the brain disengaged and you found yourself wondering whether you could make it to the pub before closing time or whether you should go to Egypt on holiday or how much the other girl had paid to have her boobs done. It was amazing how mundane your thoughts could really be, especially when the girl—perhaps it was Carol, not Caroline—was going down on you. Martina moaned right on cue. The punters never guess, of course. They are so consumed by the idea of what they are seeing—two large-breasted women devouring each other—that they don't spot the telltale signs of ennui. Wouldn't care if they did anyway.

Still, this job was slightly different than most. Usually it was played out in front of a lonely businessman masturbating before his lesbian fantasy made flesh or more profitably in front of two rich guys who couldn't wait to get involved. The lesbian bit was just the amuse-bouche for them—they couldn't wait to get stuck into the girls, riding them in tandem, silently and mutually congratulating themselves on their wealth, imagination and depravity. They were tossers to a man, but they paid well, so those gigs were always welcome.

It was much rarer for a woman to hire two girls. Especially such a well-dressed one as Cyn. Rarer still for the woman not to get involved. Most women who hired female prostitutes were happily married but sexually unfulfilled. Women who wanted the status and trappings of normal family life but yearned to be touched by another woman. For them, the show wasn't important but the contact was. Yet Cyn was different. This was her fourth time now and she'd never so much as laid a finger on them. Never touched herself either. Each encounter was the same: she'd pick them up in her van, drive them out to the New Forest and then watch as the two girls pummeled each other with strap-ons and more. They'd been a bit suss at first—was this some kind of weird voyeuristic thing?—but actually she was totally harmless. Martina often wondered what was going on in that head of hers, though. What was she getting out of it?

The final peculiarity was the payment. She'd established early on that Martina was a party girl, a clubber. And since then she'd never paid her in cash. Instead, she'd offered Martina drugs. She must have had good access because the street value of what she gave easily outstripped the cash payment she owed. Somehow she must be getting them cheap—or free, lucky cow.

They finished—a frenzy of feigned mutual orgasm—then seconds later were slipping their clothes back on. Martina's body was athletic and strong—she was tall for a girl—and Cyn ran her eyes over her form before saying:

"Something special for you today."

Cyn held out a little transparent bag of pills. Martina took it from her for closer examination. It was full of large white pills with an eagle insignia on them.

"Just in from Odense. I think you'll like them. No need for an upper with these little beauties, believe me."

Martina poured half into Caroline's eager hands; then, without hesitation, they each popped one down. Unusual taste—almondy, sweet—then Caroline asked where they were going to go tonight.

Martina was about to brush her off—she was off to visit her sister tonight—but the words wouldn't come out. She felt a sudden light-headedness. Martina swayed as if she'd got up too quickly, losing balance and coherence. She laughed and righted herself. Cyn was talking to her—checking to see she was okay—but already her voice was sounding muffled and distant. A hand was on her arm, which suddenly felt so heavy—in fact all of her suddenly felt heavy. What the hell was going on? And then there was Caroline lying prone on the floor of the van. How did she get there? What wa—

Then suddenly everything went black.

50

Helen made sure she was first in the office. Having abandoned herself so completely with Mark the day before, doubts had subsequently set in. Helen's default position of caution—the closed circle—was assailing her again. She fought it off—for once determined not to give in—but she wasn't sure how her mask would be when she first saw him, so she got in early to give herself time to prepare.

Mark came in promptly and got straight on with his work. By now most of the team were in. Helen shot a surreptitious glance Mark's way—she wondered if anyone else within the team noticed how much better he was looking these days. He'd lost weight and gained color and the whole haunted look had completely disappeared. Helen wondered if it was going to be a day of politely tiptoeing round the subtle change in their relationship, but Charlie soon put paid to that. She came round early in the day to update Helen on the latest developments.

Helen had done her old trick—keeping the suspect in custody long enough to arrange a search warrant—so that Hannah Mickery had had no time to prepare her defenses or dispose of any evidence. They'd taken her computer—she flipped at that—and most of her diaries, journals and other personal items. They obviously couldn't touch her case files—those were confidential—but there were ways of getting information on patients if one had a mind to. But that was for later.

One thing was clear straightaway. She knew an awful lot about these killings. She had all the cuttings about Sam's death, as well as Ben's, Marie's and Anna's, but also pictures. And not just those culled from local papers, which had in turn been taken from Facebook, school albums and so forth. No, these were photos she'd taken of Amy and Peter *after* the event. Helen also found Amy's phone number scribbled in her journal. Why did she have this number, when she had neither met Amy nor, according to her testimony, ever been allowed to talk to her?

She had Peter's work details, e-mail addresses and, most intriguingly, a work schedule for him, though this was from after Peter had returned to work, so, irritatingly, it couldn't in any way be linked to his abduction.

The computer was a harder nut to crack. Hannah had been asked to volunteer her password but had refused, so they'd had to do it the hard way. People think these things are secure but they are not, and although they should strictly have waited for the relevant paperwork, Helen decided to press on and the IT guys soon opened up her system.

Charlie had done most of the legwork so she sat in as Helen navigated her way through the files on Hannah's MacBook Air. Most of it was dull—business and home admin—but a treasure trove was lurking inside. Hidden away from view in the computer's Finder was a locked file, simply named "B." Tantalizing . . . but, again, it didn't take long to open.

Helen sat bolt upright as she saw what it contained. A word-for-word transcript of Amy's formal statement, as given to Helen in the custody suite. Helen's eyes narrowed, disbelieving. She clicked on the RealPlayer icon that was also in the "B" file and her worst fears were realized. There, in perfect definition, was the video footage of the traumatized Amy giving her statement to Helen. Whoever she was—whatever she was—Hannah clearly had a copper onside. A copper who had given her this footage. But to what end?

Charlie exhaled loudly. The investigation had taken an important, but potentially devastating, lurch forward. Was this corruption? Collusion? Was a cop somehow involved in these killings?

"Shut this down. And not a word to anyone."

Charlie nodded. Helen got up and quietly, discreetly went off to talk to her superior.

51

Her head was full of fog. She struggled to her feet groggily, then shivered. Her vision was still hazy, but she could smell the damp and the chill went straight through her. Where was she?

Slowly images pushed into her mind, but each one stabbed like the worst hangover pains and she had to sit down again. The floor was hard and unforgiving. She remembered the van, Cyn, Caroline . . . She looked at her watch and did a double take. Had she really slept for over twenty-four hours?

The sound of retching made her look up. And there was Caroline. She'd just been sick and was now crying into her own vomit.

Get a grip. Wake up. But this wasn't a dream. This was too weird to be made up. Had Cyn brought her here? Where *was* Cyn? Martina shouted out but received only a dull echo in response. They were in some kind of cellar—a brick-arched vault gloomily illuminated by an old lantern. Poky and rotting—the forgotten box room of some big house perhaps. It didn't make any sense. None of this made any sense.

The door was locked from the outside. Solid metal, but she beat against it nevertheless. She beat until her hands throbbed and her headache raged—she slunk back onto the ground defeated.

"Caroline?"

She called out to her and again received no response. So she picked herself up and made her way over to her. Whatever was going on, at least they were in it together. En route, Martina's foot connected with something hard, which went skittering across the floor. She cried out in pain, then realized that she was virtually standing on something else: a mobile phone.

Martina picked it up. It wasn't hers and she didn't think it was Caroline's. She pressed a button and a lurid green glow illuminated the screen. *You have one new message.*

Instinctively, Martina pressed OK.

By this phone is a gun. It has one bullet in it. For Martina or for Caroline. Together you must decide who lives and who dies. Only through death will you be released. There is no victory without sacrifice.

And that was it. Martina's eyes shot to the object she'd kicked across the room. A gun. It was a bloody gun.

"Did you do this?" she barked at Caroline. "Is this your idea of a joke?"

But Caroline just whimpered and shook her head:

"What do you mean? I don't know *what*—"

At which point Martina threw the phone at her.

"That."

Nervously, Caroline picked up the phone. Her hands shook as she read the message. Then the phone dropped out of her hand, clattering to the floor, and she hung her head on her chest and sobbed. Martina looked sickened—she obviously knew nothing.

Martina could see her breath frosting in front of her. Would it get colder in this tomb? Would they freeze to death before anyone found them?

Her life wasn't meant to end like this. She'd been through too much to die in this dank hole.

Slowly, in the fractured gloom, Martina's eyes came to rest on the gun.

52

She was being watched.

A Transit van had been parked in the same spot for days now. But there was no sign of any activity around it. It had a plumber's logo on the side, but there were never any plumbers in evidence, and, besides, she'd looked up the company name online—it didn't exist. She'd had to do this on her new smart-phone, as the police still had her computer.

Hannah Mickery scrutinized the van from between a crack in the curtains. Were they looking at her right now through the tinted glass, taking photos? Or was she just being paranoid?

There had been so many people in the house during the search, it was hard to keep tabs on them all. Would they have had time to bug the place? After they'd gone, Hannah had checked every possible hidey-hole. She'd found nothing. Perhaps it was all a bit too Cold War for run-of-the-mill plod.

But it pays to be cautious when there is so much at stake.

By now that snotty cow Grace would have pillaged her computer. She probably should have given them the password, but why not make them work a little harder for it? Anyway, by now they would know. It would be hard to pass it off as professional interest or even apologize for it as macabre gawping. But did they have anything to charge her with? Of course not.

But she'd have to be careful. The stakes were high now and a single mistake could unravel everything. So much thought and planning had gone into this. It would be criminal to fuck it up now.

Night was falling. It wouldn't be long now. Could they monitor her mobile phone calls? If it was good enough for the *News of the World*, then . . .

She hoped they had been listening. It would make it easier for her. Easier to escape. Hannah felt a thrill of excitement—when the game hung in the balance, every move was thrilling.

53

Caroline clutched her knees to her chest to ward off the cold, but she couldn't stop shivering. Was it the cold making her shake? Or fear? Caroline couldn't tell anymore. She had lost her grip on . . . everything. She had no idea if it was day or night. No real concept of how long they'd been incarcerated. She didn't know what they'd done wrong or why they were here. She just knew that it was agony.

Her stomach ached for food, her throat was parched, her bones were chilled to their marrow. When she closed her eyes, strange shapes danced in the darkness—multicolored patterns that changed into butterflies, birds, rainbows even. She was starting to hallucinate. Was this her body shutting down? If she was lucky. Perhaps it was her mind unraveling, the beginning of a slow descent into paranoia and madness. *Please, God, not that.*

Initially they'd tried to keep their hunger at bay by eating ants. Caroline had had her period, her menstrual blood clotting on the floor in the far corner of the room. Its sticky sweetness had attracted insects and Martina and she had jostled with each other to hoover them up. A day or so back, she had bagged a cockroach, thrilling to its crunch as she crushed it in her mouth. But the food was gone now. All they were left with was the awful smell. The terrible cold. And the loneliness.

Was anybody looking for them? Nobody would miss a couple of escorts. Martina kept herself to herself and had few if any friends. Caroline had a flatmate—a girl called Sharon who came from Macclesfield—but she wouldn't call her a friend. Would she have been savvy enough to call the police or would she have just put an advert out for a new roomie? The latter probably— Sharon didn't approve of what Caroline did for money and would have been glad of the opportunity to get rid of her. She was probably clearing out her room now. *Bitch.*

Martina had a sister, but were they close? Caroline had no idea. For the first time in years, she found herself missing her family. She'd had good reason to run away from home—though no one ever acknowledged that—but she regretted it bitterly now. Her mum was ineffectual but not nasty and her dad—well, he wasn't cut out to be a dad, or a husband really—but he wouldn't have wished her harm. Why hadn't she got back in touch? Their sixtieth birthdays had come and gone, Christmases, Easters— there had been plenty of opportunities to bridge the gap and effect a reconciliation, but she'd never made the effort. Would they have asked her to explain her midnight flit? Would they have been disgusted by the way she lived her life now?

Anger surged in her heart and Caroline knew exactly why she'd never got back in touch. Because she did blame them. For not noticing. For not protecting her. She was still furious at their neglect and that was why she was alone in the world. That was why there was no one looking for her now. Did she or Martina have anything—or anyone—to live for? How close was Martina to her sister? She felt like asking her, but what was the point? It wasn't a competition.

Was it?

54

Predictably, Detective Superintendent Whittaker had not taken the news well.

"What the fuck are you telling me? That a *cop* gave her this?"

The macabre nature of the killings had required an absolute information lockdown. The *Evening News* and a couple of the national newspapers had picked up on the spike in local deaths and were scratching around for more, but none had yet divined the unseen puppeteer orchestrating these terrible crimes. Forensics and other ancillary staff were unaware of the deadly ultimatum delivered to the victims. Access to that information—the phones, the interview footage and transcripts—had been kept very tight. Obviously Whittaker and Helen knew, as did Mark and Charlie and a couple of other core team officers, but that was pretty much it. So unless a data officer had been tipped off as to their content, or had stumbled on it accidentally, then they would have to look close to home to find the source of the leak. Whittaker didn't beat around the bush. Every member of the team would have to be investigated for evidence of possible corruption or collusion. It would have to be done dispassionately and it would have to be done quickly.

Helen made quick progress. These days there were no interview tapes or minidiscs—all that stuff was obsolete, long gone. The interview footage was now recorded straight onto a secure digital network. Once the interview was completed, the digital file was then encrypted and uploaded to their secure server. Stored recordings and transcriptions could be accessed only by approved users. There was only one source—the server—and anyone accessing it would leave a trace.

The interview footage had been viewed innumerable times as part of the inquiry and a long list of these viewings scrolled out as Helen delved into the search history. But on only three occasions had the actual footage been downloaded or burned onto a disc or memory stick. And for two of those, Helen had been present— moreover, she still had the downloads in her possession. Which left one unauthorized download. It was impossible to cover your tracks with these things without destroying the whole server and there it was in black-and-white: *Weds 11th January 4.15 p.m.*

It was unlikely to have been the data officers, as they were involved in industrial action that day, but perhaps that was why the thief chose that day in particular. Whittaker had been on leave, while Helen had been at the forensics lab all afternoon. The junior team officers had been doing house-to-house that day—Helen would have to double-check that—so that left two officers in the know who were in the building and had access to the secure server: Mark and Charlie.

Helen was kicking herself. She should have canceled her dinner with Mark, feigned some excuse, but he'd caught her on the hop. She couldn't back out of their dinner without offending him or acting in a way that would have aroused his suspicions, so she'd gone along with it. He'd joked with her about the effort he'd gone to to impress her, which was why they were now tucking into prawn bucatini in virtual silence. Helen was fully aware of Mark's disappointment and awkwardness—his vision of a night of passionate lovemaking in tatters—but it was impossible to stop thinking about it. Unless Helen was completely off beam, it was probable that either Charlie or Mark had grossly betrayed the team and in the process opened up their investigation to an outsider. If a corrupt officer wanted money, they'd leak to the press. So this had to be something else. Blackmail. Sex. Or something more sinister.

Helen was torn in two. She wanted to be up-front with him, but to do so would be to put her own neck on the line. This was now an internal investigation, and if she shared information with a "suspect," then she would be corrupt too. So she bit her tongue and made polite conversation.

They gave up on the meal quite quickly and moved into the living room. Helen wandered over to the mantelpiece. The pictures of the happy family and the ex-wife were long gone. All that remained were innumerable pictures of a little girl with a cute blond bob and a big smile.

"That's Elsie."

"How old is she?"

"Seven. Lives with her mother. Not far away."

But clearly too far away for Mark's liking. Helen asked some more interested questions and Mark responded as only a proud parent can. A history of Elsie's achievements and interests. Anecdotes about her idiosyncrasies and daftness. It was hard to listen to—his desolation at being apart from his daughter was so evident. A year back he was a successful copper with a loving wife and a little angel who had eyes only for him. Now he'd lost everything to another man—his wife's lover, Stephen. It was their affair that had ended the marriage and yet it was Mark who was out in the cold. He had been hurt—deeply, deeply hurt—by someone who had been cavalier about their marriage vows. She had ended up with the whole deal. He'd ended up with a rented flat and visits every other weekend.

Helen did her best to comfort him, but all the while a little voice inside her was telling her to leave. To get away from this guy who was obviously falling for her. Eventually Mark calmed down. Thanking her for listening to his ramblings, he ran his hand across her cheek—a tender, wordless thank-you. Then he tried to kiss her.

Helen found herself walking toward the front door. Mark ran after her, apologizing. As she opened the door to leave, he grabbed her arm, pulling her back. Helen spun away as if burned.

"Please, Helen, if I've offended you . . ." Mark stuttered.

"Don't beg, Mark. You're better than that."

"I don't understand what's going on here."

"Nothing's going on here."

"I thought that you and I . . . that we . . ."

"You thought wrong. We had sex. That's all."

"Am I being dumped?"

"Don't be so childish."

"Well, what, then? I thought you liked me."

Helen paused, trying to choose her words carefully.

"Mark, I'm only going to say this once, so please listen. Do *not* fall in love with me, okay? I don't want it and neither do you."

"But why?"

"Just don't."

And with that, Helen was gone. On the way down, she kicked herself for her foolishness. Her first instinct was right—she should never have come here.

55

Charlie Brooks yawned and stretched out her arms. Her joints cracked loudly—she'd been sitting in the same position for too long. She made a decision to move around more frequently, to stretch, exercise . . . then promptly banged her head on the low metal roof.

Charlie hated surveillance. The enclosed space, the junk food diet and the proximity to male officers who either fancied her or had bad personal hygiene, or both. Sometimes it brought results, but one always had the sense that the fun, the real policing, was happening elsewhere. Couldn't Helen have found some other monkey for this job? Her mood sank further as she looked across at DC Grounds, who was unself-consciously picking a spot.

Charlie had the distinct impression she was being punished—though what for she couldn't say. Helen had definitely been "off" with her recently. On several occasions Charlie had been tempted to ask her straight out what was wrong, only to pull back at the last second, concerned that she would come across as paranoid. Yet the feeling remained. Somehow she had irked Helen and perhaps the surveillance job on Mickery's house was her penance.

Hannah Mickery had hardly left the house since her release from custody. A couple of trips to the grocery store, the newsagent's, but little more. She hadn't used her landline at all and her mobile calls had been brief and mundane. Clearly she wasn't going to let the cloud of suspicion disrupt her working life, hence the visit from a client. The pair had been closeted away for an hour now—Charlie couldn't help wondering what hang-up, insecurity or peccadillo was being discussed.

Then suddenly there was movement. Charlie sat bolt upright and swung her camera into position. Only to be disappointed. It was just the client leaving her session, sheltering herself from the pelting rain with her "cheerful" yellow umbrella. Charlie sat back down, disgruntled, and watched her go.

You'd have to be a real mentalist to wear that outfit, Charlie thought uncharitably. The purple beret and the red mac—did she think she'd just stepped out of a Prince video? And the heels. They were strippers' heels, pure and simp—

Which was when Charlie noticed that the woman who'd just left the house wasn't wearing heels. She was wearing flats.

Charlie was out of the van in a flash, ordering Grounds to the house as she set off after the client. Padding fast but quietly, she gained on the woman, but then, with only forty yards to go, the woman half turned. It was only a glimpse but enough for Charlie to know for certain that this was Mickery dressed in her client's clothes. Mickery immediately broke into a sprint and Charlie gave chase—thoughts of what Helen would say if she lost her powering her forward.

Charlie thought the pursuit would be easy, but Mickery was good. She darted across the busy street without hesitation, somehow finding a path through the speeding traffic. Charlie raced after her, determined not to be beaten, but the braking cars impeded her at every turn.

They ducked down a side street. The distance between them was now about a hundred yards, and with the absence of human traffic on this quiet road, Charlie began to gain on her quarry. Eighty yards, sixty yards, fifty. Closer and closer.

The busy street loomed ahead. Hannah Mickery reached it first and launched herself across it. The beret had by now blown off and her long auburn hair trailed behind her. She reached the other side and without hesitation dived into the welcoming entrance of Marlands Shopping Centre. Charlie was seconds behind.

A sea of schoolchildren, bored and flirty. A security man picking his teeth. A couple of gawky lads in Saints shirts. But no sign of Mickery.

Then a flash of auburn. On the far escalator. Charlie set off in pursuit once more, hurdling potted plants and toddlers as she cranked up her speed. Up, up, up she sprinted—her lungs burning with the exertion. Barging a middle-aged dawdler out of the way, Charlie burst onto the mezzanine level.

The red coat. Vanishing into Topshop. No way out from there. Charlie sprinted inside, badge already on display as the security guards started to rouse themselves. Finally Charlie would be able to look Helen in the eye—a juicy prize to deliver to her.

Except—this was the wrong red coat. Right shade, wrong wearer. A singleton shopping for a date and somewhat surprised to find herself being manhandled by a sweating female copper.

"What the hell are you doing?"

"Shit!" Charlie was already moving away from her startled victim. She collared the nearest security guard.

"Did you see a woman in a red coat run past here? Did *any-one* see a woman in a red coat?"

Charlie looked at the sea of blank faces, knowing already that it was hopeless.

Mickery had got away.

56

They hadn't moved for days now. They were beaten, crushed with despair. Starvation would be their release—it was plain that there would be no escape.

Caroline had been waiflike to begin with. Now she looked like a famine victim, her ribs threatening to break through her skin at any point. Martina was the more muscular of the two, and somehow, despite day after day of starvation, she struggled to her feet now.

"Let's try again."

Martina tried to inject energy and hope into her voice, but Caroline just groaned.

"Please, Caroline, we have to try again."

Now Caroline raised her head to see if Martina was serious. It was hopeless, so why torture themselves? The door hadn't yielded an inch despite their pounding. Their shoulders were bruised, their nails broken. There was nothing more they could do.

"Someone might hear us."

"There's nobody out there."

"We have to try. Please, Caroline, I'm not ready to die yet."

A long pause. Then slowly, reluctantly Caroline dragged her weary body off the ground. Despair was easier than hope. Hope was cruel—it promised Caroline things she feared she'd never experience again: love, warmth, comfort, happiness. None of these things were possible while she was buried alive in this tomb— they were mere dreams. All Caroline wanted now was to be left alone to her despair, and if charging the door for a few pointless minutes would shut Martina up, then so be it.

Abandoning herself, she ran full pelt at the door, crashing into it. The pain was intense—a searing, burning sensation in her shoulder that slowly transmuted to a sadistic dull ache. She turned, angry.

"Aren't you going to help m—?"

Her voice gave out when she saw Martina pointing the gun at her. She'd been tricked. That devious bitch had tricked her.

"I'm really sorry," muttered Martina. Then she pulled the trigger, closing her eyes so as not to see the horror. The gunshot reverberated around the brick chamber.

But no scream came. No sound of flesh tearing. Just the dull *thunk* of the bullet burying itself in the door. She had missed.

She pulled the trigger again and again, but she knew there had been only one bullet in it. One shot at salvation.

Caroline flew through the air, knocking Martina to the

ground. They struggled fiercely in the dirt, but Martina was on the back foot and soon Caroline was on top. Her knees pressed down heavily on Martina's chest, then spread to pinion her arms. And now Caroline's raw, bloody fingers were wrapping themselves around Martina's throat.

She was wild, unhinged. But she was triumphant. And she shouted and screamed for joy as she choked the life out of the young prostitute.

She had won.

57

"Where is she?" Charlie shouted. Martha Reeves sat calmly on the living room chair, dressed in one of Mickery's dressing gowns. Despite staring down the barrel of a police charge, she seemed utterly unrepentant. Her point of view seemed to be that the police had got it wrong, were unfairly harassing an innocent woman, so if she could help her out, why not?

"She's under investigation on suspicion of *murder*. And what you've done makes you an accessory. Do you know what you get for that? Ten years. Ten years ducking the Hairy Marys in Holloway."

Cold, naked defiance.

"What do you come here for anyway?"

"Oh, come off it. Surely you don't ex—"

"What are you? A pervert? An addict? What little peccadillo needs ironing out so bad that you'll pay three hundred pounds an hour to this quack?"

DC Grounds chose this moment to step outside. He didn't like scenes and Brooks seemed to be going way over the top. For whose benefit, he wasn't sure. Whatever it was about, it wouldn't get them anywhere, so he took the opportunity to radio in—see if anyone else had had any luck.

The call had gone out, all available units had scrambled to the area, but there'd been no sign of Mickery. An eagle-eyed community support officer had found a discarded red coat in a trash can just outside Marlands Shopping Centre, but that was all. She had vanished into thin air. Cursing, Grounds headed back into the house.

"Is she allowed to do this?" Martha barked at Grounds as he entered. Charlie was busy rifling through her handbag.

"Yes, sirree. When she's like this, it's best just to sit it out."

Both women scowled at him. Mobile phone, lipstick, Black-Berry, a condom, tissues, keys on a ring with smiley family scene encased in cheap plastic, sweets, another condom . . .

"Married?"

For the first time, a moment's hesitation from Martha. But Charlie was already scrolling through the contacts list on Martha's phone.

"Adam? No? Chris, then? Colin? David? Graham? Let's try Graham . . ."

And she pressed the call button . . .

"Tom. His name is . . . Tom."

Charlie clicked off.

"Know you're here, does he?"

Martha looked at her shoes.

"Thought not. Right, let's get him to pick you up and take you ho—"

"Enough."

"It's ringing."

"I said *enough*!"

"Come on, Tom, pick up!"

"The Valley."

"I'm sorry?"

"She said she was going to . . . the Valley."

By now Tom's confused voice could just be heard from the mouthpiece, but Charlie turned the phone off.

"Continue."

"I don't know where exactly. But she said she was going to Bevois Valley and that she would be straight there and back. Wouldn't be gone more than an hour."

Charlie was out the door and running to her car. Grounds might disapprove of her methods, but nobody could say they weren't effective. The chase was back on now and heading toward its climax. Mickery had gone to Bevois Valley—home to Empress Road, Southampton's notorious red-light district.

58

Caroline was sinking deeper and deeper into hell. And the lifeless corpse of Martina was her personal demon leading the way. However much Caroline shut her eyes, turned her back, screamed, shouted, wept and wailed, the sound of Martina's silent accusation was impossible to block out.

Worse was the sound of laughter. The laughter of the evil bitch who had set this all up. She had made them a *promise*. She had said that if one of them— Caroline wept some more, but they were dry tears now. There was nothing more to give.

The whole thing had been a con. The woman was long gone. And Caroline? Caroline had killed a girl. An innocent girl. And what was her reward? Death.

Perhaps she should kill herself? A weird elation punched

through her. She stalked around the cellar looking for a means to her end. She could hang herself with Martina's clothes, except . . . there was nothing to hang from. The ceiling was smooth, the room unfurnished. There were no sharp edges and nothing to fashion into a weapon. Crazily, she soon found herself clawing at the bullet hole—*Come out, you bastard!*—before giving up and descending once more into despair.

Then, without warning, a key turned in the lock and the door swung open.

"Well done, Caroline."

She could hear her, but she couldn't see her. For a moment, Caroline was frozen to the spot. Her tormentor had reappeared and fear gripped her completely.

But nothing happened. Was the woman still there? It didn't look like it and now she couldn't hear her. Suddenly Caroline was on her feet and heading to the door. If the woman was still there, she'd wring her bloody neck. *Bring it on!* But then suddenly, in the midst of her charge to freedom, Caroline stopped. And turned.

Martina. There she was, lifeless and still. Two of them had arrived; now only one was leaving. Caroline stood on the threshold. While she remained inside she was a victim. Once she stepped outside, she was a murderer.

But what choice did she have? To live, she must embrace her crime. So she stumbled through the doorway.

She was at the bottom of a flight of stairs. Light poured down from above—through some sort of trapdoor—temporarily blinding her. Once more, she hesitated. Was her abductor waiting above? Slowly, steadily she climbed the creaking stairs. She emerged into a sea of brightness.

She was alone. Alone in the body of a decaying house. A big one. Unloved and unwanted, just as Caroline had always been. And yet, right at this moment, she loved this house. Its light, its emptiness, her liberty. She could walk in any direction, without fear, without compulsion. She was once more master of her fate.

She started to snigger. Before long she was howling with laughter—wild, raucous, crazy laughter. She had survived!

Still laughing, she marched over to the front door. Wrenching it open, she struggled up the short garden path and through the gate, back onto the bustling city streets.

59

Charlie made it to Bevois Valley in fifteen minutes flat. They could have done it in ten with the blues and twos on, but that was out of the question. They didn't want to spook Mickery. DC Grounds had been left to babysit a deeply pissed-off Martha Reeves—they couldn't discount the possibility that she would contact Mickery to warn her.

A description had gone out to uniform on the beat and Charlie immediately set about coordinating the efforts. Bevois Valley was a shabby collection of low-rent supermarkets, industrial parks and depots. It was a small place and many of the local cops were on nodding terms with the hookers and junkies who also made it their home, taking advantage of the numerous squats and abandoned houses that disfigured the streets. News could travel surprisingly fast in this enclosed community and the word was out. A good tip-off now could break the case. Could they catch Mickery in the act? Charlie felt her pulse quicken—the thrill of the chase never failed to get her heart racing. But there was more this time. This was personal—she wouldn't let Mickery escape her twice.

Five minutes. Ten minutes. Fifteen. And still no sign. In and out of the garages and body shops. The supermarkets and minicab offices. But everywhere the same—a look at the photo and a polite shake of the head.

Then a disturbance in the street. Calls for help. A woman lying prostrate on the ground. Charlie covered the distance in seconds to find a young woman in a very bad way. Crazed eyes, blood streaming from cuts on her face. But nothing to do with Mickery. A pissed-up local girl on the receiving end of her violent boyfriend's displeasure. As uniform led the protesting offender away, Charlie returned to the hunt.

Twenty minutes. Thirty minutes. And still radio silence. Charlie cursed her luck. What was it with this woman that she could disappear into thin air? She was sure Reeves wasn't lying to her about the location—she'd had to wrench the information out of her—so where the hell was she? She'd give it another thirty minutes, maybe more. *Something* had to turn up.

It started to rain. Gently at first, then big, heavy drops, then a sudden attack of hail. As the ice bounced off Charlie's sodden hair, she cursed her luck. But things were about to get a lot worse.

"Call off the search."

Charlie spun round. Helen had arrived. And she didn't look happy.

. . .

They didn't speak on their way back to the police station. No explanation about why the search had been called off, nor the expected admonishment for losing the prime suspect—twice. Charlie didn't know what was going on and she didn't like it. For the first time in her life she realized what it felt like to be picked up by the police. To be a suspect. Charlie desperately wanted to talk, to dispel her nervousness and find out what was going on. But that clearly wasn't an option. So she sat and suffered in silence, imagining a thousand dark scenarios.

They walked through the nick in silence. Helen commandeered an interview room and switched off her mobile. The two women stared at each other.

"Why did you become a police officer, Charlie?"

Fuck, it was bad. If that was the opening question, she clearly was in deep.

"To do my bit. Catch the bad guys."

"And do you think you're a good police officer?"

"Of course."

A long silence, then:

"Tell me about Hannah Mickery. And how you let her go."

Charlie wasn't going to rise to that one. Whatever was thrown at her, she must keep calm. Everything could depend on that. So Charlie told her about how Hannah had outwitted her. About how they had lost her. No point dressing things up when she was clearly already in serious trouble.

"How long have you known Hannah Mickery?"

"Known?"

"How long?"

"I don't know her. We picked her up, interviewed her, dug around her computer . . . That's it. I know her as well as you do."

More silence.

"Are you excited by her crimes?"

This was getting weirder by the minute.

"Of course not. These crimes are despicable. Abhorrent. If Mickery's guilty, then I hope they throw away the key."

"We'll have to find her first."

Low. But probably deserved. Charlie had messed up with Mickery—no doubt about that. Would there be more deaths? And would they be on *her* conscience this time?

"What did you feel when you heard Peter Brightston had killed himself?"

"What did I 'feel'?"

"Did you think he was weak?"

"No. Of course not. I felt sorry for the guy. We should all have done mo—"

"And what about Anna and Marie? Did you feel sorry for them? Or did they deserve it. They were definitely weak. What did the local lads call them? Mongs?"

"*No! Absolutely not!* No one deserves to die like that. And with the greatest of respect—"

"Do you need money, Charlie? Are you in debt?"

"No."

"Need a bigger house? Better car?"

"No. I don't need more money."

"Everyone needs money, Charlie. What makes you different? Do you gamble? Drink? Borrow money from the wrong people?"

"No! A hundred times no."

"Then why did you do it?"

Battered, Charlie finally looked up.

"Do what?"

"If you tell me now, I can help you."

"Please, I don't know what you want me to say—"

"I don't pretend to understand why you let her use you like this. Best-case scenario, she had something on you. Worst-case, you're as twisted as she is. But understand this, Charlie: if you don't tell me the truth now—every last detail—then you will go to prison for the rest of your life. Do you know what happens to bent coppers in jail?"

And at once it all fit into place.

"I didn't do it."

Silence.

"I know you think someone is helping her. Someone from this station. Someone from the team. But it isn't me."

"But I already know it's you."

"You can't. I have an alibi. You *know* I have an alibi. Yes, I was in the nick, but I was talking to Jackie Tyler in Missing Persons at that time. I was there for forty minutes at least, going through couples who'd gone missing—"

"She says you weren't."

"No, no, no—that's wrong. She made a statement saying—"

"She's retracted it. She got the timing wrong."

A heavy, bewildered silence. For the first time, tears sprang to Charlie's eyes. Helen continued:

"She didn't think it was important at first, but she now remembers that it was early afternoon that you came to her—"

"No, no—she's lying. I was there. I did spend that time with her—I can tell you the name of every couple we went thr—"

"You've let me down, Charlie. And betrayed us all. If you had a shred of decency or honesty about you, I could have helped you, but it's in the hands of Anti-Corruption now. They will be here in five minutes, so get your story straight—"

Charlie's hand shot out and grabbed Helen's.

"It's not me."

A long beat.

"I know you don't like me. I know you don't rate me. But I *swear* it isn't me. I—"

Now the tears were coming thick and fast.

"I would never . . . I couldn't. How could you think I would ever do something like that?"

Said with fierce passion. Then she broke down—deep, guttural sobs.

"It's not me."

Helen watched her, then:

"It's okay, Charlie. I believe you."

Charlie looked up, disbelieving.

"But . . ."

"Anti-Corruption isn't coming. And Jackie never retracted her statement—she's given you a cast-iron alibi. I'm sorry it had to be this way, but I've got no other choice. I need to know who's doing this."

"So?"

"You're in the clear, Charlie. Nobody need ever know we've had this conversation and it won't be on your sheet. Get yourself cleaned up and get back to work."

And with that, she was gone. Charlie buried her head in her hands. Relief and exhaustion mingled with disgust—she had never disliked Helen Grace as much as she did at this moment.

Outside, Helen took a breath. She felt sick to her stomach. Not for what she had put Charlie through, but for what her innocence meant. There was only one possible culprit left now: Mark.

60

Caroline's whole body was rigid, her ears straining for sounds of movement. It had been four days since she'd been liberated and she'd hardly slept a wink since. Visions of Martina played in her head—the gasping for breath, the bulging eyes—but it was fear that was really keeping her awake. The euphoria of survival had slowly given way to a gnawing terror. Why had she been released? What terrible fate awaited her now that she had proved herself to be a killer?

Caroline had discharged herself from the hospital as soon as they would let her and hurried back to her flat. She needed to be somewhere familiar, somewhere safe. But Sharon had taken one look at her and fled to her parents, despite Caroline's begging her to stay. Looking in the mirror later, Caroline understood why her roomie had fled. She looked crazed and inhuman, the walking dead. All life had been sucked from her—she was pale, ghostly and utterly incoherent. She hadn't been able to find the words to describe her ordeal—the endless stream of obscenities and non sequiturs had made little sense.

Left alone, her doubts and fears started to multiply. Racking her brains, she eventually summoned the memory of a guy who could fix you up with anything you wanted, and she hurried to his squat, casting fevered glances over her shoulder every five seconds. Her hand was shaking when she used the cash machine, but she'd got what she needed. Five hundred pounds was enough to get her a gun and six bullets. Walking home with the gun in her bag, she felt relieved. She would at least be armed and ready if—when—the crisis came.

The days passed slowly but without incident, and before long she was so crazed by her own company that she attempted to return to work. Her punters were clearly alarmed by her appearance, wanting to know where she'd been, why she was so skinny, so distracted, but she bullshitted them. Sold them some drab lies and tried to concentrate on the job in hand. All the time she was drinking. And drinking. Vodka, whisky, beer—anything. It's hard to give someone a handjob when your hands are shaking.

She didn't feel much guilt anymore, just fear. Cyn was still out there somewhere. The godlike Cyn who had played with her life, made her into a murderer, was still out there. Every creak of the floorboard, every door slamming, made Caroline jump. Last night, she'd been so startled by a firecracker going off that she'd started to cry in front of a client. The look of confusion on his face as he hurried out made up Caroline's mind and she legged it home—it had been a mistake to go back to work so soon.

Which was why she was now back in her flat, the covers pulled up to her neck, her hand reaching out to the gun that lay on the table beside her. Someone was trying to get into the flat. It was five a.m. and still pitch-black outside. Was this Cyn's plan? To come for her under cover of darkness? Caroline slipped out of bed—staying put was more scary than actually doing something. She opened the bedroom door, half expecting to find Cyn waiting on the other side, but the corridor was empty.

She crept out, cursing every creaking floorboard. The living room was clear, the hall was clear . . . but there it was again. A gentle *scratch, scratch*, as if someone were picking a lock or working their way in. Caroline clutched the gun a little tighter. The noise was coming from the kitchen. Steeling herself, she tiptoed toward it, teasing the door open with her foot.

It was empty, but then suddenly a noise at the window. *BANG.* Caroline fired without hesitation. Once, twice, three times. Then found herself running toward the shattered window. She looked out into the street below, determined to put her tormentor down once and for all . . . but all she saw was next door's cat sprinting away like a bat out of hell. It had been a cat. A stupid bloody cat.

Caroline collapsed to the floor, her chest heaving as the hopelessness and desperation of her situation hit home. She was alive only in name—her life was no longer hers. She was gripped by a ceaseless terror that made her victory over Martina empty and worthless. Throwing the gun in the bin, she called the police and confessed her crime.

Helen regarded Caroline across the table as she stumbled her way through her formal confession. Caroline expected to be punished.

She *wanted* to be punished. So she seemed almost disappointed when Helen reassured her that it was unlikely they would press charges—*if* her story stacked up, of course, and *if* she promised to keep quiet about her ordeal.

She took them to the house where it had happened. Bought by an entrepreneur who'd subsequently gone bust in the recession, it had been left to rot. As had Martina, who had already attracted the attention of the rats and flies. The stench—a decomposing body in a damp cellar—made you retch, but Helen had to see the body.

What had she been expecting? Some bolt of lightning? She both hoped and feared she would know the victim, to give fuel to that line of inquiry, but she'd never seen the young girl before in her life. Truth be told, she looked like any number of silicone-enhanced prostitutes who ended up in ditches. Why had the killer chosen her?

Caroline filled them in on Cyn. Who had auburn hair now, it appeared. Caroline explained in graphic detail the tricks she and Martina had performed for her pleasure. There was never any physical contact and their meetings took place in the killer's van.

"How did she contact you?"

"Online. Martina had a Web site. She e-mailed her there."

They'd look into that—see if the e-mail could be traced to an IP address. But Helen wasn't confident. The armor on this woman was too complete to allow for such a mistake. So she turned her attention back to the victims.

Caroline was nothing particularly out of the ordinary. She'd run away from home at sixteen to escape the attentions of a grandfather who wouldn't take no for an answer. She started off conning gullible punters out of cash without delivering the goods—until she encountered someone who could run faster than her. She couldn't walk for days after that, but once she could, she turned her back on Manchester and headed south. First Birmingham, then London. And finally to Southampton. Sad to say, she was a common or garden prostitute. Let down by her family, kicked by life, surviving by her wits. It was a depressing but unremarkable story.

Was Martina important in the game, then? Or had they just been chosen at random? Of the two, Martina was the more interesting. At least she would have been, if they knew anything about her. She'd arrived in Southampton only two months earlier. She had no friends, no family, no social security number. She was a blank sheet. Which in itself was interesting.

Helen took the interviews alone. Regulations said she needed someone with her, but she was paying no heed to that now. She couldn't afford any more leaks. But just as she was finishing off, news came that changed everything. Finally a chance to find out for certain who had been selling them down the river.

Mickery had resurfaced.

61

He really needed a drink. The last few days had been torture and his body, his brain, his soul ached for the release of alcohol. The first sip was always the best—you didn't have to be an alcoholic to know that—and he was straining every sinew now to resist the short walk to the liquor store.

He was out in the cold and had no idea why. Was it because he was weak? At the time crying on Helen had seemed the natural thing to do—open, honest, real—but perhaps she now despised him for his vulnerability. Did she regret sleeping with him? Or was it something else?

He hadn't seen Charlie or Helen for days. They'd been out of the station, or locked in interview rooms together. The atmosphere between them was even more troubled than usual—Helen was short with Charlie at the best of times, so something had to be going on. But at least Charlie existed in Helen's world, which was more than Mark did.

It was late now, but Mark knew Charlie never missed her boxing class at the police gym. Come hell or high water she'd be there, which was why he was now loitering in the gym car park, drawing inquisitive looks from those who passed.

And here she was. Marching across the car park toward the gym. Mark hurried over, calling her name. Charlie seemed to slow her pace a little. Was she panicking, buying herself a few seconds to work out how to deal with him? *Who cares?* thought Mark, and he dived straight in.

"I don't want to put you in an awkward spot, but I've got to know what's going on, Charlie. What have I *done?*"

A brief pause, then:

"I don't know, Mark. She's being a bitch to all of us at the moment. If I knew, I'd tell you. I promise."

She stumbled on, speaking a lot but saying very little. Mark knew she was lying. She had never been a very good actress. But why? They had always got on, always been mates. What had Helen said to her?

"Please, Charlie. However embarrassing it is, or bad it is, I have to know what I've done. This job is all I've got. If I lose it, I can kiss good-bye to seeing Elsie, to all the good things in my life, so if you know anything at all . . ."

She lied to him again, claiming ignorance while averting her eyes from his disbelieving gaze. Mark let her go—his better judgment for once mastering his rising fury. He returned to the station in a deep funk. Wherever he went now he was under a cloud, but it was safer for him in the station. Less temptation. And it was as he was sitting at his desk, mentally drafting his CV, that the call came through. It was Jim Grieves.

"Just thought you ought to know that she was a he."

"Sorry?"

"Martina, the prostitute. She may have been well stacked and all that, but there's no doubt she was a chap. Probably had the surgery in the last couple of years, and by the look of his ass, he may very well have been in this line of work before, albeit for a different clientele. I'd start looking there if I were you."

So Martina was born a boy. Immediately Mark was energized— a little crumb that, if it yielded anything, might start the process of defrosting Helen. Suddenly Mark was back in the game.

62

"Twenty Marlboro Gold, please."

Helen was smoking too much—she knew that. But she wanted to gather her thoughts before sitting opposite Mickery, and smoking had always had a calming effect on her. So she'd slipped out to the local newsagent. The owner reached back and pulled out the reassuring white-and-gold packet. He tossed them onto the counter and with a straight face told her the scandalous price.

"Let me get those."

Emilia Garanita. Another ambush. *I really must be more vigilant,* Helen thought to herself. *Getting caught out this often only encourages her.*

"No need," said Helen, handing a ten-pound note to the outstretched hand. The owner was staring blatantly at Emilia.

Was this because he recognized her from the newspaper or because of her ravaged face? For a moment, Helen felt a modicum of sympathy for her adversary.

"How are you, Emilia? You're looking well."

"Just dandy. It's you I'm worried about. How are you coping investigating *three* murders?"

"As I've said before, Ben Holland's death was an accid—"

"Sam Fisher, Ben Holland, Martina Robins. All *murdered*. This is unprecedented for Southampton. They were all remote locations; the killings were out of character. What are we dealing with here?"

The recording device was visible in Emilia's hand. Clearly she was hoping to record Helen's discomfort—or was it humiliation she was hoping for? Helen eyed her up, enjoying the tension, before replying.

"Speculation, Emilia. But I hope to have more for you very soon. We have someone in custody right now who is helping us with our inquiries. You can print that if you like. That's not speculation. That's a fact. You do still print facts, don't you?"

And with that, she left. Heading back to the station, Helen had a spring in her step. It was nice to have the upper hand for once. She drew deeply on her cigarette, savoring the thought of what was to come.

63

Mickery was saying nothing. She and Helen had been staring at each other across the interview table for over an hour now, but still she wouldn't reveal where she had been.

"It was all perfectly innocent," Mickery said, just about suppressing a smile.

"So why the disguise? The chase? A police officer ordered you to stop and you didn't. I should throw you in jail for that alone."

"I was seeing a client," Mickery retorted, "and I didn't feel it was right to bring the local constabulary down on their heads. They've got problems enough as it is, believe me."

"But that's just it—I don't."

Mickery just shrugged—she clearly couldn't give two figs what

Helen thought. Her lawyer flanked her, looking equally smug. The clock ticked by. A minute of silence. Two minutes. Then:

"Let's start again from the beginning. Where were you yesterday afternoon? Who were you meeting and why?" Helen barked.

"I've said all I'm going to say. I cannot and will not break professional confidences."

Now Helen was really riled.

"Do you have any idea how serious this is?"

The two women eyeballed each other.

"You're the prime suspect in a multiple-murder case. When I arrest and charge you, I am going to be pushing for five life sentences. Without parole and without any chance of reduction. You are going to serve every day of the rest of your life in prison, and any minor, fleeting concessions you receive will be because of what you do now. Right here in this room. If you tell me why you did it—why you killed Martina and all the others—then I can help you."

"Martina?" Mickery queried.

"Don't be cute. I want answers, not questions. And if you don't start giving me some in the next five seconds, then I am going to arrest you and charge you with five counts of murder."

"No, you're not."

"Excuse me?"

"You're not going to arrest me. You're not going to charge me. Which is why I'm going to tell you absolutely nothing."

Helen stared at her—was this woman for real?

"There's no one else in the frame, Hannah. You are the prime suspect. And you are going to be charged. There's no escape this time."

"I'm guessing you don't play poker, Inspector—otherwise your bluff would be rather better than this. Let me help you out."

Helen wanted to punch her between the eyes and Mickery knew it. She continued:

"You are currently hunting a serial killer. Let's not dress it up as anything else. But more than that, you are hunting a very rare kind of serial killer. A woman. How many female serial killers can you name? Aileen Wuornos, Rose West, Myra Hindley. It's not a long list. Which is why they are box office. Everybody *loves* female serial killers. The tabloids, filmmakers, the guy on the street—everyone is fascinated by women who kill again and again. But this one—" She paused for effect. "This one really takes the cheese. Why? Because she's so canny, so organized, yet so elusive. How does she target her victims? And why? Does she hate both of the people she abducts or just one? How can she predict the outcome? Does she care who lives and who dies? And why them? What have they done to her? Is she the first serial killer in history to get off on those who survive her crimes, rather than through those who are killed? She's a one-off, unique. And she's going to be an utter sensation."

Helen said nothing. She knew Mickery was baiting her and wasn't going to give her the satisfaction of reacting. Mickery smiled and continued:

"There are several endings to this extraordinary story. But the best one—and the one every tabloid hack and reader wants— is that the dogged cop gets her girl in the end. And then we can all have fun poring over her mug shot and reading the twelve-page special full of gory details, 'expert' opinions and thinly disguised prurience."

Mickery was warming to her theme.

"The ending that no one wants—you especially—starts with a blunder. The arrest of an innocent, respected *professional*"—she stressed that word—"which results in the story breaking before the killer is caught. The tabloids are up in arms, the man on the street is terrified, and suddenly you've got millions of eyes scanning millions of faces, driving the killer underground while flooding your incident room with a thousand bogus leads. The killer's vanished, you're hung out to dry and I get a very hefty compensation payout with which I buy that boat I've always wanted."

She paused for effect.

"So the question you have to ask yourself, Inspector," she continued, "is, are you absolutely sure I did it? And can you prove it? Because if you're not, if you can see the massive blunder you are about to make, then there's still time for you to stop. To make the right move. To let me go and get back to your investigation. I am innocent, Helen."

Her name had never sounded so much like a "fuck you." It was a good speech—no doubt about it. And it raised some pertinent questions. Could Mickery really be so pathologically unhinged and yet so convincing and articulate at the same time? Could someone with such a firm grasp on how others thought and felt really be so sociopathic?

"Am I free to go?" Mickery couldn't help rubbing it in.

Helen regarded her for a minute, then said:

"I won't be pressing formal charges over the matters we've discussed in this room yet—matters which I shouldn't have to remind you must remain confidential, as our investigation is ongoing."

Mickery smiled and gathered her things to go.

"But you did fail to stop when asked to by a police officer, and I think that warrants a night in the cells at the very least. Don't you?"

And with that, Helen left, leaving Mickery speechless for once.

64

A thousand questions spun around Helen's head. Was Mickery telling the truth? Maybe Mickery *wasn't* the killer—maybe her obsession with these killings was about something completely different: money. Mickery knew that this story was going to be a worldwide sensation when it broke and perhaps she was desperate to use her inside knowledge of the case to get ahead of the pack.

The more Helen thought about it, the more it made sense. She was probably already drafting an authoritative account of the killings, complete with psychological insights into the killer's mind-set and bona fide evidence from the police investigation. Her lucky connection with two of the victims had put her on the scent, but she was an ambitious woman and wanted more. When had she made her first approach to Mark? And why him? And where did she get the brass neck to bribe a serving officer to give her chapter and verse on the continuing investigation? If it could ever be shown that her corrupting influence had hampered police attempts to catch the killer, then she would be looking at jail time. That at least was some consolation, Helen thought grimly.

With Hannah cooling her heels in a cell, Helen had a window in which to act. But she would have to do it carefully and by the book. So her first stop was to see Whittaker. As she outlined her case, he sat there grim faced. They had to take Mark off the investigation, obviously, but could they do that without arousing his and others' suspicions? No—of course not. So they would have to suspend him and charge him. He might then go straight to the press out of revenge and a desire for profit. But Whittaker thought that a healthy payoff, perhaps even the retention of his police pension and service payments, might induce him to keep quiet. It had worked before, and Mark hardly came from a rich background. While it stuck in Helen's craw to think about rewarding Mark's treachery in this way, Whittaker was more of a pragmatist.

"Do you want me to handle it?" he asked.

"No, I'll do it."

"It's customary for the senior officer to take the lead when disciplining—"

"Yes, I know and I understand why that's the case, but I need to know what he's leaked and to whom. I think I've got more chance of getting that if I tackle him alone."

Whittaker eyeballed her.

"Do you have some special kind of pull on him?"

"No, but he respects me," Helen said quickly. "He knows I

don't bullshit and that if I offer him a deal it'll be genuine and offered in good faith."

Whittaker seemed appeased by that. So Helen departed. She'd never been so glad to get out of his office. Then again, that was the easy bit. The hard part would be facing Mark.

Helen climbed into her car and pulled the door shut behind her. For a moment, the sound of the world, with all its cares, was muffled. A moment's peace from a world that kept raining stones on her. Why had she allowed Mark to get so close to her? Why had she chosen him as her sounding board when he was obviously leaking every last detail of her investigation? She winced as she remembered their chats in the pub, in the incident room, rehearsing theories, considering suspects. Who knew? Perhaps there was some hideous caricature of her—the bumbling, ineffectual copper—already taking shape in Mickery's book. A brilliant phantom of a killer, pursued haplessly by ignorant cops.

Helen cried out in pain and looked down to see her fingernails dug into her palm. She had drawn blood in her frustration and anger. Cursing her stupidity, she tried to regain her focus. Now was not the time to be distracted by what might be. No point fighting imaginary battles. She'd done enough of that in the past. Now it was time to be calm, strong and decisive. Now was the time to act.

65

His first feeling was one of relief. Mark had been trying to get hold of Helen all day to tell her about the developments about Martina, without success. Now here she was, leaning against his front door. Satisfaction surged to something more—hope? excitement?—as she had come back to him *here*, rather than collaring him in the office. Perhaps she liked to be mysterious, hot and cold, hard to handle. But something in her expression told him this was not the case.

She said nothing as he opened the door and let her in. There was nothing for it but to play ball. See how bad things really were. So he pulled up a chair and sat down to face her. Who was going to make the first move?

"This may be the last time we meet like this. We have been

friends and more, so let's not scream or shout or accuse or lie or make this any more painful than it has to be."

As she spoke, Helen watched Mark closely, beadily, alive to his reaction.

"You've betrayed us, Mark. There's no other way of saying it. You've betrayed me, the team and the police force that made you what you are. Worse than that, you've betrayed the innocent men and women who've been murdered by this evil little—"

"I don't understand—"

"I've spoken to Whittaker," Helen interrupted, "so there's no point trying to lie your way out of it. We are about to begin an official procedure that will in all probability end in your expulsion from the police force. Your desk has been cleared, you won't be allowed access to any restricted areas and I am required to retain your badge once this discussion is over."

Mark stared at her.

"You've seen others go through it—you know how nasty it can be. But you can make it easy on yourself, Mark. I don't think you're evil. I don't think you're rotten inside and I'm sure there must be reasons—good reasons—why you would do something so awful. If you are prepared to tell me those reasons fully and cooperate in every way I ask, then there is a deal to be done here. You don't need to come out of this with nothing."

A long silence, then:

"Why here?"

Mark's response took Helen by surprise. No passionate denial, just a move in the game. It was said with real bitterness, but there was something else going on here. What was his angle?

"Why come here to tell me . . . this?" The last word was spat out. A challenge. Helen eyed him up and then responded:

"Because I want to hear it for myself before anyone else does. I want you to tell me why you did it before you have to say it on tape. I want *you* to tell *me*."

Her voice suddenly caught with emotion—her real sense of personal betrayal finally punching through. Mark just stared at her. He looked confounded, as if she were speaking Greek.

"What do you think I've done, Helen?" His tone was neutral, but it sounded mocking.

"Don't do this, Mark. Even now, you're better than this."

"Tell me. Tell me what I've done."

Helen's face hardened as her anger returned. Why had she ever allowed this arrogant bastard to get close to her?

"You gave Mickery our investigation. You sold us out."

There—finally it was on the table.

"And I want to know why."

"Fuck you."

Helen smirked, though she didn't really know why. A flash of anger from Mark and he was on his feet, as if he was going to come toward her. Helen flinched, but Mark had already turned away and now paced the room in silence. Helen had never considered that he might react violently, might be dangerous. How messed up was this guy? Perhaps she didn't know him at all.

When Mark spoke, he was plainly fighting hard to restrain his anger.

"What makes you think that I would do that?"

"Because there's no one else, Mark."

"You had access, Whittaker, Charlie, the techies . . ."

"Only Charlie and you were in the station when it was taken. The techies were on strike, Whittaker was on leave and I was out in the field."

"So it has to be *me*? What about Charlie? Have you ever thought that it might be—?"

"It's not her."

"How do you *know*?"

"Because she has an alibi. And because she looked me in the eye and told me it wasn't her. Why haven't you done that, Mark? Instead of wriggling on the line, why don't you look me in the eye and tell me you didn't do it?"

A brief pause, then:

"Because you wouldn't believe me."

The sadness in his voice was crushing. Inexplicably, Helen wanted to get up and comfort him—she fought the urge, digging her nails into her wounded hand. The pain flowed through her, calming her.

When she looked up, Mark was pouring himself a large glass of wine.

"Why the fuck not, eh?" and he drained his glass, slamming it back down on the table in front of her. Staring at her, he slammed the glass down again. And again, and again, until finally the stem snapped and the glass shattered. He tossed the remainder away across the room, then ran his bleeding hands through his hair. His anger had flared, and now seemed to dissipate.

"Why couldn't you have *asked* me first, before setting this in motion?"

"You know why. If there was any hint that I'd given you preferential treatment because I . . . because we'd . . ."

"Looking after number one, eh?"

"It's not like that. And you know it."

"You know, for a long time I genuinely thought I'd done something wrong. Offended you. Committed some terrible romantic faux pas. Then I wondered if it was the difference in rank. That you'd had second thoughts. But I didn't really believe that, so I thought maybe you were just a head case. A beautiful, unpredictable head case. And you know what? I would have been happy with that. I could have worked with that."

To Helen's surprise, he laughed. But it was brief and tinged with bitterness. She was about to respond, but he talked over her:

"But I never, ever thought that it would be this. That this was why you'd frozen me out. What makes you so convinced, so very sure that I would throw away my job, my future, my chances of being a good dad, of—fuck it—falling in love again for a backhander?"

"Who said anything about a backhander?"

"Don't be obtuse."

"I never mentioned payment."

Mark exhaled loudly. Then lowered his eyes to look at his bleeding hand.

"Did she pay you, Mark?"

There was a long silence. Then:

"You're making a big mistake."

"Did she pay you?"

"And I could sit here all day and all night and tell you exactly why I never spoke to her, why I never colluded with her, was never bribed by her, why I never did a damn thing wrong, but there's no point, is there? The train has left the station and there's no going back. And I will probably never know exactly why you've done this to me when you have no concrete proof whatsoever, whether it's a cop thing, or a head thing or an . . . I don't know what thing. But I'll tell you one thing. I'm not going to sit here and be grilled by you in *my* home without a lawyer present. You've done this by the book. Of course you've done it by the book. So you will have been to Whittaker and talked to Charlie and sent the dreaded yellow form to Anti-Corruption. So I'm going to do it by the book. I'm not going to be squeezed like some fucking . . . criminal. I'm going to sit down in interview rooms with my lawyer and my union rep and slowly, carefully unpick whatever case you think you have against me, so that I'm exonerated and you are made to look a bloody fool."

He pushed his chair back sharply and marched over to the front door, flinging it open. Helen had no choice but to obey—she was on dodgy ground being here at all.

"Should I tell them we screwed?" Mark fired at her. "Would that be good 'color'? Might explain why you're ruining my career. Perhaps I wasn't good in the sack. Perhaps you felt you'd let yourself down. Thought it might come back to you. Well, you can bet it will now."

Helen had now reached the door. She just wanted to be out of there, but Mark wasn't finished yet.

"I should hate you, you know. But I don't. I pity you."

Helen pushed roughly past and hurried away down the stairs. Why did his pity hurt her? *He's a bent copper, a rotten apple—who gives a shit what he says?* So she reasoned with herself, but it didn't cut any ice. Even amid her anger and hurt, she knew that Mark had unnerved her. He seemed so indignant, so outraged, so *sure* of his innocence. The evidence all pointed to him. She couldn't have got it so badly wrong.

Could she?

66

I remember that day so clearly. Everything that came after—the misery, the violence, the desolation—stemmed from that day. Things had been grim before that for sure, but I expected that. I hadn't been expecting this.

There had been a sort of party at ours—my uncle Jimmy's birthday. They'd been at the booze all day—someone had had a result at the bookies—and everyone was even more wasted than usual. The neighbors had already been round twice, shouting obscenities about the noise, but my folks didn't give a shit. They just cranked it up another notch—"Enjoy Yourself" by the Specials blasting out at full volume. We hung around trying to cadge the odd ciggy or can but we weren't welcome. In the end there's nothing more depressing than a group of middle-aged wankers dancing and grinding, so I pissed off to bed. My mum had passed out by that point and Dad and his "mates" would often take advantage of her insensibility to play stupid pranks on her. He pissed on her once when she was asleep—they all did—and I didn't like watching that, so I was better off out of it.

Initially, I thought he'd got the wrong room. That he was so wasted that he couldn't tell which way was up. Then I was pissed off—I'd hardly slept a wink as it was. What chance would I have of sleeping now, with him passed out next to me? But he wasn't asleep. And he wasn't interested in sleeping either.

At first I didn't move. I was just too shocked. His right hand was clamped around my right tit. Then I tried to bat his hand off, but couldn't. He tightened his grip. I remember it really hurt as he squeezed harder. Now I was struggling. I hoped this was just a stupid joke, but I think I already knew that it wasn't. Now he was climbing on top of me, pinning me down on the narrow bed.

I think I started begging now, pleading with him to stop, but his fingers were already up my nightdress, seeking an opening. His hands were rough and hairy and I remember wincing in pain as he shoved his fist inside me. I was still a virgin—only thirteen—I wasn't made for someone like him. His other hand pushed my head into the pillow. I closed my eyes and hoped that I would die. That it would stop. But it didn't—he just kept on, relentless, grunting all the while.

Eventually he got bored or ran out of puff. Wiping his hands on his jeans, he got off the bed and walked back to the doorway. I turned to make sure he was really going and only then did I realize that we'd had an audience. Jimmy and a couple of mates were watching, smiling and laughing together. My dad stumbled past them into the hallway. Jimmy let him go, then started to unbuckle his belt.

And I realized that it was his turn now and that this was just the beginning.

67

"I'm sorry. I shouldn't have spoken to you like that. I didn't mean what I said. I didn't mean to hurt you and I'm sorry that I did."

The words poured from her and Jake accepted her apology gracefully, gently nodding his forgiveness. When she'd turned up, he'd thought twice about letting her in, but after a moment's hesitation had relented. It's all very well in principle saying you're going to cut someone out of your life, but when they are there on your doorstep asking for your help, it's hard to turn them away.

"Can we go back to normal?"

It was ineloquently put but sincerely meant and it struck Jake in that moment that everybody had their own idea of "normal," each person's definition of it as weird and messed up as everybody else's. He had been wrong to judge her so quickly, even if her anger and verbal abuse had been vile and unwarranted. She had clearly suffered—he didn't know when or why—and if he made her feel better, then that was a good thing. His own journey to the life he now led had been unpredictable and individual. Born to parents who never really wanted children, Jake had been palmed off on countless grannies and aunties—each as uninterested as the rest—until eventually entering the merry-go-round of foster care. He had survived of course—but it's hard to be unloved and not feel pain. Learning to control and use that pain had been the making of him, a way of managing his anxieties and expiating his demons in ways that excited him and others. He'd tried the submissive route and after he'd got over his initial fear had enjoyed it well enough, but in his heart of hearts he liked to be in control. He knew that deep down it was his insecurities that made the choice for him, but he could live with that. He was in charge now and that was what mattered.

He had reached a place in life where things were ordered and good. Which was why he knew that he would take her back. She had hurt him but was penitent. Did she have anyone else? Jake thought not and realized for the first time that she needed him. To reject her would be cruel and dangerous.

"Yes, we can go back to normal. But I've got a client coming in five, so . . ."

She took the hint and left, but not before she had crossed the room and hugged him. Another breach of protocol, but Jake would let it go because it felt good. He watched her go, surprised at how relieved he felt. She needed him for sure, but perhaps he was now beginning to realize that he needed her.

68

Hannah Mickery had not had a good night. She had visited prisons many times in a professional capacity and had never failed to be revolted by the experience. So she'd gone to her night in the cells with real dread. And, okay, nothing bad had happened to her. But it had been a long, cold, depressing night with only a seventeen-year-old junkie for company—a junkie who'd pissed herself with fear in the middle of the night. The urine had run into the corner of the cell and stayed there, stinking out the place for the rest of the night.

She just wanted to get home, have a shower and *sleep*. She'd remained calm throughout it all, but now she felt washed-out and aggrieved. So when her lawyer, Sandy, arrived to pick her up, she breathed a deep sigh of relief. She kissed him—something she'd never done before—and asked him to take her home. Sandy, however, had other ideas.

"There's someone you should meet."

"Well, whoever it is, they'll have to wait. I'm going straight home to bed."

"It's a one-time-only offer, Hannah. I think you should take my advice on this one."

Hannah slowed her march and turned to face Sandy.

"An hour of your time—that's all I ask. I've brought clothes from your place. You can shower at mine if you're quick. The meeting starts in just under an hour. Trust me, Hannah—it's the one you've been waiting for."

At Sandy's house, the water cascaded over Hannah, reviving her instantly. The experience should have been soothing, but Hannah was too wired for that. She was full of questions, but her overriding emotion was one of girlish excitement. She had hit the jackpot. She and Sandy had pulled it off.

On the ride over, he'd outlined the proposition. It was more generous than she could have hoped for. They wanted a lot for it, of course, but she had prepared scrupulously and had all the material she needed. After the newspaper deal, they'd wrap up a publishing deal, which would lead to TV appearances and who knew what else? She would make her name, be rich and then . . . who knows? Perhaps she'd move to the States. There was enough devious criminality there to keep her busy for a lifetime.

She hadn't expected it to be a woman. And especially not such a glamorous one. Just prejudice, really—one expected every tabloid hack to be a bloke. Still, she seemed incredibly clued up, impressing Hannah with both her detective work and her barefaced cheek in getting to this point. It was all about getting ahead of the competition. The deal was hammered out quickly and generously and the three of them shook on it there and then. At which point she produced a bottle of champagne she'd brought with her—just in case. Once again Hannah marveled at her front.

Still, it was good stuff. And had an instant effect. Hannah could take her drink, so it must have been the adrenaline rush of success making her feel light-headed. By the look of things, Sandy was feeling the same way too.

69

Helen stood in front of Whittaker's desk like an errant school-girl. She knew why she'd been summoned. He knew she knew. But still he took his time, leafing through page after page of the *Evening News* before folding it up and placing it carefully on the table, the front page facing up.

CLUELESS!

The headline screamed out at her. She had read Emilia Ga-ranita's article first thing this morning and knew immediately that it would cause ripples up and down the chain. It had a few salient details about Amy and Sam, and Ben and Peter, and a couple of sketchy pointers on Martina. But it led on the release of Mickery and the suspension of "a senior officer working on the current investigation." It looked bad. Helen guessed that Whittaker had already had his ear badly bent by his superiors, such was the look of thunder he'd given her when she entered.

"I'll call her," Helen found herself saying. "See if I can get her to call off the dogs."

"Bit late for that, isn't it? Besides, there's no need. I've called her myself. She'll be here in five minutes."

Emilia entered the room looking like the cat that had got the cream. She took her time deciding between tea and coffee, indulging in small talk and so on. She had been summoned, anointed, and she was clearly going to enjoy herself.

"Do you have anything to add, Detective Superintendent? Do you still have faith in Inspector Grace's leadership of the investigation? Have there been any developments?"

"I'm not here to talk about the case. I'm here to talk about you," Whittaker fired back brusquely.

"I don't follow—"

"It's time you backed off this one. Your interventions are misleading and unhelpful and I want them to stop. No more articles until there is something genuine to report. Get me?"

Helen was amused by the boldness of his approach—no one stood between Whittaker and promotion.

"I do hope you are not trying to dictate to the press—"

"That's precisely what I'm fucking doing. And if I were you I'd heed what I'm saying to you."

Emilia was stumped for once, but she rallied quickly.

"With the greatest of respect—"

"What do you know about respect?" Whittaker barked over her. "What respect have you shown the Anderson family during their ordeal? Shouting through their letter box, calling their home night and day, sitting outside their house hour after hour, going through their bins."

"You're exaggerating. I have a duty—"

"Am I? I have a log here detailing every time your red Fiat registration number BD50 JKR has parked up outside their house. The log was compiled by Amy's father and runs to two pages. It places you there at midnight, two a.m., three a.m. It goes on and on and on. It's harassment. It's stalking. Need I remind you of the Leveson Inquiry? And the code of conduct that all journalists, whether national or regional"—he said this last word with real disdain—"have agreed to abide by?"

For once Emilia had no comeback. So Whittaker continued:

"I could demand a front-page apology to the family. I could have you fined. Fuck it, I could probably get you sacked if I really wanted to. But I'm a kind man, so I'm going to be merciful. But keep your ill-informed opinions to yourself or you'll find yourself hounded out of local journalism and—hell, there's no way back from that, is there?"

Emilia left shortly afterward, fuming but helpless.

Helen was speechless—and impressed.

"Do you really have a log of her visits?" she asked.

"Of course not," was the reply. "Now get back to work and, please, Helen, make some bloody progress. I've bought you some time. Make use of it."

And with that, she was dismissed. Helen marveled at his front and was impressed by his loyalty to the team—and to her. But as she headed back down the corridor, she couldn't help feeling that this outright attack on the grimly determined journalist would rebound on them. Emilia had survived much worse than this and always come back fighting.

70

As soon as Charlie entered the incident room, she noticed the atmosphere. When an investigation is in full cry, incident rooms are noisy, aggressive, busy places. But today it was quiet, somber even, and it wasn't hard to see why. Mark's desk was clean, his board cleared of personal photos and memorabilia. It was as if he had never existed.

Mark had been a popular member of the team and everyone felt his absence. He may have been vulnerable, a fuckup, but that was part of his charm, especially for the girls. The little-boy-lost thing. He was also bright and funny and when he applied himself he was a good copper. But now everyone was privately asking themselves whether the Mark they knew was the real one. Could he have sold them out? Had all their work been wasted, leaked?

Were his financial needs really so dire that he would betray them like this? Charlie was troubled by it—she'd always basically liked Mark—and she made a mental note to check what had happened to his personal things. She got on with her work, but the empty chair was always in sight out of the corner of her eye.

Helen entered shortly after nine a.m. and everyone made a herculean effort to be cheerful and act as if nothing out of the ordinary had happened. Helen, as was her wont, didn't mess about, calling Charlie to update her on developments. She seemed on edge and was impatient for news.

"Tell me about Martina."

"Well, she was born a he and probably had the op in the last three to five years. Scar tissue suggests it's no earlier than that."

"Did she advertise her services as a post-op transsexual?"

"No. Her line was that she liked to party and knew how to pleasure. A fun slut, that sort of thing."

"Why? You can always get more from punters for being a trannie. More exotic, more specialist. Why not advertise that fact?"

"Perhaps she didn't like the crowd it attracted?"

"Or perhaps she had something to hide?"

The question hung in the air, then:

"Was she local?" Helen continued.

"Doesn't look like it. The other girls say she started working down here a couple of months back. Her Web site confirms that— she's got a local IP address and it was set up eight weeks ago."

"What about her real address?"

Charlie shook her head. "Nothing so far. She was a bit of a mystery to the other girls, kept herself to herself."

"What about a money trail?"

239

"We're talking to the local banks, but so far no account in her name."

Helen exhaled. Nothing about this case was easy.

"Well, our best bet is the clinics, then. How many local clinics are there that do this sort of work?"

"Fifteen. We're talking to them all, though most are a little cagey about discussing their clients."

"Well, make them uncagey. Tell them what happened to Martina, show them the pictures. We need to know who she was—he was."

Charlie couldn't suppress a wry smile and for once Helen couldn't either. Was Charlie fooling herself or was their relationship improving since Helen had put her through the mill? Charlie had been enraged following the confrontation—to have someone question your integrity like that—and had even contemplated asking for a transfer. And yet she still wanted Helen to like her, still wanted her respect. Truth was, most women in the force wanted to be like her. She was the youngest female DI in Hampshire police and her progress through the ranks had been stellar. She had no husband, no family, which gave her an unfair advantage in many women's eyes, but she had still done amazingly well. She was a role model for them all.

Helen turned to face the team.

"DC Brooks will be running things today. Top priority: the clinics. I know we're a man light now and you've all got questions about that. When the time is right, I will tell you more. But for now I need you all to focus. We have a killer to catch."

And with that, she left. Charlie immediately started handing out tasks to Sanderson, McAndrew and the rest, who took them without complaint, despite many being the same rank as Charlie. Intent on appearing serious and professional, Charlie was brisk and to the point, but inside she was grinning. The first time in living memory that Helen Grace had let someone else steer the ship.

71

She'd had to call the police in the end—she hadn't wanted to, but she didn't have a choice. She'd been scared at first—Stephen wasn't at home tonight and the drunken yobs hammering on her door were bloody terrifying her—but when she found out what was really going on, she was sickened rather than scared.

She hadn't seen Mark drunk for months. He'd cleaned himself up, she'd thought, got himself together. But he was a sorry sight now. His clothes were stained, his hair unkempt, and he was slurring his words. Pathetic invective spewed from his lips as he raged at his misfortune, telling the whole street how Christina couldn't keep her legs together, that Stephen was brainless, a walking dildo. His hammering was getting louder—he would surely wake Elsie up soon—so Christina had to do something.

She opened the door on the chain a little in an attempt to appease him. She wanted to start a conversation, but this only enraged him more. What right did she have to bar his entry? he shouted. When all he wanted was to see his daughter. The daughter she'd stolen from him. Christina tried to shove the door shut, but he maneuvered his arm inside, brushing her off, ripping the chain out of its holder.

He pushed his way in and marched upstairs toward Elsie's room. Christina grabbed the phone and rang 999. She'd read about deranged guys who'd killed their kids after a divorce. Was Mark capable of that? She didn't think so, but she wasn't taking any chances. She told the operator what was going on, gave her address and then sprinted up the stairs.

She didn't know what she'd find when she entered the room, and in many ways it was worse than she'd imagined. Elsie was standing up on her bed. She was shaking with fear, crying soundlessly in shock and terror. And Mark was slumped on the floor, his body convulsing with sobs. What Christina had started Elsie had finished. The look of horror on her face was enough to stop his heart. The drink had beaten him at last, taken all that was good from him.

He was the very image of a broken man—with only a lifetime of self-pity and recrimination to look forward to. And for the first time in ages, Christina felt an emotion she'd always denied herself.

Guilt.

72

She had to be sure. She had already ruined Mark's career and probably more besides, and logically the case against him *was* sound, but . . . Helen was full of doubts. He had seemed so hurt, so outraged, so defiant—he couldn't have acted all that, could he? Having initially been stunned by the existence of a mole within the team, latterly Helen had come to hope that this rat would lead them straight to the killer. Instead, it had taken them off on a tangent, distracting them from the main prize. Helen was tempted to let it go. To turn right round and go back into the investigation room. But it was too late for that now. She had served the execution papers to the condemned man and there was a process to follow. But with the ax hovering, Helen had to be sure.

It was while reviewing the personnel files that she found

something intriguing. Helen had been at the forensics lab on the day Amy's testimony was illegally downloaded, Whittaker had been sailing at Poole and Charlie had been accounted for—in Helen's mind at least. That left Mark and the techies: Peter Johnson, Simon Ashworth and Jeremy Laing. They had all been on strike that day, so it couldn't have been one of them . . . but there was something curious about Simon Ashworth. Something Helen had overlooked previously. He had come to Hampshire police from the National Crime Unit in London, where he had been helping to construct the new database, arriving here on the back of a promotion. He had fit in well, been a good worker, but now he was being transferred back to London. Having been with them only four months. It was a sideways move and a strange one, especially as he had taken a twelve-month lease on a flat in Portsmouth. Something had happened. But not officially. Something unseen and unsettling was sending him scurrying back to London.

Helen was on the scent now and her suspicions were further aroused by the fact that Ashworth was nowhere to be seen. Sick leave—though nobody seemed to know what was wrong with him. No, that wasn't quite right. People did know what was wrong with him; they just didn't know if he was sick or not. It had taken Helen quite a while to open Peter Johnson up—to get him to talk about his colleagues—but when she did she soon discovered that Simon Ashworth was not a popular man.

He had broken the strike. Helen felt the hairs on the back of her neck stand up when he said it. Ashworth was not a union man, but still he had been expected to follow the lead of his boss and colleagues and honor the one-day walkout. But he hadn't. He was a loner by nature, socially maladjusted, and often rubbed people up

73

All she could taste was vomit. Vomit and dried blood. Her mouth felt parched, her throat torn, and her head throbbed with a dull, nagging pain. She hadn't eaten in days and she could feel the ulcers forming in her stomach. But that didn't bother her—what she really wanted, *needed*, was water. Usually she would drink liters a day, getting slightly twitchy when she suddenly found herself away from the necessary supply. What a joke those small privations felt now when she was genuinely dying of thirst. She'd never thought about that phrase before, but now she knew what it meant, what it felt like. Despair was setting in—she knew instinctively that there would be no escape.

Sandy lay inert across the way, hoping perhaps to be carried off in his sleep. A peaceful death to end this nightmare. Some hope. They were trapped. And that was all there was to it. Mickery's eyes flicked left, picking up the flight of the flies that hovered round the effluent piled up in the corner. The flies weren't there to begin with, so how did they get in? Which tiny fissure in this tin can had they penetrated? Little bastards could probably come and go as they pleased.

When she had first awoken from her stupor, Mickery had been dazed, confused. It was so dark, she couldn't tell what time of day it was, where she was or what had happened to her. She'd got the fright of her life when she heard Sandy moving. Up until that point she'd assumed she was dreaming, but Sandy's wild distress had rammed home the grim reality of their situation.

They immediately set about exploring their confines, hammering on the walls, tracing the joints in the metal, slowly coming to the crushing conclusion that they were in some kind of giant metal box. Was it a freight container? Probably, but what did it matter? It was solid and secure, and there was no way out of it. That was all they needed to know. Shortly afterward, they chanced upon the gun and the phone. And it was then that Mickery's brave attempts at denial finally collapsed.

"She's got us, Sandy."

"No. No, no, no, no. There must be another explanation. There must be."

"Read the message on the fucking phone. *She's got us.*"

Sandy wouldn't look at the phone. Wouldn't engage at all. But then again, what was there to say? It was clear that there was no easy way out—the choices were starvation or murder. It was Mickery who put these two awful options on the table. Sandy

248

was proving to be a coward, weak, unwilling to face their situation. But Mickery had made him.

They had chosen to take action. The waiting was too much to bear. The despair too crushing. Their life was now slow torture and it was time to do something about it. So they had decided to draw straws—or rather flies, as that was all they could find. So Mickery now found herself with arms outstretched, facing Sandy. In one of her hands was a dead fly. The other hand was empty. If Sandy picked the fly, he lived. If he didn't, he would be killed.

Sandy hesitated, willing his eyesight to penetrate the skin and reveal the treasure within Mickery's palms. Left or right? Death or life?

"Come on, Sandy. For fuck's sake just get it over with."

Mickery's voice was desperate, entreating. But Sandy didn't feel any pity, couldn't feel any pity. He was frozen in the moment, unable to move a muscle.

"I can't do it."

"Do it now, Sandy. Or I swear to God I'll make the decision for you."

Mickery's tone was savage and it jolted Sandy out of his paralysis. Muttering the Lord's Prayer, he slowly stretched out his arm, tapping Mickery firmly on the left hand.

A long, terrible moment. Then slowly Mickery turned her hand round and opened it for both to see.

74

It had been the strangest day. The best and worst of days. Charlie lay in bed trying to make sense of it all.

After Helen had gone, the team had hopped to it, driven on by Charlie's energy and zeal. Encouraging her guys to be brutal with the clinic managers who were evasive, hiding behind client confidentiality, the team had made good progress, working their way steadily through the list, chasing down the surgeons in the Hampshire area who had the expertise to take on a gender reassignment operation. In the end, however, they had drawn a blank. Everyone had been quizzed, but no one recognized Martina or could cast any light on who she might have been when she was a he.

So it was time to widen the search. There were several dozen clinics nationwide that did this kind of thing and they would have to contact them all. Please, God, she hoped Martina had not had the op abroad—that would be too much for their limited resources and they were desperate for a clue, something to get them back on track. Charlie left the guys at it. She was sick with fatigue and needed a moment's respite. As she drove home her mood lifted at the chance of spending a few valuable minutes with her boyfriend and cat, some decent food and, best of all, some sleep.

Road work. And a diversion. Irritating, but no more than that. But it meant Charlie had to take an unusual route home. A route that would take her straight past Mark's flat. With a sudden pang of guilt, she realized that she had momentarily forgotten about him. She had been so intent on proving to herself—and to Helen, obviously—that she could lead the team. In so doing she had shown herself to be a bad leader and an unworthy friend; one shouldn't forget the walking wounded in one's desperation to win the battle.

Kicking herself for her callousness, she pulled the car over and got out. Was this a good idea? Probably not, but she wanted to be able to sleep tonight and the only way to silence her conscience was to check on Mark. No one else from the force would, that was for sure.

What had she been hoping for? That he would be bearing up surprisingly well? He was a mess, and stunk of sweat and booze.

"Do you believe her?"

The blunt question took Charlie by surprise.

"Believe who?"

"Her. Do you think I sold you out?"

There was a long silence. There was the official answer and the true answer. In the end, the latter won out.

"No."

Mark exhaled loudly as if he'd actually been holding his breath. He looked down at the floor to hide his emotion.

"Thank you," he muttered without looking up, but his voice betrayed the strength of his feelings. Instinctively, Charlie went over to him. Seated next to him, she put her arm round him. He leaned into her, glad of the support.

"The sad thing is, I thought I was falling in love with her."

Wow. Charlie hadn't seen that one coming.

"Did you . . . ?"

Mark nodded.

"And, stupid fool that I am, I thought it could be something good. And now this . . ."

"Perhaps she didn't have a choice. Perhaps she genuinely thought . . ."

Charlie hesitated. There was no nice way to finish that sentence. The accusation of corruption was the worst thing you could throw at a copper.

"I can guess what they're saying about this at the station. But I am innocent, Charlie. I didn't do anything wrong. And I want back in. I really badly want back in . . . So . . . if there's anything you can do . . . any way you can influence her and get her to stop this . . ."

Mark petered out. Charlie couldn't think of what to say. They both knew there was no way back now. Even if he was exonerated, who would take him on, given his history of false starts and problems? In an era when no one was hiring, you didn't take bets on potential, especially if there was a hint of unreliability or dishonesty. What could Charlie say that was conciliatory but true?

"You'll get through it, Mark. I know you will."

She wasn't sure she believed it. And she wasn't sure Mark believed it either.

She left his flat, promising to pop round again shortly. Mark didn't really acknowledge her departure, descending once more into self-absorption.

As she drove home, Charlie was full of doubts. Mark wasn't the type to do anything stupid, was he? She thought not, but who could tell? He was obviously devastated. No wife or kid at home, no job to go to, a tendency to drink . . . Suddenly all these thoughts crowded in on Charlie. Her head ached; her stomach was churning. A wave of nausea hit her, so she swung the car into the shoulder, just about opening the door in time to vomit her lunch onto the pavement. She retched heavily once, twice—then it was over.

Later, at home, snuggling in the warm embrace of her boy-friend, Steve, she was assailed by doubts of a different kind. Slipping quietly out of their sleepy cuddle, she tiptoed into the bathroom and opened the bathroom cabinet. Expectation mingled with trepida-tion as she opened the small cardboard tube.

Five minutes later, she had her answer. She was pregnant. They'd been trying for ages without any joy, but there it was. A little blue cross. A second test gave the same answer. Such small things that change your life in such big ways. Steve slumbered on unaware as Charlie remained perched on the toilet, still a little in shock. Not for the first time today her eyes welled up with tears. But these weren't tears of sadness. They were tears of joy.

75

For a moment, she was staring at his eyeball. And then it was gone. Helen had tracked down Simon Ashworth's city center apartment and respectfully rang the doorbell—which showed some restraint, given her desire to hammer on the door. A long pause, no sign of movement. So she rang the doorbell again. And again. She paused, listened. Was that the squeak of a floorboard, the tiniest hint of footsteps? And then the eyeball appeared at the peephole. Helen had been expecting—hoping—for this, so was staring down the peephole herself. The eyeball immediately took fright and vanished from view. The telltale signs of footsteps padding away made Helen smile—he was busted, so why tiptoe?

A copper faces a number of choices in this kind of situation. You can go the official route, apply for a warrant, etc., but when you're working alone this almost always means that your quarry escapes while you're busy elsewhere filling in forms. You can go the patient route, feigning a departure only to take up a viewing post on the street. This usually works, as the fugitive is desperate to leave the flat having been rumbled and is often on the street within the hour. But Helen had never been very good at patience. Which was why she marched into the caretaker's office—startling him during his elevenses—and demanded he open flat 21.

He would have been well within his rights to ask for—demand— a search warrant, but it's funny how many people's brains stop working when they see a badge. Fearing censure, or excited by the drama of the moment, they usually comply. And so it was now, the flustered caretaker opening up flat 21 without hesitation. He seemed somewhat surprised and disappointed when Helen shut the door in his face—a brief smile of gratitude was all he got for his pains.

Ashworth was preparing to flee. The packed bags, the car keys—he was a man on the move. But he stood stock-still now as Helen crossed the room toward him. He looked scared, blustering about the illegality of what Helen was doing—but not in a convincing or threatening way. Putting her badge away, Helen pointed to an empty metal chair. After a brief pause as Ashworth seemed to size up both Helen and the situation, he complied.

"Why did you do it, Simon?"

Helen had never been very good at pussyfooting, so opted for a full-frontal assault. She laid out the charges—illegally downloading confidential information, compromising an active investigation for financial gain—quickly and crisply, intending to afford Ashworth no time to invent excuses or evasions. To her surprise, he offered a spirited defense of his actions.

"It couldn't have been me."

"Why not?"

"Because every technical consultant involved in something like this has their own unique access code. It's the only way in or out for us and you can always tell when we've accessed the system and how we've used it."

"There must be ways round that."

"Not for us. Tech support staff move around a lot, sometimes within the police service, sometimes outside it. In order not to compromise an investigation and to deal with the turnover of technical staff, the access system was created. If you check—"

"So why did you lie?" Helen butted in. She wasn't prepared to be lectured.

"How do you mean, lie?"

"I asked every person who had access to the investigation to account for their movements that day and you, along with all the other technical staff, claimed to have been on strike. But you weren't. You broke the strike."

"So what? I didn't agree with the strike, so I went into work briefly. I wasn't there for long, and when asked about it, I thought it better to tell a little fib so the others didn't find out."

"Didn't work very well, did it? Who told them?"

For the first time Ashworth looked rattled. *Finally, we're making progress,* Helen thought to herself.

"I don't know how they found out," he muttered, staring at his shoes.

"Are you ambitious, Simon?"

"I guess so."

"You guess so? You're very young to be at your pay grade,

you've got great appraisals. You could really go somewhere. In fact, your move to Hampshire police was a big promotion, wasn't it?"

Ashworth nodded.

"And yet, after only four months in your swanky new job, you are returning to your old job. A job which, if your application for the Hampshire posting is to be believed, you felt you had mastered and were bored with."

"We all say stuff like that in job interviews." He remained staring at his shoes.

"What happened?"

A long silence. Then:

"I had a change of heart. I hadn't really settled in Southampton, didn't have any friends to speak of, and then . . . when the lads started to cut me out because I wasn't a union stooge, I thought I'm better off out of it."

"Except you put in your transfer request before the other lads found out about your betrayal of the cause. The others were very clear about this. It was at a departmental piss-up in the Lamb and Flag on the eighteenth that you were forced to admit that you'd broken the strike. You applied to return to your old job on the sixteenth."

"They must be mistaken . . ."

"There were several witnesses to the conversation in the pub. They can't all be lying."

A longer silence.

"The truth is . . . the truth is that I just don't like it here. I don't like the people. I don't like the job. I want out."

"That's curious, Simon. Because at your three-month appraisal, you'd said how happy you were. How you were loving the increased responsibility. And you got top marks for your work, even the hint that you'd be fitted for promotion if you kept it up for a year or more. I've got a copy of your appraisal here if you'd like to read it."

Helen offered it to him, but Ashworth said nothing. The guy looked deeply, deeply miserable. Which made Helen happy. The cracks were beginning to show. She decided to put the boot in.

"You've done the police training, Simon, so I'm not going to patronize you by spelling out what the effects could be for your career if you're forced to admit to lying to a police officer who's pursuing a murder investigation. If you're forced to admit taking payment to leak confidential police material."

Ashworth sat stock-still, but his hands were shaking.

"Your career would be over. Finished. And I know how important it is to you."

Helen softened her tone now.

"I know you're a gifted guy, Simon. I know you could go places. But if you lie to me now, I will destroy you. There'll be no way back."

Ashworth's shoulders hunched and began to shake. Was he crying?

"Why are you doing this?"

"Because I need to know the truth. Did you leak the interview to Mickery? And if so, why? I can only help you if you help me."

A long pause, then:

"I thought you knew."

His voice was strangulated, cracked.

"He told me you knew."

"Who told you?"

"Whittaker."

Whittaker. The word hung in the air, but Helen still didn't quite believe it.

"What did he tell you? What should I have known?"

Ashworth shook his head, but Helen wasn't about to let this go.

"Tell me. Tell me now or I will arrest you for conspiracy to pervert—"

"Whittaker downloaded the interview."

"But he was on leave that day."

"I saw him. I went into the office. Because of the strike there was no one about. But Whittaker was there. By himself. He said he'd been going over the case material and when I looked later he'd downloaded the interview. I didn't think anything of it. He's in charge, so why not? But when I found out later that you were asking for people's movements, I realized that Whittaker had made a mistake. Got his days mixed up. I went to see him. I didn't want him to cop any flak for a simple mistake."

"You were currying favor."

"Sort of. Whittaker liked me, saw a future for me. So I just mentioned it—better safe than sorry, you know. Well, he didn't like it. Not at all. Said I was mistaken, but I knew I wasn't."

He paused, scared of saying any more.

"Go on. What happened next?"

"He said he could destroy my career with one phone call. That I didn't understand what I was getting involved with. We . . . he decided there and then that I was to be transferred back to London as soon as possible. I guess it was him that let the cat out of the bag about the strike. As a reason for my departure. He told me that you knew all this. That it was your idea."

Anger flared in Helen; then she reined it back in sharply. She had to keep calm, keep focused. Was this all for real?

"He said I was involved?"

"Yes, that you were handling it, so there was no point saying anything to you."

"What did you do next?"

"I tried to carry on but I couldn't keep it going, not with the lads on my back as well. So I signed off sick. Been hiding out here ever since, biding my time until my transfer . . ."

He tailed off as the reality of his situation hit him. For the first time that day, Helen was conciliatory.

"This doesn't have to end badly, Simon. If what you've told me today is true, then I can make this right for you. You can take the transfer, learn your lesson and start over again without a blemish on your record. You can do the things you were meant to do, achieve what you want to achieve."

Ashworth looked up, disbelief jostling with hope.

"But I need you to do one thing for me in return. You are going to come to my flat now. And when you get there you are going to write a statement putting down everything you've just told me. Then you are going to wait. You are not going to answer your phone or make any calls. You're not going to mail, text or tweet. You are going to sit still and quiet and the rest of the world need never know we've spoken, until I say the time is right. Is that understood?"

Ashworth nodded. He would do anything she told him now.

"Good. Then let's go."

76

There was no backing out now. The deal had been struck. Like it or not, it was time to follow through.

When Mickery had opened her left hand, knowing full well it was empty, Sandy had collapsed to the ground moaning. Mickery had watched, her emotions in riot. Part exhilaration, part horror, but overall . . . relief. She would live.

Shortly afterward Sandy started to beg. He said he hadn't been serious, that it was crazy, that they had to stick together, that they shouldn't let *her* win.

"What would you have done if you'd won? Would you have spared me?" was Mickery's retort. Sandy couldn't answer, which spoke volumes. He would have pulled the trigger and saved himself. He was a selfish little shit at heart.

"Please, Hannah. I have a wife. I have two daughters. You know them, you've met them. Please don't do this to them."

"We don't have a choice, Sandy."

"'Course we do. We always have a choice."

"To starve to death? Is that what you want?"

"Maybe we can get out. Force the door . . ."

"For the love of God, Sandy, don't make this worse than it already is. There is no way out. There is no escape. This is it. There is no other way."

At which point, he'd started to blub. But Mickery felt no pity now. If Sandy had won, she would have been dead by now, no doubt about it. Suddenly hatred rose up inside her—*How dare he beg for mercy that he wouldn't have rendered!*—and as he clawed at her, she pushed him sharply away. He tripped and fell, landing heavily on the dirty metal floor.

"I'm begging you, Hannah, please don't do this . . ."

But Mickery had already picked up the gun. She had never fired one before, never thought of hurting anyone, but she was cool and collected now as she prepared to execute someone she had once called a friend.

"I'm so sorry, Sandy."

And with that, she pulled the trigger.

Click.

An empty chamber. *Shit.* Sandy, who moments earlier had thrown his arms wildly in front of himself in a vain effort to shield himself from the coming pain, stopped flailing. Suddenly he was getting to his feet.

Click. Click.

Two more empty chambers—the gun must have got knocked out of sequence at some point. Now Sandy was charging at her.

Click. Click. He barreled into her, knocking the cold gun from her hands. Mickery flew backward, cracking her head on the hard floor. When she looked up, Sandy had the gun in his hand. She expected to see hatred there, but his face was a picture of disbelief.

"It's empty. It's fucking empty!" He tossed the gun to her. What had he said? Her brain couldn't keep up with developments. But he was right. The chambers were empty. There had never been a bullet inside.

A hooting to her left made Mickery start. But it was only Sandy rolling on the floor, tears of laughter rolling down his cheeks. He sounded insane. Insanely happy. What a bloody good joke it all was.

Mickery yelled. A bloodcurdling, throat-splitting yell. Long, loud and agonizing. All that for nothing. She had tricked them, made them animals, but then denied Mickery her triumph. This wasn't how the game worked. It wasn't supposed to be that way. She was meant to live. She wanted to live.

Mickery knelt on the floor, the energy draining from her. She was beaten, broken. Sandy's hideous mocking laughter rang out like a death knell.

77

Helen was back at the helm when Charlie entered the incident room the following morning. Charlie felt a slight burst of irritation—her role as team leader had lasted no more than a day—but then immediately picked up the buzz of excitement in the room and all sense of resentment vanished. Something had happened.

Two things, in fact. One good, one bad. They had found "Martina"—a gender reassignment clinic in Essex claimed to have a match. But they had lost Hannah Mickery. She and her personal lawyer, Sandy Morten, had been missing for several days now.

"Why wasn't I told?" demanded Helen angrily.

"We didn't know," Charlie replied. "Morten was reported missing a few days back, but no one reported Mickery missing. It was only when we were going through Morten's e-mails that we realized he had set up a three-way meeting for himself, Mickery and a woman called Katherine Constable. She claimed to be a journalist working for the *Sunday Sun*, but we've checked with them and there's no one of that name on their payroll."

"Constable? She's taking the piss out of us."

Helen was fuming. With herself and with the situation. She had been so intent on pursuing the mole, on running that leak to ground, that she had taken her eye off Mickery. If she had stayed with her, perhaps she would have finally come face-to-face with their killer.

She dispatched Charlie and the rest of the team to Morten's house. It was probably overkill, but this was where "Katherine" had met with Mickery and Morten—perhaps if they all went, they'd pick up a thread there, a forensic clue, a witness statement, something. In the meantime, Helen sped east to Essex.

It was good to be back on the hunt. Good too to get away from the Southampton nick—she needed time to think. Ashworth was now holed up in her flat, out of harm's way, and his statement was written and signed. Since their explosive interview, she had done some further checks. She had never questioned Whittaker's alibi before and kicked herself for that, for on close inspection it didn't hold much water. Even though conditions for sailing from Poole had been good that day—the weather had been fine and most of the pleasure boats had ventured out from the harbor—some had stayed put, among them *Green Pepper*, Whittaker's twenty-six-footer on which he lavished so much care and attention.

So Whittaker had lied to her about his whereabouts and another serving officer had placed him at the scene of the crime. Furthermore, Ashworth had gone on to accuse Whittaker of bullying, coercion and perverting the course of justice. All the time Whittaker had been protecting his own interests. His squashing of Garanita had been designed to stop her from breaking the serial killer story—it had nothing to do with protecting Helen or the team.

It was an incendiary situation and one that Helen needed to handle very carefully indeed. The success of the investigation—not to mention the future of Helen's career—depended on her making the right move.

The Porterhouse Clinic in Loughton was plush and professional. Inside, the lobby was immaculate, the staff likewise, and the whole place had a distinctly soothing feel. The clinic carried out many types of surgery but specialized in resolving issues around gender dysphoria. Therapy was the first stage on a journey that nine times out of ten ended in surgery and full gender reassignment.

The team had sent detailed information out when conducting the search for Martina. The timescale was wide enough to make the search tricky—they thought the op had been done three to five years ago, throwing up a large number of possible contenders. But still, gender reassignment wasn't massively common. And given that they could provide height, blood type, eye color and a good stab at "her" health history, the chances of a match were good. Nonetheless, Helen felt nervous as she was ushered in to see the clinic's manager. There was a lot riding on this one.

The manager, a smooth surgeon with surprisingly hairy hands, wanted to be reassured that the clinic was not going to be on the end of any unpleasant publicity in connection with "this prostitute's murder," as he put it, and Helen had to work hard to get him to play ball, but when she gently reminded him that, in a case as serious as this, he could be compelled to help them, his attitude changed.

"I think we may be able to help," he said, pulling out a file. "A young man in his mid-twenties came to us five years ago. He'd obviously been through a bad time, physically and mentally. We advised counseling to deal with his situation before committing to gender reassignment and suggested he might want at the very least to reduce his list of additional treatments. In the end we got him to drop a couple of procedures, but that was it. He was determined to have an extensive rebuild. In addition to gender reassignment, he had some buttock augmentation, leg and arm toning, and a lot of work done on his face."

"What sort of work?"

"Reshaped cheekbones, fuller lips, a streamlined nose, skin pigmentation, filler . . ."

"How much did it cost him?"

"A lot."

"Any idea why he was going to such lengths to change his appearance?"

"We asked him, obviously. We always discuss every procedure to see if it is . . . necessary. But he wouldn't talk. And we couldn't force him to."

A defensive note had crept into his voice now, so Helen decided to cut to the chase. She gestured to the file:

"May I?"

He handed it over. As soon as she saw his name, Helen felt a knot in her stomach. His picture—young, hopeful, alive—confirmed it. Her worst fears realized.

This was about her. It had always been about her.

78

She was dead. She must be dead. There wasn't enough oxygen in there for a fly to breathe, let alone a human. There was no energy, no life left in her body, and she was barely aware of her surroundings anymore. She was consumed by darkness. The heat was unbearable. There was no air.

Hannah tried to convince herself, but she knew she wasn't dead . . . yet. Death would be a sweet release from this slow torture. And there was no relief, no letup in her suffering. She had been reduced to the level of an animal, wallowing in her own misery and ordure.

How long had it been since she last heard Sandy? She couldn't remember. *Good God, what would it smell like in here if he died?* The rotting excrement was one thing, but a decomposing corpse?

If Mickery had had any tears left, she would have cried them now. But they were long gone. She was a husk. So she lay there, willing death to claim her.

Then suddenly it happened. Without any warning, a blinding light that set Mickery's eyes ablaze. She howled in agony—it was as if lasers had shot into her brain—and clamped her hands to her face. A sudden rush of cool air, freezing yet blissful, poured over her body. But the respite was temporary.

She was being dragged. It took her a while to work out what the sensation was, but she was definitely being dragged. Someone had a viselike grip on her arm and was dragging her across the floor and out into the light. Was she being rescued? Was this Grace?

She struck something metal and yelped. Now the hands were under her, hauling her up. Instinctively she knew this was no rescue, that there would be no salvation here. She landed with a thump in a small, enclosed space. Her hands felt around and slowly, gingerly she began to open her eyes.

The light was still punishingly bright, but she was lying in someone's shadow now, so could just about bear it if she snatched glimpses. She was in the boot of a car. Helpless and splayed in the boot of a car.

"Hello, Hannah. Surprised to see me?"

It was Katherine's voice—her tormentor and jailer.

"Don't be. I'm not the sadistic type, so I've decided to spare you."

Mickery looked up at her, unable to process what she was hearing.

"But I need you to do one little thing for me first."

Hannah waited. Reeling as she was, she knew straightaway

that she would do anything Katherine asked. She wanted to live more than she'd ever wanted anything before.

As the car drove off, Hannah found herself smiling. Something—she didn't know what—had happened. And she had been delivered from purgatory. Any price—any—was worth paying for that.

It never even occurred to her to wonder what had happened to Sandy. He didn't exist anymore as far as she was concerned.

79

Would she ever stop laughing at them? Mickery and Morten constituted the fifth forced abduction and still the killer didn't put a foot wrong. Sanderson, Grounds and McAndrew had supervised diligent house-to-house inquiries, hoping to find a witness to this latest abduction. Whittaker had allocated them extra uniformed officers—but all to no avail. Charlie and Bridges had spent the day at the Morten family home supervising the crime scene, but not a single shred of forensic evidence had been found. The trio had obviously been drinking champagne—two sedative-laced flutes lay where they had fallen on the floor and the imprint of another was dusted up on the coffee table—but the third glass and the bottle had vanished. Charlie fielded an angry call from Whittaker and was forced to admit she had no positive developments to give him.

Bold to do it in the victim's home. Sandy's wife had been abroad visiting relatives, but even so. Was the killer untouchable? It was beginning to look that way. The Morten house was a noisy, stressful place—the forensics circus was in town and there in the background was the wife, Sheila, who refused to go and stay with friends, feeling no doubt that her belated presence there, or at the very least her refusal to desert the family home, would somehow guarantee Sandy's safe return. It wouldn't—Charlie knew that, though she obviously couldn't say anything to the distraught wife. Sandy would return in a body bag or as a traumatized, gibbering wreck. The whole atmosphere was oppressive, and as another wave of nausea struck, Charlie hurried outside.

She'd just about made it out of sight when she hurled. A big, feisty regurgitation of her breakfast. Charlie had felt sick all day and in more ways than one. There was something profoundly odd and disquieting about bringing a new life into this dark world. She and Steve had been so looking forward to starting a family, but now Charlie was full of doubts. What right did she have to bring a baby into *this*? When there was such violence and cruelty and evil all around us. It was a profoundly depressing thought and made Charlie retch again.

As she was wiping herself down, her phone rang. Jaunty and inappropriate. She hurried to answer it.

"Charlene Brooks."

"Help me."

"Who is this?"

A long silence, an intake of breath as if the caller were summoning energy to talk, then:

"It's . . . Hannah Mickery."

Charlie stood bolt upright. It certainly sounded a bit like her. Could it really be?

"Where are you, Hannah?"

"I'm outside the Fire Station Diner on Sutton Street. Please come now."

And with that, she hung up.

Charlie was on the road within minutes. Bridges, Sanderson and Grounds were also on their way there, closely followed by Tactical Support. It was clear to everyone that this might be a trap. But pregnant or not, Charlie was going to walk into it. As they neared Sutton Street, the blues and twos went off and Tactical Support slipped round the block to watch discreetly as per usual.

Mickery looked as if she could barely stand. Her hair was matted, her red coat stood out garishly next to the deathly pallor of her skin, and she seemed to be leaning against the wall for support. Charlie was shocked by her transformation. She hurried toward her, her eyes flitting left and right, looking for any sign of danger. Oddly, now that she was here facing Mickery, she felt more vulnerable than she'd expected. Visions of the baby growing inside her flashed in her head and then were shoved back down. She had to concentrate.

Mickery collapsed into her arms. Charlie held her for a moment, running her eyes over her. She was in a pitiful state. What had she been through to be reduced to this?

Charlie called an ambulance, and as they waited for it to arrive she attempted to glean what she could from the terrified therapist. But Mickery wouldn't talk to her. It seemed as if she had instructions and was intent on following them to the absolute letter. Mickery, who had once seemed so cocky, now looked scared.

"Grace." Mickery's voice was cracked and quiet.

"Sorry?"

"I will only talk to Helen Grace."

And that was the end of the conversation.

death when she took down his crazed father. The killer, however, had made sure that James/Ben didn't have a happy ending. Helen had saved Anna and Marie from teenage arsonists, but the killer had taken care of them too. Martina had been born Matty Armstrong and was working as a rent boy in Brighton when his life went badly sideways. He'd been trapped, tortured and abused by a gang of men in a basement flat until Helen and a colleague had fortuitously heard his screams and broken down the door to end his ordeal. Again the killer had made sure he hadn't survived. Mickery was probably just a bonus, a little joke at Helen's expense—time would tell on that one—which just left Amy and Sam. They were the missing link. How were they connected to Helen? What had they done to draw themselves to the killer's attention?

Helen had received official commendations for her actions regarding James and Matty. There was a picture of her receiving her certificate in back copies of *Frontline*—easily accessible to anyone with a computer. There was no official commendation for the way she'd helped Anna and Marie, but the story had made the *Southampton Evening News* and Helen was name-checked there. Again, easy for anyone to find online. But where were Amy and Sam? Helen couldn't think of any major incidents in her career that had involved people their age. It didn't make any sense.

Helen had received another couple of commendations, the most notable of which came as a result of her quick thinking during a major traffic accident. But that was twenty-plus years ago—before Amy and Sam were born. Frustrated, Helen scrolled back to the issues of *Frontline* from that year. The details were still fresh in her mind, but she drank them in again now. On the way back from Thorpe Park a coach driver had nodded off at the wheel. His coach had swerved through the central barrier on a dual carriageway near Portsmouth and into the path of oncoming traffic. The driver was killed instantly, as were several of the drivers and passengers in the other cars involved. The resulting pileup had sparked a fire and many more of the injured motorists would have perished had it not been for the heroism of a couple of traffic cops who were first on the scene. One of those cops was a young Helen. She had been doing it for three months when the accident happened. She didn't like the job and was vocal in her desire to move on, but rules are rules and she had to do her rotation. So she did it to the best of her ability, seeing some horrible things along the way, and nowhere were her skills and bravery better demonstrated than during that accident. Along with her colleague Louise Tanner, she had pulled many shocked and injured people from the wreckage as the fire spread. Shortly after, the fire brigade roared up and the fire was extinguished. But it was clear to all present that the swift thinking of Helen and her colleague had saved dozens of lives.

Helen and Louise were mentioned in *Frontline* and the names of the local victims were listed in the *Southampton Evening News* and the *Portsmouth Echo*, but there were no details of those who had survived. Everyone was more interested in the tragedy of those who had died. Helen slumped back in her chair. Another dead end. Were Amy and Sam just random victims? Perhaps they were. And yet the killer had been so diligent in tracking down the others, there *had* to be some connection.

Helen decided to surf the archives of the national newspapers, given that many of those caught in the pileup were ferry passengers journeying to Portsmouth to start their holidays. She scrolled

81

Helen pressed the bell down and held it. It was late and she wouldn't get a good reception, but she had to persevere. Diane Anderson, hostile at first, ushered Helen inside when she realized she wasn't going away. She—the family—had had enough of the neighbors gawping at the strange goings-on at their house. She didn't want to give them anything else to enjoy.

"I'll get Richard," Diane said over her shoulder as she headed for the stairs. She couldn't face another round of questions on her own.

"Before you do, I'd like you to take a look at this."

Helen held out a printed copy of the *Today* picture that she'd run off at the station earlier. Diane paused, irritated, and returned to the living room, plucking the paper from Helen's hand. As she looked at it, irritation gave way to shock.

"Do you recognize the people in the picture?" Helen asked. There was no time to beat around the bush now.

Nothing from Diane. Shock was giving way to anxiety. Richard was only upstairs and might appear at any moment.

"Well?"

"It's me," was the mumbled response.

"So you and I *have* met before."

Diane nodded but stared at the floor.

"Did you know? When I met you after Amy had . . . after Sam had died, did you know that we'd met before?"

"Not at first. There was too much going on. But later . . . I wondered . . . I wasn't sure."

"Why the fuck didn't you say something?" Helen's anger was punching through now.

"What does it matter, for God's sake? What does it have to do with anything?"

"It matters because it linked you to the police force . . . and to me particularly. Why didn't you say anything?"

Diane shook her head, unwilling to go there.

"I need to know, Diane. If you help me now, then I promise you we will find Sam's killer. But if you don't . . ."

Diane fought back a sob, then shot a glance at the stairs. No sign of Richard—yet.

"I wasn't with Richard that day. I was driving back from Salisbury with someone else."

Now Helen got it.

"Your lover?"

Diane nodded—now the tears were coming thick and fast.

"I'd been to see him because . . . because I was pregnant. It was his. Amy was . . . is his. He wanted me to leave Richard and be with him . . . but . . . we crashed on the way back. He was killed. I couldn't get out initially. My feet were trapped. I thought I was going to burn to death, but—"

"I pulled you out."

Helen cast her eye down at the photo. If you looked hard, a bump was visible round her midriff. Helen had saved Diane's life, but, even more important, she had saved Amy's. The thought made her queasy—their killer was even more devious and twisted than she'd given her credit for.

"What's all this about? Why do you want to know about that day?"

The six-million-dollar question.

"I can't say right now, Diane, but we're much closer to understanding why Amy was abducted. I will tell you more the minute I have it. But I must ask you to keep this conversation between you and me for now."

Diane nodded—she had no problem with that.

"We will catch Sam's killer," Helen continued, "and Amy will get justice. You have my word on that. As for the rest of it, that's up to you. I've got no interest in wrecking anybody's marriage."

Diane showed her out. Helen was straight on the phone. There were several messages from Charlie, and when Helen got through to her she was brought up to speed on the Mickery situation. The game was getting stranger and stranger at each turn and Helen had the nasty feeling that things were building to a perfectly planned climax. Helen had encountered many unpleasant people during her time as a copper and her mind scrolled through them now, desperately searching for the culprit.

"I'm coming, Charlie, but I need you to do something for me first."

"Yes, boss?"

"I need you to check out the whereabouts of Louise Tanner."

82

Hannah Mickery had never been a nail biter. But her fingers were bitten to the quick now. It was ironic, really. A lot of her work had been turning hair pullers and nail biters into rational, stable human beings. But now look at her. A gibbering wreck, all sense of self-control eroded by her terrible ordeal.

Where was Grace? This waiting was slow torture. When she'd made the deal with her abductor, it had all been so simple. She would do as she was told and then she would be free. Amusing to think that in the brief heady moments after the deal she'd had a flash vision of a life beyond fear and despair. A life in which she could put her ordeal, and more specifically her recovery from it, to good use. To help others. To help herself.

Now that all seemed like arrant nonsense. A feeble flight of fancy and the product of a disordered mind. Perhaps she wouldn't get to see Grace? Perhaps she would fail? The torture wasn't over yet.

Then suddenly Grace was in the room. Mickery was filled with elation, even though Grace was visibly startled by her appearance. She was trying to do her sympathetic face, but Mickery felt like an exotic and repulsive creature being gawped at in the reptile house.

Helen, for her part, was stunned by what she saw. Mickery, cool as a cucumber in previous interviews, looked like one of the crazy ladies you see every day at the soup kitchens. Homeless women who've been so battered by life that they look completely unhinged.

"I don't want her here," Mickery snapped, casting an accusing glance at Charlie.

"DC Brooks needs to be here as a matter of proced—"

"She can't be here. Please."

Now there was a plaintive tone to her request and tears were threatening. Her whole body seemed to be shaking. With a nod from Helen, Charlie quit the room.

"What happened to you, Hannah? Are you able to tell me?"

"You know what happened to me."

"I can guess, but I want to hear it from you."

Mickery shook her head and looked at the floor.

"You're not under arrest and I've got no intention of bringing charges against you for things that you were forced to do. If you've killed Sandy . . . then tell me where—"

"Sandy's not dead," Mickery interrupted. "At least I don't think he is. And I didn't do anything to him."

"So where is he? If we can get help to him . . ."

"I don't know. We were in a metal container, a freight container down by the docks, I'd guess. I could smell the sea when I was dragged out."

"Who dragged you *out*?"

"She did. Katherine."

"Let me be clear on this. She dragged you out and spared you, despite the fact that Sandy was alive and unharmed?"

Mickery nodded.

"The gun was empty. She never intended for us to die. It was all a big fucking joke."

Helen sat back in her chair, processing this new development.

"Why, Hannah? Why did she spare you?"

"Because she wanted me to give you a message."

"A message?"

"I was to contact Brooks, but speak to you. Only to you."

"And what is that message?"

"I commend you."

Helen waited for more, but nothing was forthcoming.

"That's it?"

Mickery nodded. "I commend you," she repeated.

There was no way she wasn't giving this message, Helen thought to herself.

"What does it mean?" Hannah Mickery's question was desperate. As if Helen's answer could make sense of her terrible experiences.

"It means we're getting closer to the killer."

"Who is she?"

Helen paused. What to tell her?

"I can't be certain, Hannah. Not yet."

Hannah snorted, disbelief writ large on her face.

"And what am I supposed to do while you're playing cops and robbers?"

"We can offer you secure accommodation and personal protection if that's what—"

"Don't bother."

"I mean it, Hannah. We can look af—"

"You think anything you do will stop her? She's not going to be beaten. She's going to win. Don't you see that?"

Mickery's eyes blazed. She looked completely demented.

"Let me call you a doctor, Hannah. I really think—"

"I hope you can sleep at night." Mickery gripped Helen's arm, pinching the skin sharply. "Whatever it is you've done, I hope you can sleep at night."

Helen left the interview to seek the station doctor, with Mickery's words still ringing in her ears. Her accusation had been prophetic and troubling. Helen was so engrossed in her train of thought that at first she didn't notice that someone was calling her name.

Whittaker. She should have been expecting this. Inwardly Helen cursed herself for not having a battle plan ready for this tricky situation.

"How is she? Did you manage to get anything out of her?"

His tone was businesslike, but Helen could tell he was tense. He was a good politician, a good actor, but he was rattled. He had no idea what sort of state Mickery was in or what she was saying. She could destroy his career in a couple of sentences.

"She's in a bad way, sir. But she's bearing up and cooperating."

"Good, good." Not very convincing, thought Helen.

"What about the lawyer?" Whittaker continued. "Is he . . . ?"

"We're not sure at the moment. It looks as though she might have let them both go."

This clearly unnerved him.

"Well, keep me up to speed. We won't be able to keep a lid on this thing much longer, so . . ."

And with that, he was gone. What now? Helen knew she had little choice. It was hard to find a private space in the nick, somewhere you could talk freely. But behind the canteen bins was one such place. So she went there now and called Anti-Corruption.

"What I'm about to tell you does not leave this room, okay?"

Helen was now back in the incident room. Charlie, Bridges, Grounds, Sanderson, McAndrew—they'd all been summoned to a team briefing and were listening, tense and expectant. They nodded in unison to Helen's question and awaited more.

"So far our killer has targeted five couples. Every one of them is connected to me in some way."

A visible reaction from the team, but no one was prepared to interrupt Helen in this mood, so she carried on.

"Marie and Anna Storey. I helped save them from the mob. Ben Holland, born James Hawker, was about to be murdered by his deranged father when I intervened. Martina, our prostitute, was in fact Matty Armstrong, a rent boy who was tortured and abused by a gang of men until my colleague and I saved him."

Another murmur from the team.

"Diane Anderson, then pregnant, was in a pileup near Portsmouth. Louise Tanner and I were working in Traffic then and we helped save her and her unborn baby, Amy. Diane never came forward because she wasn't traveling with her husband at the time . . . but she's admitted it now."

"And Mickery?" Finally someone dared ask a question. Mc-Andrew was the brave one.

"Mickery and Sandy were a bonus. A little joke at our and their expense. The killer obviously thought we weren't catching on quick enough so decided to send us a message. Mickery was released on the condition that she seek me out with the following phrase: 'I commend you.'"

The phrase hung heavy in the air. No one ventured a response.

"I was given official police commendations for all but one of the incidents I just mentioned. Our killer has deliberately targeted people whom I helped and has endeavored to destroy them. It doesn't matter to her if they are killed or do the killing. They are ruined either way. She enjoys that unknown quantity—it gives the whole show an element of surprise for her."

The obvious question was, "Who's the killer?" So Helen was impressed by Charlie's response.

"Did you receive any other commendations?"

Another buzz from the team. Then Helen replied:

"Yes, one. A young Australian called Stephanie Bines. She was working as a barmaid in Southampton. She witnessed a shooting down near the docks, opted to testify, and then an attempt was made on her life. We protected her that day and the arrests we made helped send a whole gang to jail. I've already sent uniform to her last known address, but I want a couple of you on it straightaway. Not you, Charlie."

Charlie sat back down as Helen nominated two other members of the team. Then Helen pulled her aside.

"I want you to do something else for me and I want you to do it as quietly and carefully as possible. Understood?"

Charlie nodded.

"Louise Tanner was working with me the day we pulled Diane Anderson from her car and all those victims from the wrecked bus."

Helen hesitated briefly—was this the right move?—then carried on.

"She didn't . . . she didn't cope too well in the aftermath. Never went back on full duty again and dropped off the radar completely a little while later. I want you to find out everything you can about where she's been and what's she been doing, and you tell me and me alone, okay?"

"Of course, boss. I'm already on it."

"But before you go, I need to have a chat with you about something else. There's going to be the mother of all situations here soon and I need you to help me manage it."

"What do you mean?"

"Mark is innocent. He didn't sell us out."

Charlie looked at her, eyes wide. Helen had destroyed his life for nothing?

"I know who did sell us out. And it's going to tear this place apart. I'm going to need you by my side to keep everyone calm and focused. Corruption is one thing, but we've got a killer to catch. Whatever happens here, I want us to keep driving forward until the job is done. Can I rely on you?"

"Hundred percent."

And Helen knew she could. This investigation had been a nightmare and the worst was yet to come. But Charlie had proved herself during the course of their hunt and Helen was glad she would be there, or thereabouts, at the conclusion.

Which was why she felt so bad about deliberately misleading her now.

83

The crop sped through the air, biting into the firm female flesh as it found its target. She bucked, arching her body as she took in the pain, letting it flow through her. The inevitable sharp sting followed; then her body began to relax. She was fifteen strokes to the good already and she was beginning to tire, but still she said:

"Again."

Jake obliged but knew that he should call time on their session now. It had been an enjoyable encounter—almost like old times—and if they were smart they would quit while they were ahead.

"One more."

Jake raised the crop with relief, bringing it home with a little more speed and strength than usual. She groaned—a satiated,

happy groan. Jake found himself wondering if a change was taking place. Was she beginning to take sexual pleasure from her
punishment? Many of the women he beat finished themselves off
in front of him without embarrassment, brought almost to the
point of orgasm by the cruel but delicious blows he administered.
Would she allow herself to go there? Could he take her there?

Jake had found himself spending more and more time thinking about her. He had always been curious, but since their falling-
out and reconciliation, he'd found it hard to stop trying to
fathom her inner workings. Why did she hate herself so much?
In his mind, he'd rehearsed a dozen different ways to broach the
subject, but in the end the question just popped out, surprising
both of them.

"Before you go, is there anything you want to talk about?"

She paused, regarding him curiously.

"I mean . . . you know that everything that happens here is
private and discreet, so if you did want to talk there's no need to
worry. What's said here stays here."

"What would I talk about?" Her response was curious but
noncommittal.

"You, I suppose."

"Why would I do that?"

"Perhaps because you want to. Because you feel comfortable
here. Perhaps this is the ideal space for you to tell me how you feel."

"How I *feel*?"

"Yes. How do you feel when you come here? And how do
you feel when you leave?"

She looked at him strangely; then, gathering her things, she
said:

"I'm sorry—I don't have time for this."

And she was heading for the door. Jake stepped forward, gently but firmly blocking her path.

"Please don't misunderstand me. I don't want to pry and I certainly don't want to hurt you. I just want to know how I can help you."

"Help me?"

"Yes, help you. You're a good, strong person with so much to give, but you hate yourself and it doesn't make any sense. So please let me help you. You've got no reason to beat yourself up like this and perhaps if you would talk to me . . ."

He petered out, such was the ferocity of the glare that she directed at him now. It was a toxic mixture of anger, bile and disappointment.

"Fuck you, Jake."

With that, she pushed him out of the way and was gone. Jake slumped onto the chair—he had played it all wrong and would now pay the price. He knew with absolute certainty that he would never see Helen Grace again.

84

Everyone has a tipping point. A line that must not be crossed. I was no different. Had the stupid bastard been sensible, then none of this would have happened. But he was dumb and greedy and that's why I decided to kill him.

I was a wreck by this point. I'd given up on life—I knew that it was my lot to be damaged and discarded. I'd made my peace with that—after all, that's what happened to the girls I knew. None of them made it out the other side. Look at my mother—a sorry fucking excuse for a person. She was a doormat, a punching bag, but worse than that she was an accomplice. She knew what he was doing to me. What Jimmy and the rest were doing to me. But she did nothing. She ignored it and just carried on. If he kicked her out, she'd *probably die in the streets—no one else would have her. So she took the easy way out. If anything, I hated her more than I hated him.*

At least that's what I thought until that day. When I saw him come into our bedroom and hesitate. Normally he just charged in and took his fill—he liked things to be brief and violent. But that day he paused, and for the first time his gaze drifted to the top bunk.

I knew what that gaze meant, what evil thoughts were spinning round his head. Strangely, he backed off, walked out. Maybe he wasn't quite ready to go there yet. But I knew it was only a matter of time. And in that moment my mind was made up.

I decided there and then that I was going to kill the fucker.

And what's more, I was going to enjoy doing it.

85

"It's not difficult to do. Do you want me to show you how?"

Simon Ashworth had some color in his cheeks for the first time in days. Hiding out in Helen's flat, he'd become a nervous, fidgety creature, eating little and smoking a lot. But now that Helen had some work for him—and proper detective work at that—he had perked up. He loved a chance to show off his technical expertise and Helen had just handed him an opportunity on a plate.

He'd been surprised by her sudden arrival. She burst in and started firing questions at him without asking him how he was or bothering to update him on the Whittaker situation. She seemed agitated, distracted, and as she filled him in on the details of the investigation, he could see why. He took it all in, but still it was mind-blowing. Progress had clearly been made, however. DI

Grace had worked out why the victims were targeted; now she wanted to know how the killer did it. How did the killer know her victims' movements so well that she could be on hand at the perfect moment to offer them a lift and then abduct them?

Some of them, such as Ben Holland's weekly meeting, were easy for any ordinary stalker to work out. And Marie and Anna never left the flat. But what about Amy? Or Martina? Their movements were impulsive and unpredictable. How could you climb inside their minds?

"Presuming they don't post their movements in advance on social media sites and so on, the best way to monitor their plans is to hack into their communications," Simon began.

For once Helen was silent and Simon relished the brief shift in power.

"Hacking into their phone communications is tricky, as it requires you to lay your hands on their phone and insert a chip. Possible, but risky. Much easier to hack into their e-mail accounts."

"How?"

"First step is to go to their Facebook site, or anything similar that has personal information on them. Normally you can get their e-mail address from there—Gmail, Hotmail, whatever—plus loads of info about their family, date of birth, favorite holiday destinations, et cetera. Then you call up their e-mail service provider and tell them that you can't access your e-mails anymore as you've forgotten your password. They will ask you a number of fairly standard security questions—your mum's maiden name, name of a pet, significant date, favorite place—most of which you should be able to answer if you've done your homework properly. They will then tell you the old password and ask you if you want to keep it or change it. You tell them to keep it as is, leaving the actual account holder none the wiser and meaning you can now access all their e-mails on your own device. Simple."

"And would we be able to tell if someone's account was being accessed by more than one device?"

"Sure. Their account provider would be able to tell you, if you could persuade them. They are a bit funny about that, but if you tell them it's a murder inquiry they'll probably play ball."

Helen thanked Simon and headed back to the nick. He had proved to be crucial to this case in ways she could never have predicted. Amy had e-mailed her mum giving her the exact details of when she'd be hitchhiking home. Had the killer accessed these e-mails and lain in wait? Similarly, Martina had e-mailed her sister—the one person from her old life that she still kept in contact with—asking if she could pay her a visit, get away from Southampton. Was this how the killer had traced Matty? And was this why "Cyn" abducted them when she did, fearing that if Matty/Martina departed to her sister's in London the opportunity would be lost?

More questions than answers, but finally Helen felt she was getting closer to the truth.

86

"Stay away from me."

Mickery hissed out the words, but Whittaker ignored her, advancing upon her.

"You lay one finger on me and I'll scream this whole place down."

She'd been put in the station infirmary overnight. There she could rest while being protected twenty-four/seven. The callow PC on duty for the late-late shift hadn't picked up anything unusual in being allowed a cigarette break by the station chief. It was yet another sign of what a good bloke he was. Whittaker knew he had five minutes max and intended to make the most of it.

"I need to know what you're going to do."

"I mean it. Don't come any closer."

"For God's sake, Hannah—I'm not going to hurt you. It's me, Michael."

He attempted to reach out to her, console her, but she pulled away sharply.

"This is your fault. This is all your—"

"Don't be ridiculous. You came to me."

"Why didn't you find me?"

The vulnerability in her voice shocked him.

"I was in hell, Mike. Why didn't you find me?"

Suddenly all his anger dissipated and he was filled with pity. He felt a lump in his throat, a sudden welling of sadness. He had first met Hannah in the aftermath of the botched shooting that ended his frontline career. She had counseled him, healed him, and the pair had fallen in love. He'd kept her existence secret because he didn't want the world to know he had a shrink, but his feelings for her were sincere.

"We tried, Hannah, my God we tried. We threw everything at it. Every uniform I could spare without arousing—"

Hannah looked up sharply.

"Without giving yourself away?"

It was said with real bitterness.

"I tried, believe me. I really, really tried. But there was no trace of you. Or Sandy. You'd vanished off the face of the earth. I don't know if this killer is human . . . or a bloody ghost. But we couldn't pick up her trail. I am so, so sorry. If I could have swapped places with you, I would have, believe me . . ."

"Don't say that. Don't you *dare* say that."

"What do you want me to say?"

The question hung in the air. Whittaker knew he had only moments left—everything was telling him to leave.

"I want you to tell me it never happened. I want to have never met you. I want never to have fallen in love. I want you to have kept your killer to yourself. I want it all to go away. I wish I wasn't here anymore. I wish I didn't exist."

Whittaker stared, lost for words in the torrent of her despair.

"But you needn't worry. I'm not going to tell them about you. I'm going to keep quiet. I'm going to do as I'm told and then maybe I will live."

She returned to her bed and faced the wall.

"Thank you, Hannah."

It was inadequate, grossly so, but time was pressing, so Whittaker slipped out. Moments later, the young PC reappeared, stinking of cheap cigarettes. Whittaker slapped him on the back and departed. Back in his office, Whittaker exhaled. The original plan had been to retire together with millions in the bank. That was screwed now, but at least he was in the clear. It had all gone horribly, horribly wrong, but he was going to be okay. He'd been up all night and was shattered, but as the sun began to rise, Whittaker felt a surge of energy and optimism.

Which was when there was a sharp knock on the door. Before he had a chance to respond, Helen entered—flanked by two officers from Anti-Corruption.

87

Stephanie Bines was nowhere to be found. Itinerant workers are particularly hard to locate, especially those who work in bars. It's a promiscuous profession in which the promise of a few bucks more prompts people to jump ship all the time. Stephanie Bines had worked in most of the bars in Southampton—she was attractive and funny, but also flighty and temperamental—and no one had seen her for a while.

After the court case, she'd considered going back home, but she'd run away from Australia for a reason and the idea of returning there with her tail between her legs—still broke and unattached—didn't appeal. So she hopped from Southampton to Portsmouth and did what she did before: work, drink, screw and sleep. She was a piece of driftwood washed up on the south coast.

There was no response at her last known address. Sanderson had paid a visit, but it was a come-and-go place where you paid by the week, and Stephanie hadn't been seen there for ages. The owner, suspicious of the police and uncertain who or what might be discovered in his cheap rooms, was not keen to help, demanding a warrant before he'd open any doors. The team immediately applied for one, but it would take time. So they resumed their search in the city center clubs and bars, the local hospitals, cab firms and more. But still there was no trace.

She had vanished.

88

Whittaker eyeballed Helen. Neither was speaking—Anti-Corruption was formally laying out the accusations—but Helen felt she was being interrogated nevertheless. Whittaker's glare bore into her skull as if he was trying to divine her thoughts.

"I must say, I'm surprised at you, Helen. I thought you had more sense than this."

DS Lethbridge from Anti-Corruption came to an abrupt halt, surprised by the sudden interruption.

"I thought we'd cleared this matter up," Whittaker continued, "and now I find it landing on my doorstep. I don't have to remind you that there is an active investigation going on that should have your *full* attention."

Helen refused to drop her gaze, refused to be intimidated. Lethbridge started up again but Whittaker just talked over him.

"I can only assume that this is about ambition. Perhaps you felt that you weren't moving up the ladder quick enough. Perhaps me promoting you to be the youngest female DI this nick's ever had wasn't sufficient reward. But let me tell you something— maliciously stabbing senior officers in the back is not the way to get ahead. As you're about to discover."

He never took his eyes off her. Helen broke the stare first—a pang of conscience, guilt—though why she should be feeling guilty was beyond her. This was classic Whittaker: reminding her of what she owed him while delivering a veiled threat. He was adept at not crossing the line while nevertheless intimidating and neutralizing anyone who threatened his position. It was true that Whittaker had "spotted" her, plucked her out as a promising DC and helped her slide up the promotion chain all the way to inspector. And then she had turned on him. But what he had done was so bad—not just his relationship with Mickery and his leaking of crucial information, but his scapegoating of Mark and Simon Ashworth—that in reality she should feel nothing but contempt.

Helen was glad when the interview concluded after only twenty minutes. They would have to reconvene with Whittaker's police representative and lawyer and Helen would be excluded from the process from now on. Whittaker predictably had said little, denying all the charges. Would he crack?

There was simply too much smoke for there not to be a fire. Charlie seemed innocent. Hand on heart, Mark had put up a convincing case too. And Simon Ashworth had been so compelling in his account. It all pointed to Whittaker's guilt. But Helen knew that senior officers were very seldom hung out to dry publicly. And it was even less likely in this case, as the investigation that he had compromised was so sensational. These corruption cases tended to drag on behind very closed doors for months, even years. And what was the betting that at the end of it he would be pensioned off without any real censure or punishment? Helen hated the realpolitik of it all.

The process would take time to play out, but two things were immediately apparent. First, that Helen would take over Whittaker's role in an acting capacity. And second, that she wanted Mark back on the team.

Helen took a deep breath and rang his bell. This wasn't going to be easy, but there was no time for hesitation. Charlie was still chasing down Louise Tanner, there was no sign of Stephanie Bines and they were no closer to ending this nightmare. She needed all her best people round her.

"Come on, come on," Helen muttered as she listened for signs of life. A minute ticked by. Then another. She was about to cut her losses and go when she heard someone fumbling with the lock. She turned just as the door swung open to reveal Mark. Or what was left of him at least.

He was a sorry sight. Unshaven, red eyed and unsteady on his feet. A daytime drinker with nothing—or no one—to make him stop. He was wearing a tracksuit, but exercise was not in the cards. He had shut down. Helen felt a pang of regret. She had offered to save Mark, then driven him to the bottle once more.

He stared at her with a mixture of surprise and contempt, so Helen jumped straight in:

"Mark, we've been through too much together for me to beat around the bush or try to dress things up, so I'm just going to say it straight. I know that you are innocent of everything I threw at you. I know I fucked up big-time. And I want you back on the team straightaway. If you don't have the energy or can't face being in the same room as me, I would understand, but I want to find a way to get you back in—you're too talented a copper to be thrown on the scrap heap. I was wrong. But I've nailed the right guy now and I want to make amends."

A long silence. Mark looked stunned. Then:

"Who?"

"Whittaker."

Mark whistled, then laughed. He was incredulous.

"We don't know yet if it was a financial relationship with Mickery or a romantic one, but I'm totally convinced it was him. He lied about his alibi, pressured other officers to lie . . . It's a big mess."

"So who's taking over?"

"I am."

"Well, congratulations."

He had been polite until now, but the first hints of sarcasm were creeping in.

"I know I upset you, Mark. I know I betrayed our . . . friendship. I didn't want to hurt you, but I did it all for the right reasons. I just got it wrong. Badly, badly wrong."

She drew breath, then carried straight on.

"But things have developed and I need you back. I know now

that the killer is motivated by a personal hatred of me. We're getting closer, Mark, but I need your help to get me over the line."

She swiftly explained the situation—the victims, the commendations. Mark took it all in, passively at first, but then slowly he ventured questions, becoming more and more engaged in the narrative. The old instincts were awakening, Helen thought to herself.

"Have you told the rest of the team? That I'm innocent," Mark fired back, wresting the initiative from Helen.

"Charlie knows. I'll tell the others later today."

"That's the very *minimum* that has to happen before I will even think about what you've said today."

"Of course."

"And I want you to apologize. I know you're not very good at tha—"

"I'm sorry, Mark. Truly, truly sorry. I should never have doubted you. I should have listened to my instincts. But I didn't."

Mark stared at her, surprised by the comprehensive nature of her apology.

"I know I drove you to this, but I want to make amends. Clean yourself up and help us catch her. Please."

He wouldn't commit there and then. Helen knew he wouldn't, though there was a part of her that was hoping he might. Instant forgiveness is always desirable, if not very probable. So she left him pondering and got back on the job. Had she left it too late to repair the damage? Time would tell.

89

Charlie Brooks didn't like alcohol. Never had. So pubs that opened at nine a.m. certainly weren't her natural habitat. But she was trawling them today, taking a step into a different, darker world. There are some pubs where you go to woo your lover. There are others where you go to stand on the tables and sing. And there are others where you go to drink yourself to death. It was still early morning and yet the Anchor was already pretty full—of pensioners, alcoholics and those who'd rather be anywhere than on their own.

Despite the smoking ban, there was a strong smell of cigarette smoke. Charlie wondered what else they turned a blind eye to in this insalubrious establishment. For years the council had tried to get these portside pubs closed down, but the might of the breweries was strong and pubs that sell strong beer at £1.99 a pint will always be popular with the punters.

It had already been an exhausting search. There were plenty of dodgy drinking dens near Southampton docks and Charlie would have to visit them all. Eyes darted and ears pricked up the moment she entered. Despite dressing down, she was still too attractive, too fresh for these places and the clientele was instantly intrigued or in some cases on their guard. No one afforded her a warm welcome and she was starting to get disheartened when finally she got a break.

Louise Tanner, or Louie as she was known locally, was a regular at the Anchor. She'd be here at some point. All you had to do was sit and wait.

Was this progress? It was better than nothing, so Charlie bought herself a drink and took a corner seat at the back. It afforded her a good view of the entrance without revealing herself and would be a good vantage point.

She tried to imagine what Louise might look like. They had only her official police association photo to go on, and that was years old. Then she was a muscular officer, with blond hair tied tight back in a ponytail and a slight gap between her front teeth. Not attractive, you'd say, but nonetheless an imposing and impressive character. Her physical strength had come in handy when she and Helen had pulled those people to safety, but the aftermath revealed a distinct lack of mental strength. You can never tell how you might react to a traumatic experience, but whereas Helen Grace had managed to bottle it up or clamp it down or deal with it in some way, Louise Tanner hadn't. Was it the burn injuries on some of the young victims? Was it the driver crushed between bus and pillar? Was it the heat, the smell, the fear, the darkness? Whatever it was, Louise struggled to shrug off the aftereffects. She had counseling, halved her hours and had all the support you would expect, but a year later she'd quit.

Colleagues and friends tried to stay in touch, but Louise became increasingly aggressive and bitter. People said she drank too much, even speculated that she might be involved in petty crime. And one by one they broke contact with her, until in the end there was no one, not even her family, who could positively vouch for where she was. Her life could not have contrasted more unfavorably with Helen's, who had shot to the top of her profession and now enjoyed the money and status that came with the rank of detective inspector. Tanner somehow blamed Helen for her problems, hence the hate mail she occasionally sent to Southampton nick. Helen had let it go, but it proved useful now, the Southampton postmark revealing that Tanner still lived locally. There had been the occasional Southampton sighting, and Helen's gut instinct was that Louise wouldn't stray far from what she knew. Which was why Charlie was now clutching a tepid orange juice at the back of one of the nastiest pubs she'd ever been in.

Time crawled by. Charlie started to wonder if this was an elaborate joke. Had the owner somehow tipped Louise off? Perhaps they were both chuckling now at the dimwit DC wasting her time on a pointless stakeout.

But then movement by the entrance. A woman in a Puffa and tracksuit bottoms half pimp-rolling into the place. Clearly a regular. A glimpse of the face and a wisp of lank blond hair. Was it Louise?

She sashayed up to the bar and cracked a joke with the owner.

A couple of words in response and she immediately turned to look at Charlie. The owner had obviously said something and there was no doubt as she peered toward the gloom at the back of the bar that it was Louise. Her eyes met Charlie's, a split-second appraisal of the situation—then Louise Tanner turned and fled.

Charlie was swiftly after her. Louise was thirty yards ahead and running for her life. Down the narrow cobbled streets that crisscrossed this once medieval area, then across the main road and toward the freight warehouses on the western docks. Charlie redoubled her efforts, her lungs already starting to burn. Louise was clearly not in a good way—she had a weird lolloping run that suggested a historic injury of some kind—yet despite this she was surprisingly fast, driven on by desperation.

Charlie was only ten yards behind her when Louise suddenly darted right and into warehouse 24, a repository for Polish freight where the containers were packed sky-high. Charlie changed course and charged inside. But Louise was nowhere to be seen.

Charlie cursed. She had to be almost within touching distance, but with so many tiny alleyways between the containers and so many corners to hide in, where on earth should she start? She dived left, then pulled up short. She listened. Yes, there it was again. A muffled cough. Louise was a heavy smoker and the sprint would have done her smoker's cough no good. Creeping round the back of the nearest container, Charlie padded along softly, guided in by the concealed but persistent coughing. And there Louise was, with her back to Charlie, trapped now—if Charlie could only get to her.

Charlie was ten yards from her when Louise spun round, wild eyed and desperate. Which was when Charlie saw the knife—a stubby but nasty-looking thing that Louise thrust toward her. Charlie instinctively stepped back, for the first time realizing the danger she had put herself—and her unborn baby—in.

Now Louise advanced upon her. Charlie sped up her retreat, furiously backpedaling while urging calm.

"I just want to talk to you, Louise."

But her quarry said nothing, pulling the hood back over her head as if to hide her identity from her pursuer. Closer, closer, Charlie's eyes were locked on the approaching blade.

Bang! Charlie thudded into the metal wall of a container. She turned round and too late realized she had walked into a dead end. There was just time to turn and raise her arms in capitulation as Louise grabbed her by the collar, thrusting her back. With the knife poised at Charlie's throat, Louise began to search her for valuables. A look of fury turned to disgust when she came across the police badge and radio. She tossed them on the floor and spat on them.

"Who sent you?" Louise barked.

"We're conducting an inquiry—"

"*Who* sent you?"

"Helen Grace . . . DI Grace."

A moment's pause. Then Louise broke into a gappy-tooth grin.

"Well, give her a message from me."

"Sure."

At which, Louise slashed the knife across Charlie's chest, narrowly missing her throat. Blood seeped from the long wound just above her breasts. Charlie stood transfixed in shock, before being brought back to earth by the sinister sound of Louise's chuckling.

"Not enough for you?"

Suddenly a huge burst of static erupted from Charlie's discarded police radio. Louise shot a glance sideways, fearful of interruption, and Charlie flicked her left arm sharply up, batting the knife from Louise's hand. Charlie launched herself forward, but as she did so Louise's flailing left fist caught her in the throat. It felt for a moment as if her larynx had been crushed. She choked, couldn't breathe, had to steady herself on the wall. When she looked up, Louise was already out the door and legging it to freedom. Charlie started to pursue her, then immediately pulled up short and vomited. She couldn't go another step.

Charlie radioed for backup, then walked slowly to the entrance. The shock was kicking in and she needed fresh air. She breathed in deeply, filling her lungs with sea air, and momentarily felt better. Then she raised her eyes and was surprised to see uniformed officers already hurrying toward her. Beyond them she now glimpsed a police incident scene in the vicinity of warehouse 1. It hadn't been used for years, or so they'd thought. Something had been going on there and as uniform tended to Charlie they filled her in. Truant schoolkids had found a middle-aged man earlier that morning—not dead but getting there—lying comatose in an effluent-smeared freight container.

They had found Sandy Morten.

90

The local probation service was based in Southam Street in what was once a school. Sarah Miles, an old colleague from the police training college at Netley, worked there and it was to her that Helen hurried now. She hated deceiving a good friend, but there was no other way. She couldn't be transparent about her suspicions until she was absolutely sure. There would be plenty of time for explanations later. If there was a later.

She'd asked to see what they had on Lee Jarrot, a serial petty criminal who Helen suggested may have breached the terms of his probation. It was a mean trick to play on Sarah, and probably Lee too, as he had to Helen's knowledge done absolutely nothing wrong, but there it was. As Sarah swiped into the records department in the basement, Helen followed. It wasn't allowed for nondepartmental officers to be down there, but Helen often accompanied Sarah to gossip and chat. They were halfway to the Js, walking on and on past the endless lines of files, when Helen realized she'd left her mobile in the car.

"I said I'd be contactable twenty-four/seven. Do you mind bringing the file back up with you?"

Sarah rolled her eyes and carried on walking. She was a brisk lady who didn't like to waste time.

Which meant Helen would have to move fast. Heading back to the entrance, she veered off left sharply. Her eyes scanned feverishly—where the hell were the Cs? Sarah's clip-clop heels could be heard slowing down. She must be near to Jarrot's file.

C. There we are. Faster, faster, Helen flicked through the files. Casper, Cottrill, Crawley . . . Sarah was on her way back now. Helen had only seconds left when . . . there it was. In any other circumstances she would have hesitated to touch it—even the thought of it was traumatic. But now Helen grabbed it and thrust it into her bag.

When Sarah returned to the entrance, Helen was waiting for her.

"Was in my bag all along. Honestly, I'd forget my head if it wasn't screwed on."

Sarah Miles rolled her eyes again and the pair exited, Helen breathing a short, secret sigh of relief.

weakness by a woman—however justified—would be pounced on by her male colleagues. You'd be labeled as a weak link and treated accordingly. And God help you if you put babies before the job. As soon as they had you down as a mother hen, they wrote you off. If you wanted extended maternity leave or to work part-time, you might as well ask for a transfer to Administration. Nobody likes a part-timer on the front line.

There was no place for sentiment—it was all or nothing. That was why everyone respected Helen Grace: because she was never off duty, never allowed her home life to interfere. In short, she was the perfect female officer. She made it damn hard for the rest of them, set the bar too high, but that was the way it was. So Charlie stayed. Even though she was shaken to the core, she wasn't going to let people write her off after she'd worked so hard to get there.

Mark bided his time, waiting for the crowd to disperse, before crossing the room to give Charlie a big hug. She knew why he was hanging back—there were doubters in the room, people who would take a while to trust Mark again, so it wouldn't do for him to be at the front of the queue. *Screw them,* thought Charlie, holding Mark in a bear hug for longer than was strictly necessary. She wanted to make a point to the rest of the team. Perhaps some of her saintliness would rub off on him and speed up his redemption.

Soon they would have to swallow their suspicions about Mark and quit the innuendos—Mickery was talking. Charlie shouldn't know that, of course, but walls have ears and Mickery had hardly left the police infirmary since she'd been picked up. It was her sanctuary and she had all her discussions with Anti-Corruption there. Charlie had enough friends among the bored and gossipy female officers who had to keep an eye on Mickery.

They passed on what they picked up and the word was that Mickery had had a romantic relationship with Whittaker after he had used her professionally. Were they still sleeping together when the killings started? And who was it that came up with their scheme to enrich themselves? It didn't matter really. Mark was going to be in the clear—that was what mattered.

The big question was, how would Mark react when Helen was in the room? If they could find a way to get along, then his resurrection would be assured. If they couldn't, he was in big trouble.

Right on cue, Helen entered. She didn't acknowledge Mark's return, instead calling everyone together so she could allot tasks.

"So we now know that Sandy Morten had a stroke," she began. "He wasn't harmed by Mickery; his body just couldn't cope with the conditions. He's in ICU and fighting hard, but believe it or not, he was lucky. If those boys hadn't found him when they did, we'd have another corpse on our hands. Doctors think he'll pull through. What does this tell us?"

"That he wasn't part of the plan," replied DC Bridges.

"Exactly. She spared Mickery and Morten. Was never serious about killing them. They were just her little joke. Her way of hurrying the game along."

Helen scanned the team and was pleased to see anger mingling with determination. Police officers hate being goaded.

"So it's time for us to push up a gear, be one step ahead of her for a change. Top priority is to find Stephanie Bines. She's the obvious next victim and I do not want her death on our consciences. Charlie, can you coordinate efforts on this? Use whoever, whatever you need—we have to find her. Mark, I need you to focus on finding Louise Tanner. She's highly dangerous, has a particular animus against me and has already attempted to kill one of our own. So pick a couple of guys and get on her, okay?"

Mark nodded, the eyes of the team upon him. He was playing it just right, Helen thought—straight, unembarrassed, determined. He was making a superhuman effort with his colleagues, with his appearance—okay, he still looked like shit, but he was clean and sober—and with her. She felt massively grateful to him and pleased that he had decided to trust her once more.

The team sprang to life. Now that Helen was acting station commander, her officers were even more determined to win her approbation, and there was a sense that the man or woman who brought the killer in would be in pole position to succeed Helen as DI. So everyone redoubled their efforts, scenting glory.

Helen retired to the privacy of Whittaker's office. Even though he was currently suspended and in reality would never be returning to this nick, it still felt like *his* office. So Helen avoided sitting in his chair for now, standing next to his desk as she once more leafed through the file she had just stolen.

She picked up the phone, rang Social Services and soon had the address she needed.

The rest of the team was out hunting down Bines and Tanner, so Helen had a few hours' grace. But that still wouldn't be enough and she had a long way to go, so she cranked the throttle and sped on her way. The M25 was its usual snarled-up self and so it was with some relief that she peeled off onto the M11. Soon she was on the A11 and heading toward Norfolk.

Following the signs for Bury St. Edmunds, Helen found herself in unfamiliar territory. As she zeroed in on her destination, she realized that she felt nervous. This was an uncomfortable place for her and returning to it was like opening Pandora's box.

The house was a pleasant-looking bay-fronted house with well-kept gardens. Technically it was a probation hostel, but it looked much nicer than that. Locals knew to be wary of it, but a passerby would think it an attractive, welcoming place.

Helen had called ahead so was swiftly ushered in to meet the hostel manager. She confirmed her credentials, presented the most recent photo and trotted out her cover story with assurance. She knew it was a long shot, but nevertheless she felt deflated when the manager told her that Suzanne Cooke had not been seen for over a year. She had never really fit in, the manager confided, never seemed interested in engaging with their programs. They had obviously alerted the probation services after she'd vanished, but what with the cutbacks and reorganization, they never spoke to the same person twice and her case was never followed up.

"We'd love to do more, but there's only so much we can do. We have our hands full here as it is," the manager concluded.

"I understand—it's tough. Tell me a little more about Suzanne. What did she do when she was here? Did she have friends? Anyone she confided in?"

"Not that I know of. She didn't really join in. Kept herself very much to herself. Mostly she liked to exercise. She's very well built, muscular, athletic. She did a lot of bodybuilding, and when she wasn't in the gym she was helping out with the culling. She was stronger than most of the blokes, they said."

"Culling?"

"In Thetford Forest. It's only a couple of miles away and every year we allow some of our residents to help out with the summer cull if they want to. It's strictly supervised, obviously, because of the firearms, but some people like it—it's hard manual labor and you get a whole day out in the fresh air."

"How so?"

"It's mostly red deer in Thetford. They are shot early in the day, usually in remote areas of the forest. It's pretty impassable for vehicles, so draggers have to get them back to the nearest track so they can be loaded up."

"How?"

"Using a deer harness. You tie the deer's legs together, then clip a canvas cord round the bind. The cord is attached to a harness—bit like a mountaineer's harness—that you put on round your shoulders. Then you drag the deer along behind you. Much easier than trying to carry it."

Another piece of the jigsaw had fallen into place.

92

Charlie stared at the computer screen, her stomach knotted with tension. Skype was making its trilly ring tone and Charlie was praying someone would answer. The fate of Stephanie Bines hung in the balance.

It had been an exhausting search, but Charlie had never given up hope. Accompanied by DCs Bridges and Grounds, she'd trawled every low-rent pub, café and nightclub in Southampton and beyond. The conversation always went the same way:

"Yeah, we know Stephanie. Used to work here few months back. Very popular, especially with the fellas."

"And do you know where she is now?"

"No idea. Just didn't show up for work one day."

Initially this had made Charlie extremely nervous. Any mention of sudden disappearances was likely to do so in this case, but slowly Charlie formed a picture of a naturally itinerant young woman, not comfortable in herself, who didn't form strong attachments to people or places. She was a traveler who had dropped anchor on the south coast, but something told Charlie that this was only a temporary mooring. So she'd stopped pounding the streets and returned to the incident room to run a check on international travel. The last trace of her in Southampton was in September, so she started there. Aided by her DCs, she bashed the phones to Qantas, British Airways, Emirates before eventually hitting the jackpot with Singapore Airlines. October 16, Stephanie Bines, one-way ticket to Melbourne. Further checks revealed that Stephanie had a sister living in a suburb of Melbourne and Stephanie had now been traced—alive and well, seemingly—to her home there.

But Charlie was taking no chances, hence the Skype hookup. The killer's ability to mislead and deceive was such that Charlie wouldn't—couldn't—relax until she'd seen Stephanie with her own eyes.

And there she was. More tanned than before, blonder than before, but definitely Stephanie. A small victory for Charlie, Helen and the team. They had saved one at least. Had Stephanie's sudden decision to return home spoiled the killer's best-laid plans?

Stephanie didn't need much encouragement to get traveling again. She'd been at home only a few weeks, but already was feeling suffocated and belittled. Charlie had to think on her feet, inventing a mild security risk connected to the gangland trial Stephanie had helped to conclude. She was calm and reassuring, but suggested it might be best for Stephanie and her family if she took a little trip—to Queensland, the Red Center, wherever—while they got to the bottom of things over here.

Charlie ended their Skype session with a sense of optimism—perhaps the killer wasn't so invincible after all.

Her attention was suddenly caught by Mark, gesturing to her from across the incident room. She hurried over.

"Station has just taken a call. Tanner's been spotted begging near the old kids' hospital on Spire Street."

"When?"

"Five minutes ago. Mum with a buggy called it in. She'd given Tanner a quid and nearly lost her whole purse into the bargain."

They were on the road and heading to the city center. Was Tanner their killer? They would soon find out. Charlie felt her pulse quicken as she and Mark sped to the scene. It was good to be back in the saddle together and closing in for the kill.

93

There are countless moments in the average life when you have to decide whether to open yourself up or bury yourself deep. In love, at work, among your family, with friends, there are moments when you have to decide whether you are ready to reveal your true self.

Helen had deliberately made herself an enigma. She had a thick carapace that she presented to the world and it defined her— she was tough, resilient, incapable of doubt or regret. She knew that was far from the truth, but it was amazing how many others bought it. We always question ourselves more than we question others and most of her colleagues and occasional lovers seemed to buy the image of a tough, committed career copper who could not be shocked, frightened or intimidated. The longer she kept it up, the more people believed it, which was why she had taken on an aura of invincibility, especially among uniform.

Helen knew all this and paused for breath now as she stood on the verge of smashing the idol she had created. Letting others in now was the right thing to do and could save lives, but it came at a cost to Helen, dredging up events and decisions that had been buried deep.

DC Bridges entered, breaking Helen's introspective trance. He was carrying the case files she'd requested. As they pored over the pages together, discreetly tucked away in her office, Helen was constantly evaluating each link in the chain, double- and triple-checking her assumptions. There could be no room for doubt.

Then suddenly her heart stopped.

"Go back."

"To personal effects? Or—"

"The forensics report. From Morten's house."

In the wake of Sandy Morten's disappearance, Forensics had scoured his house. They knew the abductor had been there, had drunk champagne with Morten and Mickery, so they had searched long and hard for any traces of her.

"Nothing there, boss. Forensics found lots of DNA from Mickery, Morten, his wife, all the main—"

"The second page."

"Just the incomplete samples, most of which we've signed off—"

Helen snatched the report from him and stared at it. There could be no doubt now. She knew who the killer was and why she was killing.

. . .

Tanner was nowhere to be seen. But a discarded handbag near the boarded-up children's hospital suggested she had been here recently and perhaps bagged the prize she was after. They were about to leave when they heard something that made them stop in their tracks. A sharp metallic *clunk* from within the derelict building, as if something had been dropped.

Mark gestured to Charlie. Instinctively they both turned off their radios and phones and crept toward the building. One of the boards on the windows was loose—this could be the perfect hiding place for someone who wanted to come and go unseen.

Charlie and Mark climbed inside, levering themselves over the rotting windowsill as quietly as possible. Inside, the place was crumbling and deserted, a shell of the busy and vibrant place it had once been before the new city center hospital sealed its fate. Charlie removed her baton from her belt and readied herself for action. Her hand was shaking—was she ready for this? Too late now. They crept forward, expecting to be jumped at any moment.

Then a sudden movement. Tanner in hoodie and trackies bursting from her hiding place and through some swing doors. Mark and Charlie gave chase, busting a gut to get into the corridor and after their prize. *Bang!* They crashed through the doors but were already twenty yards behind Tanner.

Bursting into the stairwell, they looked up to see Tanner taking the stairs three at a time. They sprinted after her, Mark pulling ahead in his determination to bag her. Up, up, up. Then another crash.

By the time they caught up, they were on the fourth floor. Had she gone left or right? The swing doors to the left swayed slightly. Left it was. Mark eased the doors open and they slipped inside.

Empty. But there were doors at the other end—none of them moving—and four rooms off. She could be in any one of them. If she was, she was trapped now. They tried one, then another. Then another. Only one left.

Bang! It all happened so quickly that Charlie's brain could hardly process it. A metal pipe crashed onto Mark's head from behind and he crumpled to the floor. Charlie swung her baton hard at Tanner—it connected with the metal pipe with a harsh clang. She thrashed at her again and again as Tanner parried the blows.

Except it wasn't Tanner. This should have been apparent by the way she'd leapt up the stairs during the chase. And from the cunning she'd demonstrated in getting them to choose the wrong corridor before sneaking up behind them. It wasn't Tanner. It was their killer, and Charlie was now face-to-face with her.

It was time to take the fight to the enemy. Ordering the startled Bridges to assemble the team, Helen pulled out her mobile phone and dialed Charlie's number. Voice mail. Cursing, she rang Mark's. Voice mail again. What the hell were they playing at? Helen left a hurried message, then headed for the incident room.

She didn't like kicking off without her two best officers, but she had no choice. Even without them, the team was twenty strong and she could rely on McAndrew, Sanderson and Bridges to marshal the team's efforts effectively.

Helen wanted everything out on the table as fast as possible, so she dived straight in.

"The woman we are looking for is called Suzanne Cooke."

The team passed the photos of Suzanne along the line until everyone had one.

"Attached to the back, you'll find her charge sheet. She's a convicted double murderer who served twenty-five years. She went AWOL from her probation hostel twelve months ago. She was in the Norfolk area, but I believe that she is now in Hampshire and may be responsible for these killings."

A buzz went around the incident room. Helen paused, then continued:

"I believe she is deliberately targeting *me* through the choice of her victims. Stephanie Bines seems fine for now, but I want full liaison with our Australian counterparts so we can keep her safe. She's the last possible person on the list, but as the abduction of Mickery shows, Suzanne has got an imagination and is capable of deviating from the plan. So I want every available person on this. I'll handle the press—I want you lot to focus all your efforts on finding her. DC Bridges, can you inform uniform? I want everyone out on the street asking questions. Suzanne Cooke is now our number one suspect and I want every eyeball in the county looking for her. Understood?"

"Why you, boss?" replied DC Grounds, asking what they were all thinking. "Why is she deliberately targeting you?"

Helen hesitated. The time for secrecy was over, but even now she took a deep breath before replying:

"Because she's my sister."

Charlie tensed herself for a fight to the death. But her adversary made no move toward her, instead releasing her grip on the metal pipe in her hand. It clattered to the floor, the sound echoing around the deserted building. Charlie froze, suspecting a trick. But the killer merely slipped off her hood, revealing a hard but attractive face. For a moment, Charlie had a weird flash of recognition. But it was gone as quickly as it had come. Who was this woman? She was well built, with prominent shoulder muscles, but had a thin, attractive face, even though it was unadorned by makeup. Presumably this was to make her look as much like Tanner as possible.

"I don't know why you've brought us here, but we can end this peacefully. Turn around and place your hands on the wall."

"I'm not going to fight you, Charlie. That isn't why we're here."

Hearing her name in the mouth of this killer was profoundly unsettling. But worse was to follow. Smiling, the killer now casually pulled a gun from her pocket and pointed it at Charlie.

"You know what one of these can do, don't you? If memory serves, you trained using a Smith and Wesson, didn't you?"

Inexplicably, Charlie nodded. This woman had a strange power—was it personality or simply the fact that she knew everything about you?

"So put down your baton and take off your belt. If you're going to pull your colleague downstairs, you'll want to travel light."

The killer threw some sort of harness at her and gestured to her to put it on. Charlie just stared at her. Couldn't move.

"Now!" the killer bellowed.

Charlie dropped the baton to the floor. They had walked into a massive trap. It was presumably *she* who'd called the station with the "sighting" of Tanner. And they'd fallen for it.

Facing Tanner had been bad, but this was something infinitely worse.

The team assaulted Helen with questions—some of them angry, some of them curious—and Helen stood her ground, answering as honestly and calmly as she could.

"How long have you suspected?"

"How long have you *known*?"

"What does she want?"

"Will she target you directly?"

But there was still so much Helen didn't know, and speculating would only get them so far. So after a frantic half hour, she called time on the discussion. She needed them out there searching for Suzanne.

As she walked down the corridor toward the awaiting press, Helen realized her hand was shaking. She had buried her past for so long that revealing it now was like opening an old wound. Would her team still follow her? Still believe in her? Helen prayed that they would—she had a nasty feeling that the worst was yet to come.

94

"Is the public at risk, Inspector?" Emilia Garanita made sure she got her question in first. With journalists from the national tabloids and broadsheets in attendance, she wasn't going to miss this opportunity to twist the knife. Whittaker's attack on her was still very fresh in her mind.

"We don't believe that the general public is in danger, but we would urge people not to approach the suspect. She may be armed and her behavior is unpredictable. If anyone sees Suzanne Cooke, they should dial 999 immediately."

"What is her connection with the recent deaths in Southampton?" The killer question from the *Times*.

"We are still trying to establish the full facts of the situation," Helen replied, noting Emilia's cynical eyebrow rise in response, "but we believe she may have been actively involved in inciting the murders of Sam Fisher and Martina Robins."

Helen tightened a notch internally. It had been a tough call whether or not to mention Martina in the briefing. If the press got onto this and tracked down Caroline, the game would be up. There was no way she would be able to hold back telling them chapter and verse about Suzanne's diabolical role in these murders.

"Is it true that you've been promoted, Inspector?" Garanita forced her way back into the conversation. "Rumor has it that Detective Superintendent Whittaker has been suspended and is facing possible corruption charges."

At this point the room erupted—question after question raining down on Helen. It was a sustained assault, but Helen had no choice but to weather it, however damaging or provocative the questions were. She needed the public to be vigilant, so she needed the press onside. It was a bitter pill to swallow, but the situation was critical now. Sometimes in life you have to feed the hand that bites you.

95

Pain seared through him. Mark closed his eyes as the agony took hold and then he collapsed to the ground. What the hell had happened to him? Instinctively his hand went to the back of his head and he winced as his fingers probed the deep, bloody wound. His head hurt like hell, but in truth so did the rest of him—it felt like he had sustained a prolonged, savage beating.

Slowly it came back to him. The hunt for Tanner, the chase through the hospital, and then . . . a nasty blank. He vaguely recalled a nanosecond of alarm, a sense of something or someone behind him. Stupid bastard—he must have turned his back on Tanner and paid the price.

He scanned his surroundings. The place smelled antiseptic, but also musty. He tried to lift his head again, acclimatizing his eyes to the gloom. He was in some kind of boiler room. Was this the basement of the hospital? If so, how had they got down here?

"Mark."

Charlie. *Thank God.* Mark craned his neck round slowly, ignoring the shooting pains that accompanied every movement, to see Charlie huddled in the corner. She was cradling a battered camping light, which was their sole source of illumination.

Even as he began to take in this strange image, mental alarm bells started to ring.

"She's got us, Mark."

"Tanner?"

But Charlie just shook her head and buried her head in her hands. Eventually, she muttered:

"It was a trap. *She's* got us."

Suddenly Mark was staggering to his feet, scanning the room. But he'd got up too quickly, saw stars, then felt himself falling to the floor with a bump.

When he came to, his head was in Charlie's lap and she was blowing on his face. He was hot and cold, sweaty—and his throat raged sore. He was glad of the comfort of Charlie's touch. He looked up to thank her, but saw she was crying.

"She's got us, Mark."

It had been an illusion. There was no comfort here.

96

The Glock felt snug in her hand. It had been a while since Helen had held a gun, but it felt powerful and reassuring to be gripping one now. She signed it out and moved on to pick up her assigned ammunition. On the request sheet, she'd put that it was for personal protection given the possible threat to her life. But was it? Or was there a darker need pushing her to arm herself now?

Protocol decreed that she no longer work alone, given the threat level, but this wasn't a journey she could share with another, so she lied, saying she was required at regional HQ to brief them on the unfolding situation. The team bought it, but others weren't so easily fooled—as Helen sped north, she noticed Garanita's red Fiat purring along behind her. Not too obvious—she wasn't an amateur—but obvious enough. Helen felt anger surge inside her and she pulled the throttle back hard. She shot through the forty-miles-per-hour zone at over seventy, challenging her civilian pursuer to follow her. Thankfully, Emilia saw the hopelessness of breaking the law in pursuit of a copper, so gave up the chase. Once out of sight, Helen did a U-turn, heading back toward the ring road and then toward London.

The list of Helen's childhood haunts was a short one and once she'd discovered that Chatham Tower was scheduled for demolition, she'd decided to head there first. Given Suzanne's MO, this was the perfect place to use. It had to be significant. Funny how she kept thinking of her as Suzanne, as if this were somehow less painful than using her real name. That said, Helen herself had comfortably inhabited her new name now—she had chosen the name Grace because of its redemptive associations and Helen because of her maternal grandmother—and it would feel profoundly odd and unsettling to have anyone call her by her real name now.

Helen realized she was driving ninety-five miles per hour and eased off the throttle. She had to try to stay calm. Helen had no idea how this game was designed to end, but she would have to keep her wits about her if she was to end it on her terms.

She realized now that for a long time she had been in denial, repeatedly pushing away the thought that her sister could be involved in the killings. She hadn't communicated with her in over twenty-five years and that was the way she'd liked it. Out of sight and out of mind. But when she'd seen the forensic report from Sandy Morten's house, she could deny it no longer. Forensics had found a compromised element of DNA, a fragment of a fingerprint. They'd managed to lift something of it, and as it seemed to match Helen's DNA sequence, they'd signed it off as hers. They always do this to avoid wild-goose chases prompted by police carelessness at crime scenes. But there was just one problem. Helen had never been to Sandy Morten's house. This anomaly had been overlooked—but to Helen it had leapt off the page, confirming all her very worst fears.

She was now in the shabbier suburbs of South London. Before long, Chatham Tower came into view. It was designed as a sixties utopia, but was now earmarked for demolition. The dream had turned sour. Arrow Security, which kept the site secure, had been contacted, but even so Helen had to wait for someone to arrive with the key. The grumpy guard unlocked the wooden site door while Helen quizzed him about security breaches to the wooden boards that surrounded the derelict building. He insisted there hadn't been any—kids were too busy stabbing each other at the local shopping center to bother coming out here—but even so Helen did a full tour of the perimeter fence, probing for gaps or weaknesses. Eventually, she conceded it was secure and they headed inside. Could someone scale the boards with a ladder? Possibly.

The lift was off-limits, so they walked to the eleventh floor, Helen marching, her companion trudging behind. Before she knew it, Helen was standing outside number 112. She put her hand on the wall to steady herself as the security guard tried the door. It wasn't locked and swung gently open. He was about to enter when Helen stopped him.

"Wait here."

The security man looked surprised, but relented:

"Knock yourself out."

And without another word, Helen stepped into the flat and disappeared from sight, swallowed up by the darkness inside.

97

"We've got to keep strong, Mark. If we keep strong, if we keep united, she won't win."

Mark nodded.

"She's not going to beat us. I won't let her," Charlie continued.

Mark clambered to his feet, aided by Charlie, and together they explored their surroundings. If they were at the hospital, there was no way anyone would hear them. The council had been trying to flog the building to developers for years with zero success. It stood alone in a run-down, forgotten part of town.

They were surrounded by concrete walls. There were no windows and the door had been recently and extensively strengthened—renovation that sat at odds with the otherwise dilapidated room. They tried to get at the hinges, but without a tool of some kind it was hard to gain any purchase. Still, it was something to work at. If they could somehow loosen the hinges . . .

Mark ignored his pounding head and rising temperature to work away at the hinges while Charlie battered at the door with her fists. She punched it again and again. Harder and harder, screaming all the time at the top of her lungs, begging for help. She was making enough noise to wake the dead—but was anybody listening?

Already great swirls of dust were kicking up, enveloping them both, creeping into their ears, their eyes, their throats. Charlie's voice was cracking but she didn't give up. On and on they went, challenging each other not to give up, but after over an hour of fruitless exertion, they collapsed to the floor, exhausted.

Charlie refused to cry. They were stuck in the middle of the worst nightmare they could possibly imagine, but they had to keep their spirits up. That was crucial if they were to have any chance of surviving.

"Do you remember Andy Founding?" Charlie said as brightly as she could, her cracked voice belying her jaunty tone.

"Sure," Mark replied, confused.

"Apparently he's suing Hampshire police. Claiming he's been the victim of sexual harassment by female officers."

Mark snorted a brief laugh in response. Andy Fondling, as he was affectionately known, was a desk sergeant in Portsmouth whose wandering hands were legendary, especially where junior female officers were concerned. Charlie continued her anecdote, and though Mark craved sleep, craved some peace, he responded to Charlie's offering, knowing too that they must fend off despair.

As they swapped stories, neither of them mentioned the gun that lay on the floor between them.

98

I was sure they would wake up and stop me from having my fun, but it's amazing what seven pints of cider will do. My father had always been a heavy drinker—beer, cider, anything he could get his hands on, really—and Mum had followed suit. It made the beatings more bearable and stopped her thinking. If she'd been sober long enough, she'd have realized what a cesspit her life was and put her head in the oven. I wish she had in some ways.

I'd planned this moment so many different ways. In my dreams, I always used a knife. I loved the idea of severed arteries, of blood splattering the walls, but in reality I didn't have the nerve. I was worried I'd mess it up. Not strike hard enough, miss an artery. When I did it, I had to do it right or I would be dead and no *mistake. Bastard would take his time too—God knows what he'd do to me—so I had to get it right.*

I found some gaffer tape stockpiled in the caretaker's office and took three rolls. In the end I only used one but I was nervous and wanted to be sure I didn't run out. I did him first. I picked up his wrist and wrapped the tape gently round it. It almost felt affectionate, as if I was binding a wound. Round and round it went . . . Then I lifted his arm and placed it next to the iron bedhead, looping the tape round and round the metal post until his arm was securely tethered to it. I then did the same with his other arm.

My heart was beating fit to burst. My dad was already stirring, getting uncomfortable, so I had to work fast.

I did my mum's left arm quickly, but while I was doing her right arm, she woke up. Or at least I think she did. She opened her eyes and looked straight at me. I like to think she saw what was happening and gave in to it. Agreed with me. Whatever—she closed her eyes again quickly and I had no more trouble with her.

They were both now secure, so I ran to the kitchen. It didn't matter if I was noisy now. It was all about speed. I grabbed the cling film and jogged back into their bedroom. I'd seen this in a film and always wondered how it would be for real. I pulled off a large sheet of it, then double- and triple-strengthened it with some more. Then I climbed onto the bed, straddling my sleeping father's torso, and gently lifted his head. I slipped it over his face, then quickly passed it round the back, again and again, until his eyes, nose and mouth were completely encased in the springy, tense plastic.

And now he started to struggle like fuck. He opened his eyes and stared at me as if I was mad. He tried to shout, tried to wrench his hands free. I had to fight hard to stay on as his body cavorted, but I wasn't going to be denied my triumph. I pressed down harder. His eyes were bulging now, his face puce. Next to him my mother was slowly rousing, irritable and sleepy.

Now the fight was going out of him. I pressed down even harder. I was gripping the edges so hard my hands were aching. But I had to make sure it wasn't a trick. Had to finish the old man off.

Then suddenly he was still. My mother was awake now and was looking at me with a look of complete confusion. I smiled at her, then pressed the cling film over her face. Only one sheet this time. I wasn't expecting much of a fight there.

It was all over pretty soon. I got up and realized I was drenched with sweat. I started to shiver. I didn't feel happy, which was disappointing—I'd thought I would have. But it was done. That was all there was to it.

99

She was standing in the bedroom, looking at the devastation around her. The tatty posters and secondhand furniture that used to be here were long gone—now there was just the detritus of the vagrants and junkies who had passed through since the building was condemned.

There were so many memories in this room. Good, bad, horrific. Every time she pictured this room in her mind's eye, Helen remembered her fear, her confusion, her sense of helplessness as she lay stock-still, listening to her sister being raped on the bunk bed below. These thoughts swirled around Helen. She had been so powerless, so helpless for so long as a child that it felt profoundly weird to be standing here now as a grown-up woman—a grown-up woman with a gun in her hand. How she could have done with her older self *then*. Someone who could create order, ease suffering and administer justice. Maybe all this could have been avoided if someone—anyone—had listened to her cries for help.

The bunk bed had been rammed into the far corner. There was nothing there now, just a tattered Britney Spears poster, recently defiled with a felt-tip pen. Helen found herself marching across the room, tearing the dog-eared poster down. Running her hand over the rough plaster behind it, she found what she was looking for: *J.H.* Her initials. She'd carved them into the wall with a school compass all those years ago. It was a mark of the awful desperation of her childhood that she'd done so— hoping that they would survive there even if she didn't.

Dark thoughts crowded in on Helen and she hurried from the bedroom. She dived into the other bedroom, the fetid kitchen, the mildewed lounge. But it was already clear that there was nothing here for her. She had been so sure that a visit here would yield results, but she'd come up empty-handed.

This would be the last time she saw this place. She paused for a second to take it all in. Funny how they had never had any problem renting it out, even after what happened that night. When you're poor you can't afford to be squeamish or superstitious. There was a new family in within the week. And slowly over the years the fabric of this home had frayed and torn, until it was fit only for animals. A fitting end perhaps.

Helen hurried away from the block of flats, the guard grumpily trudging back to his cold cup of tea. She sat for a moment on her bike, pondering what to do next. Her instincts had always served her well, but they'd let her down here. Nothing for it but to pursue the other possibilities. Chase down every link.

She switched her phone on and was immediately alarmed by the number of missed calls. Alarm turned to horror when she picked up the first of many messages from DC Bridges.

Mark and Charlie had disappeared.

100

For a moment she was free. She was in a shopping mall running toward the escalator. Her mother stood at the top of it talking to a security guard, lecturing him on his responsibilities. She'd never been so pleased to see her mum and sprinted toward her. As she approached, the security guard turned to her, but oddly he was unable to speak—he just stared at her, moaning, moaning, moaning . . .

Charlie woke with a start, the grim reality crashing in on her. Mark was lying on the floor next to her, moaning, moaning, moaning . . . Charlie suppressed a flash of anger—it wasn't his fault. His head wound was a nasty one and they had been unable to treat it. Initially Charlie had used spit and a shirtsleeve to clean it, but she worried now she'd succeeded only in rubbing more dirt into it. Mark was in a bad way even before they'd been abducted—too much booze, too many sleepless nights—and the blood loss had weakened him still further. Now he had a nasty wound that was in the first stages of full-blown infection. Fever seemed to be taking hold. What would she do if he became seriously ill?

Pushing this thought away, Charlie checked her watch. How long had she been asleep? Not long enough. Time moves so slowly when you've given up hope. That first morning they had both been active, even hopeful, intent on fashioning a way out of this tomb. They'd resolved to sleep at night and work by day. The second morning, they'd used their belt buckles to try to make an impression on the heavy hinges of the door. But in the end the buckles snapped, and by the second afternoon of their captivity, listlessness and despair were already taking hold. It's hard to keep going when all your efforts are to no avail.

Never had Charlie felt so dirty, so disgusting, so utterly helpless. The small confines of their prison were already becoming repellent. They had made a pact to defecate and, in her case, vomit in the far corner of the room. Charlie had stuck religiously to this, hurrying over to empty her guts onto the reeking floor when her morning sickness struck. Mark, it seemed, was already too weak or too careless to honor their agreement. He had just soiled himself and the stench filled Charlie's nostrils.

Immediately, nausea gripped her and she hurried over to the dirty corner, heaving up a long string of acidic bile. Her stomach convulsed again, then again, before finally coming to rest. Suddenly her throat raged—an all-consuming punishing thirst. Charlie charged round the room looking for any source of moisture, all the while screwing up her eyes, trying to cry so she could lap up the salty tears. But nothing. She was already cried out. All was los—

Movement. Out of the corner of her eye, she saw movement. Terrified to look, scared of what she might find, she turned her head, inch by inch. And there it was. A big, fat rat.

It had appeared from nowhere. To Charlie, it was a miraculous vision of hope, an oasis in the desert. *Food.* Mentally she was already sinking her teeth into it, ripping the flesh from its bones, silencing the pangs of her groaning stomach. There might be enough for both of them, given its size.

Careful now. Not too fast. This could be the difference between life and death. Charlie slipped her jacket from her shoulders— not a brilliant net, but it would have to do.

One step forward. The rat looked up suddenly, peering into the gloom. Charlie froze. Then, after a quick sniff, the rat returned to his nibbling, greed winning out.

Another step forward. This time the rat didn't move.

Another step. Charlie was close now.

Another. Now she was virtually on top of it.

Charlie sprang forward, bringing the coat down on its head. The rat struggled furiously as Charlie rained down blows on the wriggling bulge. Finally it stopped moving. Had she done it? She gave it another whack to be sure, then loosened her grip a notch to check. The rat darted out of the coat in a desperate bid to escape. Charlie snatched at its tail, almost snagging it, but it slipped through her hands and away. Through a crack in the wall to safety.

Charlie hauled herself to her feet. It was so desperate it was almost funny. Her stomach ached for food; her throat was on fire. She had to have something. Some relief. Some sustenance.

She gave in and did what she had vowed she wouldn't stoop to. Dropping her knickers, she urinated into her cupped hand, then drank the warm liquid down in one go.

101

Was it her imagination or did they blame her? Charlie and Mark had been missing for over forty-eight hours and the team's anxiety was morphing into shock and distress. Now, as Helen marshaled the team's hunt for their missing colleagues, she began to see accusing stares everywhere, as if they had collectively decided that this was all her doing.

Phone triangulation last placed Mark and Charlie on Spire Street. This tallied with the anonymous tip-off about Tanner that had prompted them to head to that area. But after that the trail went cold. They had turned off their mobiles and radios and hadn't been in touch with any of their police colleagues. Initially the team had hoped that the spotting of Tanner was genuine and that somehow—somewhere—Charlie and Mark were still working the case. But slowly it had become obvious to all that the phone call was bogus. There had been no attempted mugging—Mark and Charlie had been deliberately guided to this location. It smacked of a trap. Everyone was thinking the same thing—had *she* got them?

Spreading out from Spire Street, they investigated every building, spoke to every shop owner and passerby, and on the second circuit of the former children's hospital a sharp-eyed constable had spotted a loose board on one of the windows. There was fresh mud on the sill as if someone had climbed through it recently. Helen wanted to get officers inside immediately, but her superiors had refused to let her do so without tactical support.

It had taken a frustratingly long time to mobilize an armed unit, but Helen had knocked heads together and was now speeding toward the old hospital with a SWAT team in tow. It was a big building with multiple exits and she didn't want to allow Suzanne to slip through their fingers—if she was there, of course.

They effected their entry as carefully and as quietly as they could. The SWAT team took point, with Helen, DC Bridges and a dozen PCs right behind them. It was a massive area to search, but, fanning out, they could cover it fairly quickly, keeping in constant touch via radio.

Helen's whole body was tense. She knew she had to try to control her nerves—excessive nerves led to bad decisions, especially when you've got a Glock in your hands. It was a blustery day and the wind that whistled through the broken windows made the whole place feel unearthly, even haunted. *Get a grip,* she told herself—she mustn't see shadows or phantoms where they didn't exist.

But it was hard to relax when there was so much at stake.

This *was* all her fault. Not just because she had inspired the killings, but because she had pleaded with Mark to return to the job. If she'd only left him alone, he would have been a sad but *safe* fuckup. He had returned to work without a hint of recrimination or anger. Because he believed in what he did and because—in spite of everything—he believed in her. And what a bitter harvest he had reaped for his dedication.

She crept upstairs, breaking with protocol by peeling off on her own. She peered in the first room. It was lonely and forgotten, a dark, dusty place. Helen released the safety catch on her weapon. Instinct told her that her sister would not be careless enough to walk into a SWAT unit. It was Helen she was after. She raised her gun as she darted her head into the next doorway, convinced she would soon be face-to-face with her nemesis.

A sudden squawk on the radio. DC Bridges. He sounded excited rather than alarmed. He had heard noises. Coming from downstairs. He was on his way there now to investigate. Helen immediately turned tail and sprinted down the stairs.

Running fast in the direction of the banging, DC Bridges was surprised to see Helen pull ahead of him. He had always prided himself on his speed, but his DI was a woman possessed. She was trying to keep it all in, but Bridges could see she was a coiled spring. Now, driven on by fear, apprehension and anger, she was making this story hers. She wanted to be the one to end the nightmare.

As they reached the bottom of the stairs, the corridors splintered off in four directions. The radio squawked again and Bridges turned it down, silenced by a venomous look from Helen. They strained their ears to hear.

Straight ahead. The noise was definitely coming from the corridor right in front of them. They sprinted forward. The first door was locked, but the sound was from farther up. They were on the move again. There was the sound, repetitive and insistent—*bang bang bang*. From the room next door. The door was locked. But they would get through. They had to get through.

As Helen screamed through the door hoping for a response, a PC hared off to get a crowbar. He was back in under a minute, bringing more officers with him. Putting his shoulder into it, he worked the lock on the heavy metal door. Back and forth, back and forth until eventually with a protesting crack the door gave way. Shoving him out of the way, Helen and Bridges tore inside.

To find an empty room.

A broken window, half off its hinges, beat an insistent rhythm on the metal window frame as it flapped angrily in the wind.

102

He wanted to die.

For Mark death would be a blessing now, a relief from the pain that racked his body. He had tried to fight the fever, to concentrate on the here and now, to try to work out how he and Charlie could effect some sort of escape, but that made his brain ache even worse than usual. So he'd succumbed to lethargy instead.

How long does it take to die of starvation? Too long. He had lost track of time but was certain they'd been in their prison for the best part of three days now. His stomach cramped constantly, his throat was swollen and raw, he barely had the energy to lift himself up. To pass the time he tried to conjure memories of his childhood, but thoughts of school bled into thoughts of *Paradise Lost*, the poem he'd studied—hated studying—in secondary school. He felt like a character in that nightmare vision now, endlessly tortured by the freezing cold at nights and the awful sweats that gripped him during the never-ending days. There was no release.

He knew his fever was getting worse. He had good moments and bad moments. Moments when he was lucid and could talk to Charlie, others when he knew he was babbling incoherently. Would he lose the plot completely at some point? He pushed that idea from his mind.

His hand reached round to the back of his head to explore his wound. The gash was wide and deep and his dirty fingers probed it now.

"Leave it, Mark." Charlie's voice penetrated the gloom. Even after three days of purgatory, she was still looking out for him. "You'll only make it worse."

But Mark ignored her, for something was moving against his finger. His wound was alive. He pulled his fingers out and brought them up to his nose. Maggots. His wound was infested with maggots.

He held his fingers up to his mouth and swept the little worms into his mouth with his tongue. It felt strange as they slipped down his throat. Strange but good. He plucked a few more from his wound and crammed them into his mouth.

Charlie was already wandering over. She lowered herself to the ground beside him. Mark paused, their friendship and common decency kicking in once more. With an effort he turned his head, offering himself to her. Hesitantly, she plucked two fingers worth of maggots out of his wound and dropped them into her mouth. She savored them, letting them dissolve on her tongue, then took a fingerful more.

Too soon it was over. The maggot meal was finished. Now their stomachs pulsed with hunger, the tiny morsels they'd consumed only reminding their innards how utterly empty they were. *More. More. More.* Their stomachs wanted more. *Needed* more.

But there was nothing more to give them.

103

They had pored over every inch of land within a two-mile radius of the old hospital, but there was still no sign of Mark or Charlie. What they had found was fresh blood, in a corridor on the fourth floor of the hospital. Tests had subsequently confirmed that it was Mark's. DC McAndrew was in tears and she wasn't the only member of the team who was visibly distraught. Helen hadn't realized until now how popular he was within the team. No wonder they hated her.

So Mark and Charlie had been tricked into the hospital, attacked and then taken elsewhere. There was no CCTV in the immediate vicinity of the hospital. CCTV on busy streets nearby had picked up numerous Transit vans in the area at about the right time, but which one was *their* one? Where had she taken them?

There were certainly plenty of disused buildings and warehouses in the area. Uniform were already working their way through them, aided by the dogs Helen had demanded. They were canvassing every potential witness and passerby and doing extensive house-to-house interviews. Anyone acting suspiciously would have their house searched from top to bottom—torn apart if need be.

Helen was gambling all on the idea that they would still be close by. Suzanne might have moved them elsewhere, but these were police officers who would be on their guard, a harder proposition than her other victims. She wouldn't want to mess things up—surely she would play it safe now. They needed eyes and ears—as many as possible—scouring Southampton, Portsmouth and beyond. Helen had already requested extra officers from neighboring forces, pulled in auxiliary Community Support officers and canceled leave for everyone at Southampton Central. But still it wasn't enough.

There was one more obvious play to make. Emilia Garanita had got wind of the aborted raid on the former children's hospital. Annoyed at not having been tipped off in time, she'd been plaguing Helen with calls, desperate to know what the raid was about and why there had been so much activity since. Were they searching for Suzanne? Or for more victims?

It was a risky move, but Helen had no choice. It was day four of their search and they still had nothing. So she picked up the phone and dialed Emilia's number.

104

Emilia Garanita loved her job. The hours were long, the pay was rubbish and many in authority were openly rude to reporters from the local rag, but none of that mattered to Emilia. She was addicted to the adrenaline, the unpredictability and the excitement that her job provided on a daily basis.

Then there was the power. As dismissive as politicians, coppers and councilors were, they were all terrified of reporters. They were so reliant on the goodwill of the public for career advancement—and it was reporters like Emilia who told the public what to think. Emilia felt that power now as she sat opposite Helen Grace. Emilia had chosen the venue—not Grace—and it was she who was setting the agenda now. Grace needed her help, so there would be no more lies or obfuscations.

"Two of our officers are missing," Grace began briskly. "Charlie Brooks and Mark Fuller—you know them, I think. They may have been abducted and we need your help—your readers' help—in our search for them."

As Grace continued, Emilia felt that familiar tingling. This was the other great thing about being a reporter: at any given time a juicy story, a real whopper, could fall into your lap. These were the days that you grafted for. All those lost hours spent covering cases at the magistrates' courts—the vandalism, the fights, the burglaries—were the price you had to pay to earn yourself a *real* story. And when one did come along, you'd better be ready.

Emilia couldn't write quick enough, even though she was using shorthand. The developments in this story were astonishing; she could already see the spread in her head. And to think she was ahead of the nationals on something like this!

Emilia promised to do all she could, and Grace departed. The DI said she was pleased with the outcome of their "chat," but she looked rather green around the gills, Emilia thought. Not a woman who was comfortable asking for help or playing second fiddle to another girl. So much for the sorority.

Emilia sped back to the office. The nervous excitement she'd felt earlier had dissipated now and she felt oddly calm. She knew exactly what she would do.

Throughout her working life, she had used journalism as a weapon—to expose, harm or destroy those who had it coming.

This time would be no different.

105

It was six thirty a.m. and the sun refused to rise. A thick, dank fog hugged Southampton—the perfect embodiment of Helen's mood. She slammed the front door shut behind her, mounted her bike and raced off toward the city center, gunning the throttle unnecessarily hard.

Another thirty-six hours had passed and still no news. No, that wasn't true—there'd been plenty of "news," but none that had been helpful. Ever since she'd left Emilia, Helen had been kicking herself, fearing she'd made a bad mistake. She hadn't really had much choice—the press *had* to be informed—but still, she had only made things worse. She had met Emilia late at night, so the following morning's story was sensational but light on the details. Today's offering from the *Evening News* promised to be a rather different affair.

A copy of the paper was lying on Helen's desk when she arrived. A member of the team being helpful or someone making a point? Helen skipped the lurid headline and went straight to the details on the inner pages. It was awful. Torture porn in all but name. In exhaustive and prurient detail, they took their readers through the various stages of starvation and dehydration, speculating on which officer would hold out longer and what were the possible causes of death. For the cloth-headed reader, they even had a helpful graphic—a schedule of physical and mental decline—outlining how Charlie and Mark would feel on Day One. And Day Two. Three. Four. Five. A big question hung over the days beyond, but it meant only one thing.

Buried in among all the prurience was a police hotline, the alleged point of the exhaustive coverage. Predictably, it had been ringing off the hook. The sense of excitement generated by this extraordinary story ensured that. The majority of the calls were desperate, attention-seeking stuff—it made Helen seethe with anger.

When she sat down with Charlie's boyfriend and Mark's parents, Helen had little solace to offer. The sensational reports in the *Evening News* had made them frantic with worry and they vented their anger on Helen. She'd had to be frank with them about their loved ones' chances of survival while promising to do everything possible to bring them home. They were shell-shocked and could barely take it in, as if this were some grim nightmare from which they'd soon wake.

Helen was desperate to give them something, some good

news to end their misery, but there was no point lying. She knew Mark and Charlie would be strong, but no one had seen hide or hair of them for almost a week now. Who knew what state they were in? How long could a human being hold out after all?

The clock was ticking now and every minute counted.

106

Charlie tried to get up. But as she pulled herself upright, her head swam. She felt light-headed, drunk, and collapsed back down onto her bum. Turning her head away, she retched once more. But there was nothing to bring up—hadn't been for a couple of days now.

She was starving. It was a phrase she had used so many times casually—now she was learning its full awful meaning. Repeated bouts of diarrhea, spasming joints, red blotches all over her torso and maddening cracked skin around her mouth, elbows and knees. It was as if she were molting—disintegrating. In time she would be little more than a skeleton. The maggots were long gone. Mark would probably be dead before they returned.

Across the room, Mark started mumbling "I had a little nut tree" by way of accompaniment. He had been mangling nursery rhymes for a few days now—perhaps his mother had sung them to him, or perhaps he sang them to his daughter.

The words were all wrong, though, the tunes all mixed up. He was just making noises, really, proving to himself that he was still alive.

Charlie scanned their prison for the umpteenth time. And the same four walls stared back at her. The smell was six days of excreta, sweat and vomit combining into a hideous cocktail. And they were getting awfully cold. Charlie had tried to wrap Mark, whose teeth chattered with fever, in boiler insulation, but it scratched and annoyed him and fell off anyway.

Charlie had considered eating it, but she knew it wouldn't stay down and she couldn't face any more unnecessary vomiting. So she just sat and thought dark thoughts.

She rested her head against the hard, cold wall. For a moment, the coolness of the stone soothed her. This, then, would be her tomb. She would never see Steve again. She would never see her parents. Worst of all, she would never see her baby.

There would be no salvation now. She was no longer expecting the rescue party. All they could do now was wait for death.

Unless. Charlie kept her head pressed tight to the wall, her eyes screwed shut. She knew the gun was close by but she refused to look at it. It would be so simple just to walk over and pick it up. Mark couldn't stop her—it would all be over quickly.

She bit her lip hard. Anything to distract her from that thought. She wouldn't do it. She couldn't do it.

But suddenly it was all she could think about.

107

It was an annihilation. Other police officers might have shrunk from the task, sending some scapegoat to field the shitstorm. But Helen knew this situation was of her making, so she had no choice but to be the sacrificial lamb.

Flanked by two huge close-ups of Mark and Charlie, Helen briefed the national press, urging anyone who had suspicions to get in touch. Emilia's spread in the *Evening News* had started a stampede. Every major tabloid and broadsheet from the UK was represented in the packed briefing room, as well as journalists from Europe, the U.S. and beyond.

There was no hiding anymore. They were hunting a serial killer. This was the public admission that Emilia Garanita had been waiting for and she piled on the agony now, calling for

Helen to resign. She demanded an official inquiry into Helen's leadership during this case. The *Evening News* was running another big spread, cataloging the lies, half-truths, evasions and incompetence that had in their view characterized the investigation so far. Helen let the assault ride over her—as long as she got the message out there, the professional cost was of little importance.

She had intended to stay at the coalface all night, to work off her anger and frustration, but her concerned team finally prevailed on her to go home—for an hour or two at least. They had all worked themselves to the bone, but she was running on empty.

Helen biked home, keeping her speed steady—she was still shaky and emotional. Once home, she showered and changed. It was good to feel clean and immediately she felt a surge of energy and, even more ridiculously, hope.

For a brief exhilarating moment, she felt sure she would find them alive and well.

But as she stared out the window at the gloomy nightscape, this brief spasm of optimism started to evaporate. They had looked *everywhere* and they had come up empty-handed. While Hampshire police tore Southampton apart in their hunt for the missing officers, Helen had contacted her colleagues at the Met. Perhaps there was something personal in her sister's choice of location? Perhaps she'd chosen somewhere "fun" to have the last laugh? There were the derelict warehouses where they used to go to smash the windows, the cemetery where they used to get drunk, the schools that they truanted from, the underpasses where they watched the boys skateboarding. She had asked for them all to be investigated.

108

The baby wouldn't stop shouting.

Charlie kept picturing it inside her. Somehow she knew it was a girl. And when she pictured her baby, it was already human with a personality and needs, rather than just a bunch of cells. She pictured her baby screaming for food, confused and distressed about why she wasn't getting anything from her mother. This wasn't how it was supposed to be. Was her tiny stomach cramping with hunger as Charlie's was? She might not even have a stomach yet, Charlie thought, but it was an image she couldn't get out of her head. *I am starving my baby. I am starving my baby.*

Mark and Charlie had put themselves in this situation. They were to blame for it. But her baby was innocent. Pure and innocent. Why should her baby pay the price? Her anger at their stupidity fired her spirit. Her will at least wasn't diminished, unlike her emaciated, useless body.

She tried to swallow her fury. She tried to sleep. But the night was long. And cold. And quiet. Charlie tried to sleep but her baby wouldn't stop shouting.

Shouting at her to pick up the gun.

109

The team had been briefed and dispatched. While Bridges, Sanderson and the rest of the team had fanned out across the county and beyond, Helen remained behind in the incident room. Someone had to coordinate the massive search, and, besides, Helen had the nasty feeling she was missing something and wanted to review the evidence again.

She had chased up every tiny lead. Every council in southern England had been contacted and the clerical staff were now poring over the list of brownfield sites that were awaiting renovation or demolition. The port authorities had been contacted—a list of warehouses and craft that were out of action was being compiled. Rental properties were being chased down, but they could process only the most recent rentals and who was to say Suzanne hadn't rented a place weeks ago?

The search was massive and all-encompassing, but nevertheless Helen was gripped by a sense of the futility of it all. If the location where they were being held had been chosen randomly, then what were the odds of finding it? Driven by fear of failure and a sense that the answer was under her nose, Helen went back over the key sites of the childhood she'd shared with her sister. She'd always looked up to Marianne, who was the stronger of the two, and who had followed her around like a shadow. If you could find Marianne, you would find Jodie—that's what they used to say. Changing her name, changing her life, Helen had tried to step out of that shadow, but it fell on her now once more, bringing darkness and despair with it.

It was while reading her file on Arrow Security that Helen had felt that first shiver of excitement and exhilaration that heralds a new lead. In this age of gender equality, the presence of a female security guard on their lists shouldn't have stood out. But how many female security guards did you really see? More important, this female guard had joined Arrow only two months ago. She had been assigned to help keep an eye on the properties around Croydon and Bromley, as that's where she lived. But her references looked shaky—forged—and a quick check by the clerical staff had shown her home address to be fake.

Helen faxed Marianne's original mug shot and the computer-generated image of an "older" Marianne over to Arrow and the alarmed company had responded promptly. The woman in the images could be their new employee, who went by the name of Grace Shields.

Grace. There could be no doubt about it. But was it a "Fuck you" or "Come hither"? Helen opted for the latter and was now once more speeding toward Chatham Tower. She couldn't be sure if—or when—her sister had meant her to find the link, but her mind was made up. Either Marianne was somewhere in Chatham Tower or Mark and Charlie were, and she was going to find them.

Helen felt a surge of hope inside as she sped north. The endgame had begun.

110

It was raining when they took me away.

I hadn't noticed it when they'd dragged me out to the cop car, but as I sat in the back like a common criminal I noticed the pulsing blue lights reflecting in the puddles on the street.

I felt numb. The psychologists would say it was shock after the killings, but I never believed that. It was shock all right, but not about that. They'd tried to get me to talk to them, but I wouldn't—couldn't—give them a word. I was already shutting down. It was the beginning of the end for me.

I looked up and saw her staring at me from the doorway. She was wrapped in a blanket and there was a social worker fussing around her, but she just stared straight ahead, as if she couldn't believe what was happening. But it was happening and she had made it happen. It was she who tore the family apart, not me.

I got all the bad press, got a stretch, was spat at and vilified. But she committed the real crime and she knew it.

I could see it in her eyes as they drove me away. She was a Judas— no, she was worse than Judas. He only betrayed his friend. She betrayed her sister.

111

Do it quickly now. Get it over with.

Mark urged himself to move, to summon his last reserves of strength and do the deed. But his fever raged, his body ached and he found it hard to move his legs. But needs must—he willed himself into action.

Charlie lay across the room. She was crying and shouting now. Was she losing her mind? Normally so calm, so warm, now she was full of fury and violence, a hissing harpy on the road to madness. Who knew what was going through her mind?

The gun was equidistant between them. Mark couldn't keep his eyes off it. Now that they had exhausted all attempts to escape, the gun was the only solution for them.

He pulled himself up onto his elbows. Immediately they

collapsed beneath him and he fell to the floor, his chin connecting sharply with the cold stone. Furious, he tried again, straining every muscle to raise his skeletal frame from the ground. This time he managed it, pressing home the advantage by bringing his knees up and tucking them underneath his chest. Sharp pains arrowed around his chest, his legs, his arms—his body was rebelling against him, but he wouldn't let it win.

He stole another glance at the gun. *Easy does it now—no sudden movements.* He moved slowly up onto his bum so he was sitting up again. Suddenly being upright made his head pound and unbidden a memory shot forth—of Elsie laying a cold flannel on his head to soothe away a New Year hangover. *My little angel.*

The gun was five feet away. How quickly could he cover the ground? Once he had committed to doing it there must be no turning back. A moment's delay and his resolve would fail him. A moment's indecision and his body might fail him. He had made his decision now and mustn't let any last-minute doubts stop him.

He scrambled across the floor on his hands and knees. The pain was excruciating but he managed to keep moving forward. Charlie heard him and turned quickly, but it was too late. Mark had got there.

He snatched up the gun and cocked it. It was time to kill.

112

It was raining hard now—a storm had broken and the falling water lashed Helen as she raced toward the tower, the skies filled with the same fury that drove Helen onward.

The water running off her visor blurred the view, so when Helen first saw her, she appeared ghostly, like a vision of some kind. At first she thought it was the Arrow rep coming to meet her—but then she realized it was a woman. Immediately she tensed, slowing the bike and reaching for her gun.

Then suddenly she couldn't breathe. She clamped her eyes shut, then opened them again, willing herself to be wrong. But she wasn't wrong. She skidded to a halt, jumped off and ran over to the drenched and seminaked figure.

Charlie lurched past as if she didn't recognize her. Helen

grabbed hold of her arm, hauling her back toward her. Charlie turned and with savage anger in her eyes tried to bite Helen on the face. Helen pushed her off, slapping her hard. The blow seemed to stun Charlie, who now sank to her knees. Bedraggled and unclothed, she was a nightmare version of the perky officer Helen had once known.

"Where?" Helen's question was blunt and uncaring.

Charlie couldn't look at her.

"He did it. It wasn't me. He did it to save me—"

"Where?" Helen roared.

Tears were now pouring down Charlie's face. She lifted her right arm and pointed to Chatham Tower.

"The basement," she said, her voice cracked and feeble.

Helen left her where she knelt and sprinted toward the tower. She released the safety catch on her gun as she burst through the unlocked site entrance. There was no place for strategy or caution here. She had to find Mark.

She pushed the possibility that he was already dead to the back of her mind—surely there was time to save him? There had to be. In an instant, Helen realized that she *had* had feelings for Mark. Not love yet, but something warm and good that could have grown. Maybe they'd been brought together for a reason. Maybe they were supposed to save each other and repair the damage of their pasts.

Inside, she scanned wildly about her. Then she was sprinting across the atrium, kicking open the door next to the lifts. Down, down, down she went, taking the stairs three at a time.

Now she was in the basement. She kicked open the first door to find . . . an empty cupboard. No, that wouldn't be right, the door wasn't strong enough to hold anyone inside, she would have needed . . . Then Helen saw it: the reinforced metal door swinging on its hinges. Helen raced down the corridor and hared inside.

As she entered, her knees gave way and she collapsed to the ground. She had seen Mark. And she had seen the worst. Slowly she raised her head, but it was no better on second sight. Mark lay in a pool of his own blood. Mark was dead, the gun that killed him still clutched in his hand. Helen scrambled across the filthy floor to him, cradling his head in her arms. But he was cold and still.

A loud bang and Helen looked up. Who had she been expecting? Charlie? Bridges? It was Marianne, as she knew it must be.

"Hello, Jodie."

She smiled as she locked the door behind her.

"Long time no see."

113

There was no victory. No happiness. There wasn't even a sense of relief. Charlie had survived. She would live. Her baby would live. But the old Charlie was dead and buried. There was no coming back from this.

She lay on the pavement, the rain pouring down on her. Her brain was reeling. Shock mingled with loathing. Slowly exhaustion took hold. She closed her eyes and opened her mouth. The rain tumbled into her parched, bleeding mouth. A momentary sense of relief, of life flooding through her and then oblivion. Her eyes closed, her brain drifting, she felt herself being sucked underwater, pulled into a darkness that was comforting as well as debilitating.

Then a voice. A weird, distant, mechanical voice. Charlie

tried to pull herself out of the abyss, but exhaustion gripped her. There it was again. The voice, urgent and insistent. She managed to open one eye. But there was no one there.

"Where are you? Please respond." The desperate voice was becoming clear now.

Charlie opened the other eye, managing to lift her head off the ground.

Helen's police radio, lying on the floor by her discarded bike. And the voice . . . the voice was DC Bridges. Searching for her.

Perhaps it wasn't all over. Perhaps Charlie did have a shot at redemption after all. She knew she had to try. She hauled herself up, then collapsed to her knees. Her body was shaking, her teeth chattering. She was seeing double. But she had to make it to that radio somehow.

114

"How could you?"

Marianne laughed. There was a beautiful irony to Jodie's question. It was exactly what Marianne had said to *her* all those years ago. A broad grin spread across Marianne's face—could *she* have even predicted it would all work out so perfectly?

"It was simpler than you might think. The men were easy—you know what they're like with a pretty face. And the girls—well, they were very . . . trusting. I'd like to say it was hard work, but as you can see I got others to do the heavy lifting."

She shot a glance toward Mark's body.

"Did you see Charlie, by the way?" she continued. "How is she doing? She ran straight past me when I opened the door, so I didn't really get a proper look at her."

"You've destroyed her . . ."

"Oh, don't be so melodramatic. She'll be fine. She'll get better, be with her boyfriend, have her baby. Whether she'll be able to look the kid in the eye's a different matter, but she won. She survived. I thought she was going to do it, but Mark took it out of her hands."

"Why didn't you just come for me?" Helen demanded.

"Because I wanted you to suffer."

There it was. Bald and unadulterated.

"I did the right thing. I'd do it again." Helen's voice was getting louder as her fury took hold. And for the first time, there was a flash of something—anger?—in Marianne's eyes.

"You never really cared how much I suffered, did you?" she spat back.

"That's not true."

"It wasn't that you wanted me to suffer. It's just that you didn't care if I did, which is worse."

"No, that was never what I felt or wan—"

"I was inside for *twenty-five years*. They tried to break me in juvie and then tried all over again in Holloway. I wrote to you, so don't pretend you don't know what I'm talking about. The bottlings, the abuse, the beatings. I told you all about it *and* how they paid for it. I ripped one girl's eyeball right out of her fucking head in Holloway—do you remember? 'Course you do. But still you didn't write, you didn't visit. You didn't help me *at all*, because you wanted me to rot. To shrivel up and die. Your own sister."

"You stopped being my sister a long time ago."

"Because of what I did to them? At least I had some fucking balls, you ungrateful little bitch." Venom was seeping through now. "I *saved* you. You were next in line. They would have *destroyed* a little girl like you."

The truth of Marianne's accusation scythed into Helen's conscience.

"I know that. I know you felt you were helping me—"

"We *could* have been happy together, you and me. We could have gone somewhere, lived off the street, got something going. They would never have found us. If we'd've stuck together, we'd still be fine now."

"Do you really believe that, Marianne? Because if you do, you're more far gone than I thought—"

Suddenly Marianne was marching across the room toward Helen, fire in her eyes. Helen immediately raised her Glock and Marianne paused, checking her march. There were only three feet between the pair now.

Helen took in her sister's face. So familiar in its shape and lines, but so alien in its expression. As if a monster had climbed inside her and was eating its way out.

"Don't you dare look down on me," Marianne hissed. "Don't you dare . . . judge me. It's you who's on trial here, not me."

"Because I did the right thing? The *decent* thing? You murdered our parents, Marianne. You murdered them in cold blood."

"And did you miss them? Afterward? Did you miss those rapists?"

For a moment, Helen was at a loss for words. She had never asked herself that question. She had been so caught up with Marianne in the aftermath, so involved in her own bewildering journey through foster homes and Social Services that she'd never really had space to grieve.

"Well, did you?" Marianne demanded. A long silence, and then:

"No."

Marianne broke into a smile. A smile of victory.

"There you are, then. They were nobodies, worse than nobodies. And they deserved a worse fate than they got. I was kind to them. Or have you forgotten what they did?"

She tugged off the blond wig she was wearing to reveal her scalp. The hair had never grown back on the spot where her father had held her head to the space heater, leaving a strange and disfiguring bald patch on her crown.

"These are just the scars you can see. He would have killed us in the end. So I did what had to be done. You should be bloody grateful."

Helen watched her sister—the same defiance, the same anger that she'd displayed during her trial was still there all these years later. There was truth in what she said, but it still sounded like the ravings of a madwoman. Helen suddenly felt a strong desire to be out of this awful room and away from this burning hatred.

"How does this end, Marianne?"

Marianne smiled, as if she'd been waiting for this, and then: "It ends as it started. With a choice."

And now it all started to make sense.

"You made a choice all those years ago," Marianne continued. "You chose to betray your sister. Your sister who'd helped you. Who'd killed for you. You chose to save yourself and throw me to the wolves."

"And all your victims faced a choice," Helen countered, as the horror of Marianne's scheme became perfectly clear.

"You think people are good, Jodie. You're one of life's optimists. But they're *not*. They are mean and selfish and cruel. You proved that. And so did every one of the selfish little shits I abducted. In the end, we are all just animals scratching each other's eyes out to survive."

Marianne took a step closer—instinctively Helen gripped the trigger of her gun. Marianne paused and smiled, then raised a Smith & Wesson to Helen's eye level.

"And now you have another choice to make, Helen. Will you kill or be killed?"

So that was it. Helen and Marianne were to be the last players in her deadly game.

115

DC Bridges left Charlie where she lay and sprinted toward the building. SWAT was on its way in full flak gear and the paramedics were racing to the scene, but he didn't have time to wait. Helen was in there with the killer—Suzanne, Marianne, whatever the hell she was called—and he didn't fancy her chances of survival. This was a scheme that was always designed to end in bloodshed.

He burst through the lobby. The lifts were dead, but the door to the basement was ajar, so he ran toward it. Down the stairs and along the corridor. He wasn't armed but what the hell? Every second was crucial now.

And there it was. The locked metal door. He hammered at it and Helen's voice rang out clear, telling him to back off.

Bugger that, he thought, scanning around desperately for a tool of some kind.

The corridor was empty, but the last door at the end was a store cupboard, still littered with half-used bottles of bleach and disinfectant. Lying discarded on the floor was a fire extinguisher. One of the old-fashioned seventies ones, heavy and thick. Bridges hauled it off the floor.

Sprinting down the corridor, he was back in front of the metal door in seconds. He paused, gritted his teeth, then launched the fire extinguisher at the lock.

116

The door shuddered with the impact, a roaring metallic scream echoing down the corridor, but Marianne didn't blink. Her eyes were trained on her sister, her finger caressing the trigger of her gun.

Crash. Another heavy blow to the lock. Whoever was outside was obviously determined. The door moaned under the sustained assault.

"It's decision time, Jodie." Marianne smiled as she spoke. "I will fire the second that door opens."

"Don't do this, Marianne. It doesn't have to be this way."

"It's too late to call off the dogs. He's coming through. So make your choice."

The door was starting to buckle. Bridges was making progress.

"I don't want to kill you, Marianne."

"Then the choice is made. Pity, really—I thought you'd jump at the chance."

The door creaked ominously—there were only seconds left now.

"I want to help you. Put the gun down."

"You had your chance, Jodie. And you washed your hands of me. You saved all those people. All those *strangers*—but you washed your hands of *me*."

"And don't you think I felt guilty for that? Look what you've done to me. What you still do to me."

Helen had ripped off her shirt to reveal the scars on her back. For a moment, Marianne paused, shocked by what she saw.

"I eat myself up with guilt every minute of every day. Of *course* I do. But I was thirteen years old. You'd killed two people. Killed my mum and dad in their bed, for God's sake. You murdered our parents! What was I supposed to do?"

"You were supposed to protect me. You were supposed to be pleased."

"I never *asked* you to kill them. I never *wanted* you to kill them. I never wanted any of this. Can't you see that? You did this all to yourself."

"You really believe that? Do you *honestly* believe that?"

"Yes, I do."

"Then there's nothing more to say. Good-bye, Jodie."

Just then Bridges burst through the door and a single shot rang out.

117

Through the driving rain, Charlie glimpsed two figures. A man leading a woman away from the tower. Charlie had never been a religious woman, but she'd been praying for the last ten minutes, hoping against hope for a miracle. And now she would have her answer.

Pushing the attending paramedic aside, she rushed forward. She made it only ten yards before her legs gave way. She fell to her knees on the sodden ground. Shielding her eyes from the rain, she strained to see through the gloom—was Bridges helping the woman or restraining her?

Then suddenly the sun broke through and for a moment the gloom lifted.

It was Helen. She had survived. Already the paramedics were

rushing to her, her colleagues surrounding her. But she pushed them away. Charlie called out to her, but Helen walked past without hearing.

Shrugging off Bridges, Detective Inspector Helen Grace walked alone through the rain. It was over. She was alive. But she hadn't won. Her ordeal was only just beginning. For as Marianne knew only too well, there is no peace for those who shed the blood of those closest to them. It was Helen's turn to live with that stain now.

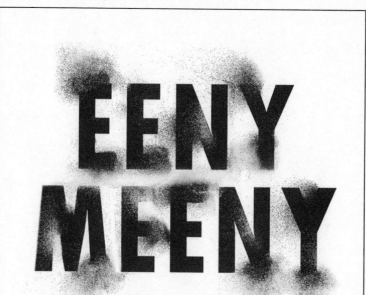

M. J. ARLIDGE

A CONVERSATION WITH M. J. ARLIDGE, AUTHOR OF *EENY MEENY*

Q. After years focused on your career in television, why did you decide to write your first novel?

A. I have always been a huge fan of crime fiction, especially works by the great U.S. thriller writers Thomas Harris, Patricia Highsmith, James Patterson, and others. I felt I might have a novel in me, but like most aspiring writers didn't want to share that conviction with anyone else, in case it turned out I didn't! Screenwriting is extremely collaborative; novel writing much less so, so I was drawn to the latter as it meant I could write my first novel in secret.

Q. What aspect of Eeny Meeny *came to you first—the compelling premise, the fascinating protagonist, or something else?*

A. The concept. We live in a competition culture. Hit shows like *Big Brother*, *Survivor*, and *The X Factor* have helped create a society in which we are constantly judging other people. Who's hottest? Who's most talented? Who do we *like* more? Who do we want to evict from the house? I thought it would be interesting if a serial killer posed these questions, raising the stakes so it became a matter of life and death.

Q. What are the main differences between writing for the screen and the page? The similarities?

A. The similarities are obvious. You have to have great characters, a great concept, and a punchy hook. The differences are largely to do with the process of writing—you have much more creative control writing a novel, whereas a TV show has to take account of the opinion and talents of your cast, your director, your producers—and the experience of reading. Despite the growing popularity of tablets and smartphones, screen viewing (be it movies or TV) is still often a group activity, shared with your partner, your family or friends. Reading is a solo experience where the author talks directly to you. That is its enduring power and strength.

Q. Detective Inspector Helen Grace is an intelligent, engaging, and complicated character with an intensity that leaps off the page. Who is she and what makes her tick?

A. Because of her background, Helen always fights for the underdog. She is passionate about gaining justice for the weak, dispossessed, or vulnerable. Also, because of past sins, she feels a huge need to atone, to work harder, longer, and better than anyone else.

Q. *Explain the different ways Helen Grace leads her personal and professional lives.*

A. These two worlds seldom combine. She is a strong, visible leader, driving her team forward, inspiring them to be the best they can be. But her private life is kept just that—private. She is obsessively secretive and seldom lets anyone get close to her.

Q. *What sort of research did you do to write* Eeny Meeny? *Did you explore abandoned diving pools, grain bins, or any of the other eerie locations included in the book?*

A. Good question. I always like to research and spent many happy hours in Southampton plotting dark deeds. But in the end it is the flight of your imagination that creates the most memorable and surprising things, so having done my research I just closed my eyes and let my mind wander. . . .

Q. *People seem to be fascinated by serial killers and serial killer stories—why do you think that is?*

A. We are fascinated by the question of why people commit acts that they know to be harmful or immoral. Serial killers are the ultimate—and scariest—example of this human desire to transgress, hence our enduring fascination with them.

Q. Close relationships—mother and daughter, boyfriend and girl-friend, coworkers—play an important part in the plot of Eeny Meeny. *What made you choose the relationships of the victims and how do their connections shape the narrative?*

A. I wanted to choose pairings where the strength of the relationship differed. Of course you wouldn't kill your own child to escape death and you hope you wouldn't kill your lover or partner. But what about a work colleague? How would you feel then? I wanted to steadily push the reader into asking themselves questions that were not easy to answer.

Q. Eeny Meeny *raises an interesting moral question for many readers. Kill or be killed—how would you choose?*

A. Depends who was standing in front of me! We all like to think we'd do the right thing, but I suspect there is something innate in all of us which would want to survive, no matter what the cost.

Q. What can we expect next from you and Helen Grace?

A. There is plenty more to come from Helen Grace, as she continues to battle evil in all its forms. I'm completely in love with Helen and hope to write about her for many years to come. She seems to inspire ideas in me, so much so that when I first sat down to discuss *Eeny Meeny* with possible publishers, I verbally pitched them the first seven novels in the Helen Grace series!

DISCUSSION QUESTIONS

1. This novel asks some very difficult questions about moral choices. The lines between right and wrong, guilt and innocence, are constantly blurred. Discuss the choices that the various characters make. Do you think that their decisions are justifiable? If you were put in the same situation, what would you do? What might you have done differently?

2. Discuss the character of Helen Grace. Some think she's damaged; others think she's the perfect, dedicated cop. How do you see her? How do you think she sees herself? Did your opinions about her change as the events of the novel unfolded?

3. The topic of female cops comes up quite a few times. What do you think the story is saying about the ways marriage and motherhood can define women's professional lives, or what people expect from women, as wives, mothers, or unmarried women? How are the lives and actions of the various female characters influenced or restricted by their role in society as

women? Compare and contrast Charlie's and Helen's experiences, for example.

4. Several times throughout the novel, Helen is forced to contend with the dogged reporter Emilia Garanita. What role is she meant to serve? How does her presence affect Helen's investigation? Do you think that Emilia's investigative methods are ethical? Do you think the media help or hinder the police in solving crimes?

5. Discuss Helen's complicated relationship with Mark. Do you think she really cares for him? Why do you think she was so quick to believe that he'd betrayed the team? If she had chosen to believe him, how might the investigation have turned out?

6. Discuss Helen's past. How has what she has been through affected her character? Do you think she could have become the brilliant detective she is without those experiences? Do you think they provide her with some kind of edge or insight the other detectives don't have?

7. How does the book deal with the divide between perception and reality, or the difference between public image and private lives? Which characters are most skillful at navigating this divide, and how?

8. The novel includes the following observation: "We always question ourselves more than we question others." Do you think this sentiment is true? Are we always our harshest critics?

9. Discuss why Helen chose the name "Grace" for her new persona. What do you think she's trying to remind herself of? Or is she trying to convince herself of something?

10. Were you surprised by the twist in the story regarding the villain? Why or why not? Do you think Helen should have caught on sooner? Do you think she was in denial?

11. Do you think the villain was ultimately successful in what she had set out to do? How do you think this experience will affect Helen in the future? Do you think she will be able to move on from it?

12. Discuss the story's ending. Why do you think Helen made the decision she did? Do you agree with her choice? Was it a satisfying conclusion to the story?

DI Helen Grace's next case begins now.
Turn the page for a sneak peek.

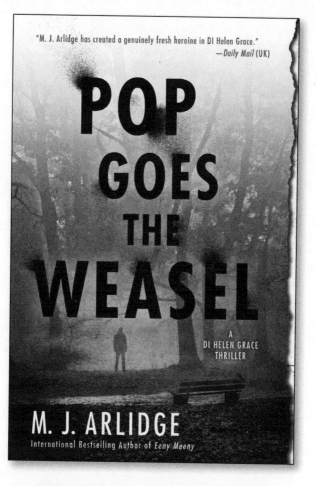

"M. J. Arlidge has created a genuinely fresh heroine in DI Helen Grace."
—*Daily Mail* (UK)

POP GOES THE WEASEL

A DI HELEN GRACE THRILLER

M. J. ARLIDGE

International Bestselling Author of *Eeny Meeny*

AVAILABLE OCTOBER 6, 2015

1

The fog crept in from the sea, suffocating the city. It descended like an invading army, consuming landmarks, choking out the moonlight, rendering Southampton a strange and unnerving place.

Empress Road Industrial Park was quiet as the grave. The body shops had shut for the day, the mechanics and supermarket workers had departed and the streetwalkers were now making their presence felt. Dressed in short skirts and bra tops, they pulled hard on their cigarettes, gleaning what little warmth they could to ward off the bone-chilling cold. Pacing up and down, they worked hard to sell their sex, but in the gloom they appeared more like skeletal wraiths than objects of desire.

The man drove slowly, his eyes raking the line of half-naked junkies. He sized them up—a sharp snap of recognition occasionally punching through—then dismissed them. They weren't what he was looking for. Tonight he was looking for something special.

Hope jostled with fear and frustration. He had thought of nothing else for days. He was so close now, but what if it was all a lie? An urban myth? He slammed the steering wheel hard. She *had* to be here.

Nothing. Nothing. Noth—

There she was. Standing alone, leaning against the graffiti-embossed wall. The man felt a sudden surge of excitement. There *was* something different about this one. She wasn't checking her nails or smoking or gossiping. She was simply waiting. Waiting for something to happen.

He pulled his car off the road, parking up out of sight by a chain-link fence. He had to be careful, mustn't leave anything to chance. He scanned the streetscape for signs of life, but the fog had cut them off completely. It was as if they were the only two people left in the world.

He marched across the road toward her, then checked himself, slowing his pace. He mustn't rush this—this was something to be savored and enjoyed. The anticipation was sometimes more enjoyable than the act—experience had taught him that. He must linger over this one. In the days ahead, he would want to replay these memories as accurately as he could.

She was framed by a row of abandoned houses. Nobody wanted to live round here anymore and these homes were now hollow and dirty. They were crack dens and flophouses, strewn with dirty needles and dirtier mattresses. As he crossed the street toward her, the girl looked up, peering through her thick fringe. Hauling herself off the wall, she said nothing, simply nodding toward the nearest shell of a house before stepping inside. There was no negotiation, no preamble. It was as if she was resigned to her fate. As if she *knew*.

Hurrying to catch up with her, the man drank in her backside, her legs, her heels, his arousal increasing all the time. Already he could hear her screams in his head, her cracked voice begging for mercy. As she disappeared into the darkness, he picked up the pace. He couldn't wait any longer.

The floorboards creaked noisily as he stepped inside. The derelict house was just how he had pictured it in his fantasies. An overpowering smell of damp filled his nostrils—everything was rotten here. He hurried into the sitting room, now a repository for abandoned G-strings and condoms. No sign of her. So they were going to play "Chase me," were they?

Into the kitchen. No sign. Turning on his heel, he stalked out and climbed the stairs to the second floor. With each step, his eyes scanned this way and that, searching for his prey.

He marched into the front bedroom. A mildewed bed, a broken window, a dead pigeon. But no sign of the girl.

Fury now wrestled with his desire. Who was she to mess him around like this? She was a common whore. Dog shit on his shoe. He was going to make her suffer for treating him like this.

He pushed the bathroom door open—nothing—then turned and marched into the second bedroom. He would smash her stupid fac—

Suddenly his head snapped back. Pain raged through him—they were pulling his hair so tight, forcing him back, back, back. Now he couldn't breathe—a rag was being forced over his mouth and nose. A sharp, biting odor flared up his nostrils and instinct kicked in too late. He struggled for his life, but already he was losing consciousness. Then everything went black.

2

They were watching her every move. Hanging on her every word.

"The body is that of a white female, aged between twenty and twenty-five. She was found by a Community Support officer yesterday morning in the boot of an abandoned car at the Green-wood Houses."

Detective Inspector Helen Grace's voice was clear and strong, despite the tension that knotted her stomach. She was briefing the Major Investigation Team on the seventh floor of Southampton Central Police Station.

"As you can see from the pictures, her teeth were caved in, probably with a hammer, and both her hands have been cut off. She is heavily tattooed, which might help with ID'ing, and you should concentrate your efforts on drugs and prostitution to begin with. This looks like a gang-related killing, rather than common or garden murder. DS Bridges is going to lead on this one and he'll fill you in on particular persons of interest. Tony?"

"Thank you, ma'am. First things first, I want to check precedents . . ."

As DS Bridges got into his stride, Helen slipped away. Even after all this time she couldn't bear being the center of everyone's attention, gossip and intrigue. It was nearly a year since she'd brought Marianne's terrible killing spree to an end, but the interest in Helen was as strong as ever. In the immediate aftermath, friends, colleagues, journalists and strangers had rushed to offer sympathy and support. But it was all largely fake—what they wanted were *details*. They wanted to open Helen up and pick over her insides—were you abused too? Do you feel guilty about all those deaths? Do you feel *responsible*?

Helen had spent her entire adult life building a high wall around herself—even the name Helen Grace was a fiction—but thanks to Marianne that wall had been destroyed forever. Initially Helen had been tempted to run—she'd been offered leave, a transfer, even a retirement package—but somehow she had caught hold of herself, returning to work at Southampton Central as soon as they would allow her to do so. She knew that wherever she went the eyes of the world would be on her. Better to face the examination on home turf, where for many years life had been good to her.

That was the theory, but it had proved far from easy. There were so many memories here—of Mark, of Charlie—and so many people who were willing to probe, speculate or even joke about her ordeal. Even now, months after she'd returned to work, there were times when she just had to get away.

"Good night, ma'am."

Helen snapped to, oblivious to the desk sergeant she was walking straight past.

"Good night, Harry. Hope the Saints remember how to win for you tonight."

Her tone was bright, but the words sounded strange, as if the effort of being perky was too much for her. Hurrying outside, she picked up her Kawasaki and, opening the throttle, sped away down the West Quay Road. The sea fog that had rolled in earlier clung to the city and Helen vanished inside it.

Keeping her speed strong but steady, she glided past the traffic crawling toward St. Mary's Stadium. Reaching the outskirts of town, she diverted onto the motorway. Force of habit made her check her mirrors, but there was no one following her. As the traffic eased, she punched her speed up. Hitting eighty miles per hour, she paused for a second before pushing it to ninety. She never felt so at ease as when she was traveling at speed.

The towns flicked by. Winchester, then Farnborough, before Aldershot eventually loomed into view. Another quick check of the mirrors, then into the city center. Parking her bike at the Parkway NCP, Helen sidestepped a group of drunken squaddies and hurried off, hugging the shadows as she went. Nobody knew her here, but even so she couldn't take any chances.

She walked past the train station and before long she was in Cole Avenue, in the heart of Aldershot's suburbia. She wasn't sure she was doing the right thing, yet she'd felt compelled to return. Settling herself down amid the undergrowth that flanked one side of the street, she took up her usual vantage point.

Time crawled by. Helen's stomach growled and she realized that she hadn't eaten since breakfast. Stupid, really—she was getting thinner by the day. What was she trying to prove to herself? There were better ways of atoning than by starving yourself to death.

Suddenly there was movement. A shouted "Bye" and then the door of number 14 slammed shut. Helen crouched down. Her eyes remained glued to the young man who was now hurrying down the street, punching numbers into his mobile phone. He walked within ten feet of Helen, never once detecting her presence, before disappearing round the corner. Helen counted to fifteen, then left her hiding place and set off in pursuit.

The man, a boyish twenty-five-year-old, was handsome, with thick dark hair and a full face. Casually dressed with his jeans hanging around his bum, he looked like so many young men, desperate to appear cool and uninterested. It made Helen smile a little, such was the studied casualness of it all.

A knot of rowdy lads loomed into view, stationed outside the Railway Tavern. Two pounds a pint, fifty pence a shot, and free pool, it was a mecca for the young, the skint and the shady. The elderly owner was happy to serve anyone who'd hit puberty, so it was always packed, the crowds spilling out onto the street. Helen was glad of the cover, slipping in among the bodies to observe undetected. The lads greeted the young man with a cheer as he waved a twenty-pound note at them. They entered and Helen followed. Waiting patiently in the queue for the bar, she was invisible to them—anyone over the age of thirty didn't exist in their world.

After a couple of drinks, the gang drifted away from the prying eyes of the pub toward a kids' playground on the outskirts of town. The tatty urban park was deserted and Helen had to tail the boys cautiously. Any woman wandering alone at night through a park was likely to draw attention to herself, so Helen hung back. She found an aged oak tree, grievously wounded with scores of lovers' carvings, and stationed herself in its shadow. From here she could watch unmolested as the gang smoked dope, happy and carefree in spite of the cold.

Helen spent her whole life being watched, but here she was invisible. In the aftermath of Marianne's death, her life had been picked apart, opened up for public consumption. As a result people thought they knew her inside and out.

But there was one thing they didn't know. One secret that she had kept to herself.

And he was standing not fifty feet away from her now, utterly oblivious to her presence.

3

His eyes blinked open, but he couldn't see.

Liquid oozed down his cheeks as his eyeballs swiveled uselessly in their sockets. Sound was horribly muted, as if his ears were stuffed with cotton wool. Scrambling back to consciousness, the man felt a savage pain ripping through his throat and nostrils. An intense burning sensation, like a flame held steady to his larynx. He wanted to sneeze, to retch, to spit out whatever it was that was tormenting him. But he was gagged, his mouth bound tight with duct tape, so he had to swallow down his agony.

Eventually the stream of tears abated and his protesting eyes began to take in their surroundings. He was still in the derelict house; only now he was in the front bedroom, lying prostrate on the filthy bed. His nerves were jangling and he struggled wildly—he had to get away—but his arms and legs were bound tight to the iron bedstead. He yanked, pulled and twisted, but the nylon cords held firm.

Only then did he realize he was naked. A terrible thought pulsed through him—were they going to leave him here like this? To freeze to death? His skin had already raised its defenses—goose bumps erect with cold and terror—and he realized how perishingly cold it was.

He bellowed for all he was worth—but all he produced was a dull, buzzing moan. If he could just talk to them, reason with them . . . he could get them more money, and they would let him go. They couldn't leave him here like *this*. Humiliation seeped into his fear now as he looked down at his bloated, middle-aged body stretched out on the stained eiderdown.

He strained to hear, hoping against hope that he was not alone. But there was nothing. They had abandoned him. How long would they leave him here? Until they had emptied all his accounts? Until they had got away? The man shuddered, already dreading the prospect of bargaining for his liberty with some junkie or whore. What would he do when he was liberated? What would he say to his family? To the police? He cursed himself bitterly for being so bloody stu—

A creaking floorboard. So he *wasn't* alone. Hope flared through him—perhaps now he could find out what they wanted. He craned his neck round to try to engage his attackers, but they were approaching from behind and remained out of view. It suddenly struck him that the bed he was tied to had been pushed out into the middle of the room, as if center stage at a show. No one could possibly want to sleep with it like that, so why . . . ?

A falling shadow. Before he could react, something was passing over his eyes, his nose, his mouth. Some sort of hood. He could feel the soft fabric on his face, the drawstring being pulled taut. Already the man was struggling to breathe, the thick velvet resting on his protesting nostrils. He shook his head furiously this way and that, fighting to create some tiny pocket of breathing space. Any moment he expected the string to be pulled still tighter, but to his surprise nothing happened.

What now? All was silent again, apart from the man's labored breathing. It was getting hot inside the hood. Could oxygen get in here? He forced himself to breathe slowly. If he panicked now, he would hyperventilate and then . . .

Suddenly he flinched, his nerves pulsing wildly. Something cold had come to rest on his thigh. Something hard. Something metal? A knife? Now it was drifting up his leg, toward . . . The man bucked furiously, tearing his muscles as he wrenched at the cords that held him. He knew now that this was a fight to the death.

He shrieked for all he was worth. But the tape held firm. His bonds wouldn't yield. And there was no one to hear his screams.

ABOUT THE AUTHOR

M. J. Arlidge has worked in television for the last fifteen years, and he lives in England. *Eeny Meeny* is his debut novel, and has been sold in twenty-five countries. Visit him online at twitter.com/ mjarlidge.